Max punched the button for the camera in the kitchen and fast-forwarded through the tape, searching for the right spot. There he was. Just entering the kitchen. The camera had a perfect shot of his face, his thin mouth and close-set, beady eyes. He seemed completely unaware that he was being caught on camera. He crossed the room and knelt down in front of the gas cooker. He pulled open the oven door and took an object out of his pouch. Max couldn't see clearly what it was, but he realized suddenly what the man was doing.

He spun round and raced across the basement and up the stairs. 'Chris! Chris, where are you?' he yelled. He burst into the kitchen, glancing across at the cooker, then sprinted down the hall. 'Chris!'

Chris leaned over the banisters on the first-floor landing. 'What is it?'

'We have to get out.'

**Praise for the Max Cassidy Adventures:**

'Written in clear, punchy prose . . . somewhere Charlie Higson fans might go next'
*Sunday Times*

'Pacy and exciting . . . Fans of high-octane adventure are going to enjoy reading about Max Cassidy'
*www.bookbag.co.uk*

'Hits all the right notes for a rip-roaring adventure'
*Sunday Business Post*

# attack

## at dead man's bay

## PAUL ADAM

CORGI BOOKS

ATTACK AT DEAD MAN'S BAY
A CORGI BOOK 978 0 552 56034 4

Published in Great Britain by Corgi Books,
an imprint of Random House Children's Books
A Random House Group Company

This edition published 2012

3 5 7 9 10 8 6 4

The Random House Group Limited supports The Forest Stewardship
Council (FSC®), the leading international forest certification organisation.
Our books carrying the FSC label are printed on FSC® certified paper.
FSC is the only forest certification scheme endorsed by the leading
environmental organisations, including Greenpeace. Our
paper procurement policy can be found at
www.randomhouse.co.uk/environment

MIX
Paper from
responsible sources
FSC® C016897

Printed and bound in Great Britain by Clays Ltd, St Ives PLC

Set in 12/16pt Lomba by
Falcon Oast Graphic Art Ltd.

Corgi Books are published by Random House Children's Books,
61–63 Uxbridge Road, London W5 5SA

www.kidsatrandomhouse.co.uk
www.totallyrandombooks.co.uk
www.randomhouse.co.uk

Addresses for companies within The Random House Group Limited
can be found at: www.randomhouse.co.uk/offices.htm

THE RANDOM HOUSE GROUP Limited Reg. No. 954009

A CIP catalogue record for this book is available from the British Library.

*For R and J*

Escapologists like Max undergo years of training before they can try the dangerous stunts like the ones in this book. Random House Children's Books would like to make it clear that we do not recommend you try any of these stunts yourself.

# ONE

The view from the west walkway of Tower Bridge had to be the best in London. There were higher viewpoints, more central ones, but few of them gave such a magnificent panorama of the city.

From where Max stood, he could look down on the Tower of London, the union flag gusting in the breeze above the White Tower, then as his eyes scanned west, following the north bank of the Thames, he could see the shimmering glass skyscrapers of the financial district, the dome of St Paul's Cathedral and, far away on the horizon, the tall, thin shape of the Telecom Tower, its top hazy in the summer heat.

The south bank of the river was less impressive – the circular skeleton of the London Eye just visible in the distance, then nondescript office blocks and apartments until you reached City Hall, with its curving glass façade that was like a huge car headlight beaming out over the Thames.

But what was unique about Tower Bridge, that made its view so special, was that you were directly over the river. Max could look upstream to where HMS *Belfast* was moored, then beyond that to London Bridge and Cannon Street Bridge, across which a locomotive, appearing no bigger than a child's model train, was pulling a long line of carriages.

He diverted his gaze to the banks of the river. The north embankment, by the Tower of London, was crowded with people, and there were more on the approaches to the bridge and on the south bank, clustered tightly together on the lawns and steps outside City Hall. There were people out on the water too, lining the decks of tourist cruisers and pleasure boats which had formed a flotilla stretching right across the Thames. In all, there must have been five or six thousand spectators. Max felt a flutter of nerves in his stomach as he reminded himself that they were here to see him – to see Max Cassidy, the Half-Pint Houdini, perform one of his spectacular stunts.

He craned his neck out of the walkway window and looked straight down at the cloudy, brown waters of the Thames, forty metres below him. He braced himself mentally for what was about to happen. In just a short while, he was going to be handcuffed, sealed inside a large wooden crate and lowered into the river. Not for the first time in his escapology career, Max wondered whether he was quite right in the head.

'Max, are you ready?'

He turned and saw his Spanish stage assistant, Consuela, coming towards him, her long, dark hair swinging around her shoulders, the light catching the sequins on her vivid red and gold top. She studied him closely.

'Are you all right? You look tense.'

'I've just had enough of this waiting around,' Max said. 'I want to get on with it.'

'The waiting's almost over,' Consuela replied. 'They've got the crate finished and the mayor is on his way across from City Hall.' She smiled at him and gave his arm a reassuring squeeze. 'Everything's going to be OK, don't you worry.'

Max nodded, trying to smile back, but feeling too much on edge to manage more than a brief twitch of the lips. He wasn't enjoying this experience, wasn't really sure he should be performing such a high-profile stunt at this time. After all the terrifying things that had happened to him over the past few weeks he knew it would be wiser to keep out of sight and avoid trouble. But he'd agreed to the stunt nine months earlier and signed a contract to do it. Tower Bridge had been closed to traffic, the event had been widely publicized, it was going to be on television and all those spectators down below had come to see him. If he pulled out now, he would probably be sued for thousands of pounds. Worse, he'd be letting down the public and tarnishing his image. The bad publicity would almost certainly finish his career as a performer.

But there was another reason why Max wanted to carry out this stunt, despite his fears for his own safety. He saw it as a gesture of defiance to his enemies, the people who'd tried to kill him. It was his way of showing them that he wasn't afraid, that he wasn't going to hide.

'Shall we go?' Consuela asked softly.

Max took a deep breath. This was the moment he'd been preparing himself for over the past few years. All those hours he'd spent in the basement of his house, practising picking locks, getting out of handcuffs, keeping fit: this was where that hard work paid off. Everything had been building towards this one important day, when he finally got to show the whole world what he could do.

He nodded. 'OK, I'm ready.'

They headed along the walkway together, a television cameraman with a handheld camera filming them as they climbed out through an access door onto the platform that had been specially constructed on the outside of the bridge.

Max felt the cool breeze buffeting his body and

glanced over the edge of the platform. The river looked a long way down, the water choppy, broken by waves as the wind cut across the surface. Ripples and eddies and tiny whirlpools could be seen in the centre of the channel, where the incoming tide collided with the outgoing flow of the river. The stunt had been timed to coincide exactly with high tide, when the Thames would be at its deepest beneath the bridge. Max needed that depth, and the silt and mud churned up by the currents, to hide his actions under the water.

A cheer went up from the crowd on the embankments as the pictures from the platform were relayed to two enormous screens on either side of the river. Max gave a wave, the people just a blur of faces and bodies far below him, and saw thousands of arms raised to acknowledge his gesture.

There was a television presenter stationed on the platform: a young, blonde woman named Mandy Nelson, who was shivering in a low-cut dress and high-heeled shoes which seemed terribly inappropriate, hazardous even, for such a precarious position – a four-metre-square metal frame suspended out over the river with no guard rail. One stumble and she'd be over the edge and tumbling down into the Thames.

'Hi, Max, it's good to see you,' Mandy said brightly, and sincerely. She was overjoyed to see him. She'd been out on the platform for the past half hour, watching the carpenters constructing the wooden crate in which Max was going to be sealed, and she was freezing, her bare arms and legs covered with goose pimples. 'How are you feeling?' She pushed her microphone under Max's nose.

'I'm feeling good,' he replied. 'I'm looking forward to it.'

'So are we,' Mandy said. 'So are all the spectators down there and millions of viewers watching at home. We've seen this crate being put together from scratch by local craftsmen, so I can vouch that there's nothing funny about it. No hidden doors or secret escape hatches. It's a good, solid wooden crate. Now we just need to handcuff you and put you inside. And for that we are—' She paused, fingering the radio receiver in her ear. 'I'm just getting word, the mayor has arrived. And here he is . . .'

A shambling figure in a crumpled suit climbed out onto the platform, his blond hair flopping across his face.

'Golly, there's a bit of a gale blowing up here, isn't there?' he exclaimed good-humouredly. 'I say, what a splendid view. I'll have to get my office moved over this way.'

'Thank you for coming today,' Mandy said.

'I wouldn't have missed it for the world. Let me shake your hand, young man.' The mayor grabbed Max's hand and pumped it up and down. 'You're an extremely brave young chap. I admire you tremendously for your pluck. Well done!'

'Mr Mayor,' Mandy said. 'If you'd like to search Max, make sure he's not got any tools or keys hidden on him.'

The mayor frisked Max thoroughly, going through his pockets and patting his arms and legs. 'Nothing there, as far as I can tell,' he confirmed. 'The chap's as clean as a whistle.'

'Everything's ready for you, Max,' Mandy said. 'This is the point of no return – your last chance to pull out. Are you sure you still want to go ahead with this stunt?'

'I'm sure,' Max replied firmly.

'Where are the handcuffs?'

Consuela unclipped a pair of steel handcuffs from her belt and handed them to the mayor. Max held out his arms. The mayor snapped the cuffs over his wrists and tested them.

'Locked tight,' he said. 'If he can get out of those, well, he's a better man than I am.'

Max lifted his arms to show the crowd down below, then stepped across to the wooden crate, Consuela by his side. He looked at her. She smiled at him, her eyes warm, affectionate. Max smiled back. There were too many strangers around him today. Thank goodness Consuela was also there; he'd be lost without her.

He paused for a second. All the talking was over. The show-business hype, the celebrity presenters, the mayor of London faded away into the background and Max took centre stage. The crowd had fallen silent. All eyes were fixed on the tall, fair-haired boy standing high on the platform above the river. Max was no longer nervous. He was in control now. Whether he succeeded or failed was entirely in his own hands. He felt confident, exhilarated. This was going to be fun.

He climbed up onto the small wooden block that had been placed next to the crate. Consuela held his arm to steady him, and for an instant their hands touched. Then Max swung his leg over the top and dropped nimbly down inside the crate. The cameraman zoomed in on him, the pictures showing on the big screens by the river and on millions of televisions around the world. Max held up his cuffed hands again and grinned. Then the wooden lid was slid into place and he disappeared from sight. It was a sombre, slightly chilling moment. If anything went wrong with the stunt, this was the last time anyone would see Max Cassidy alive.

One of the professional carpenters who had constructed the crate came back out onto the platform and expertly nailed the lid to the base. To make absolutely sure it couldn't be removed, a thick rope was fastened around the crate and knotted on the top like a gift-wrapped box tied up with ribbon.

Consuela pressed a button on the small crane at the back of the platform and a metal hook descended and was attached to the rope around the crate. Consuela adjusted the controls. The crate was lifted into the air and swung round away from the platform so that it was suspended above the river.

She waited. Down below, at the foot of the south tower, a man with a walkie-talkie gave a command to the bridge's main control room and the bascules – the two lifting halves of the roadway – began to tilt back and rise upwards. When the bascules were fully raised, there was now nothing to stop the crate going straight down to the river.

Consuela closed her eyes briefly, praying silently for Max, then pressed the button on the crane. Very slowly, the cable began to unwind.

Crouched inside the crate, Max felt the box start to descend and he knew he had only a few seconds before it hit the water. He was already out of the handcuffs. The moment the lid had been nailed in place, he had reached up behind his right ear and removed the key that was taped underneath his thick hair – a place the mayor hadn't thought to search; no one ever did – and unlocked the cuffs. That was the easy bit. The hard part was still to come: getting out of the crate while it was underwater. But for that, too, he had come prepared.

He opened his fingers and looked at the small pair of nail-cutters that were hidden in the palm of his hand – the nail-cutters that Consuela had so slickly passed him as she helped him climb into the crate. Max smiled at the memory. They'd done it right under the noses of the mayor and Mandy Nelson, not to mention the spectators and television viewers, and no one had noticed. He looked down, sensing the Thames drawing nearer, and got himself ready for the next stage of the escape.

Up on the platform, Consuela was watching the crate carefully, gauging its distance from the river. When it was five metres above the surface, she slowed the winch right down so that the impact, when it came, wouldn't jar Max too much. Four metres ... three ... two ... one ... The base of the crate touched the river with barely any more force than a feather. At that exact moment, Consuela clicked the stopwatch around her left wrist to begin timing. There was a clock up on the television screens too – a digital display registering the seconds ticking by – so that the audience could see how long Max had been underwater.

Consuela could feel her heart pounding. They'd practised this stunt many times, but that didn't make it any less dangerous. She knew Max could do it in a tank of water, but conditions were different today. He was in the river. There were the currents and tide to deal with, the cold, dirty water, a massive crowd of onlookers. The pressure was enormous. Max had nerves of steel, but inevitably he would be feeling the weight of expectations on his young shoulders. He would be tense, and that might affect how long he could hold his breath. Timing was critical. Consuela had to judge it exactly right – to prolong the stunt for as long as possible, but not so long that Max drowned.

Inside the crate, Max was on his knees, waiting until the base was underwater before he began his escape. Water was seeping in through two holes the carpenters had drilled in the bottom of the crate. It was a few centimetres deep now, creeping around Max's feet and lower legs, soaking his trousers and cooling the skin underneath. It was cleaner than he'd expected, but still brown and cloudy with particles of mud. He didn't fancy swallowing any of it.

The water got deeper. Max's legs were submerged now. He gripped the nail-cutters in his right hand and leaned over into the corner, slipping the cutters down to where the side planks of the crate were joined to the base. There was a narrow gap along the joint into which Max slid the cutters, searching for the nails holding the planks together. He found the first nail, encircled it with the jaws of the cutters and squeezed. The sharp blades sliced easily through the soft metal. He moved on to the next nail – there should have been only two per plank – and cut through that too.

The water edged up his thighs. The crate was filling quickly, sinking deeper into the Thames. Max knew he had to get a move on. He slid the cutters along the joint to the next plank, feeling for a nail. It took him a few seconds to locate it, then a couple more to snip through it. The water was up to his waist now, cold enough to make him catch his breath. He paused for a second, forcing himself to slow his breathing. That was important. When the water finally closed over his head, he needed his body to be completely relaxed, to be using as little oxygen as possible.

He found the next nail and sliced through that too. One more plank to go. The water crept up over his chest. It was so murky he couldn't see his hand. He had to rely on his sense of touch to find the joint in the planks. The cutters encountered an obstacle – a nail. Max sliced quickly through it, then moved along to the last nail, severing it with another squeeze of the cutters.

He was only just in time. The water had reached his

neck and was swirling around his throat. He took a few breaths, exhaling hard to flush out his lungs. He knelt up as high as he could go, so his hair was touching the underside of the lid, and waited until the water was almost over his chin before he tilted back his head and took an enormous breath. Then he clamped his lips tight shut and ducked down under the water.

He felt good. Everything was going according to plan. The ends of three side planks had been detached from the base. There was enough flexibility in the timber for Max to bend them out, creating a gap through which he could squeeze. But before he did so, he had to wait for the crate to descend deeper into the river. At least four or five metres below the surface to make sure his escape was concealed from the spectators on the bridge and the embankments.

Five seconds passed . . . ten . . . fifteen. The pressure on his ears increased. He had to be at least four metres underwater by now. Max pushed on the loose planks. Two of them moved. One didn't. Max pushed harder, an alarm bell jangling inside his head. Something was wrong. The plank still seemed to be attached to the base. How could that be? He'd cut through six nails. He applied more force. The plank gave a little, but didn't bend out. He could think of only one explanation. The carpenters had put in more than two nails.

He reached down with his cutters again, trying to find the joint at the bottom of the plank. But the joint had closed shut under the pressure of the water outside. Max put his elbow to the plank, opening up a tiny gap, and jammed the cutters in, sliding them along until he hit an obstacle. Was it a nail? He couldn't see, even if he put his eyes right down next to the wood. It had to be a nail. He hooked the cutters around it and squeezed. Nothing happened. This nail was tougher than the others. He squeezed harder – and felt something snap. He pushed on the plank again and was relieved to feel it flex away from the base.

How long had he been submerged? A minute? Maybe a bit longer. That was cutting it fine. Max could hold his breath for three minutes, but he had a lot to do before he got his next gulp of fresh air. He applied his shoulder to the three loose planks, bending them outwards. *Careful now*, he told himself. *Bend them too far and they'll snap, then everyone will know how you got out. Take it gently, a bit at a time.* He increased the pressure and slowly the gap widened. Ten centimetres . . . fifteen . . . twenty . . . When it got to thirty, he jammed his head and shoulders into the opening and pushed back with his hands, propelling himself out into the river.

Looking up, he saw only a glimmer of light through

the dark, foggy water and knew he would be invisible to the watchers above. He twisted round and grabbed hold of the crate to stop himself floating to the surface, then pushed the planks back into place. They wouldn't go completely. They kept springing out, leaving a gap of a few centimetres, but Max was ready for that. He felt behind his left ear and removed the three nails he'd taped beneath his hair earlier. He put one nail against the bottom of the first plank and, using the flat back of the nail-cutters like a hammer, knocked it home. Then he did the same with the second nail and the second plank. A close inspection of the crate would reveal the deception, but there wasn't going to be a close inspection. What counted was that when the crate re-emerged from the river there should be no obvious signs that it had been tampered with, no planks hanging loose.

One plank left. Max was feeling the strain. He'd been holding his breath for more than two minutes and he hadn't been at rest during that time – he'd been working his muscles, and that required oxygen. He felt slightly dizzy, there was a claw around his chest that was getting tighter with every passing second. He had to finish the job and get to the surface.

He took the third nail between his forefinger and thumb and pressed it into the last plank, getting ready to strike with the nail-cutters. Then something happened. He fumbled, his fingers lost their grip for an instant and the nail slipped away, tumbling down towards the river bed.

Max threw himself after it, kicking hard with his legs, his arm outstretched. He saw a flash of metal in the gloom and snatched at it instinctively, felt the nail hit his fingers and bounce off. But fortunately his other hand was there below it, waiting. The nail sank into his palm and he closed his fingers firmly around it, relief flooding through his body.

The claw squeezing his chest was digging in harder. His lungs were burning, his head and heart pierced with sharp stabs of pain. Swimming rapidly back to the crate, he held the nail against the plank again, his fingers shaking. He hit it once with the nail-cutters, then again, and again. The nail sank in all the way, holding the plank in place. Max let go of the nail-cutters, so they'd sink down into the mud at the bottom of the river, and hauled himself up the side of the crate. *Now, Consuela*, he screamed silently to himself. *Now!*

Forty metres above him, on the platform over the river, Consuela was gazing intently at her stopwatch. It was almost three and a half minutes since the crate had entered the river. Allowing thirty seconds for it to fill completely with water, that meant Max had been under for nearly three minutes, the maximum he could manage. Was he out? She couldn't see anything in the water below – no outline of the crate, no shape that might have been Max. She couldn't wait any longer. She just had to trust in him and hope.

She hit the 'start' button on the control panel and stared down anxiously as the cable began to reel in. One metre . . . two metres . . . Couldn't it go any faster? The crowd was watching apprehensively too. They could all see the clock on the big screens. Some spectators had their eyes closed, unable to watch, others were holding their breath, sharing the ordeal with Max. He seemed to have been underwater for an eternity.

The surface of the river began to churn, the cable emerging slowly from the depths. Then Consuela caught a glimpse of something, a shadow in the water. Was it him? She stared, unblinking, as the shadow began to take on human form. It was him. It was Max!

His head broke the surface. He was standing on top of the crate, one hand gripping the wire cable. Consuela saw him gulp in the air, then heard a deafening roar boom out across the river as six thousand people cheered and applauded. Max grinned and held up his arm to wave. His hair was slicked down, water running off his sodden clothes. He looked pale and drawn, but he was alive. Consuela felt tears of joy and relief well up and trickle down her cheeks.

Max looked around as the crate rose up from the river, seeing a sea of bodies, of waving arms. He felt jubilant, delighted to have pulled off the stunt. Yet he was also feeling uneasy. The knot of nerves in his stomach had returned. Escapology was a dangerous business, but not half as dangerous as real life. He could make out no individual faces in the cheering crowd, but he wondered who was out there watching him, biding their time. He was safe for the moment. This was too public an event for anyone to attempt a move against him. But he knew that moment wouldn't last. His enemies would try to kill him again, Max was certain of that. The only question was when.

# TWO

Max wanted nothing more than to get out of his wet clothes, take a shower and go somewhere warm with a hot drink. But it wasn't his choice. There were other people around him who had a say in what he did next. He had responsibilities, things that were expected of him. Six thousand people had made the effort to come to Tower Bridge to watch him perform, and many more had watched his stunt on television. He couldn't just slope off afterwards and pretend that they didn't exist, that he didn't owe them some kind of duty, at the very least the courtesy of a final appearance and a few words to camera. That was the deal. That was show business. You put yourself out there in the public arena and the public expected a piece of you, they expected to get their money's worth. If Max wanted to continue performing, he knew he had to get used to that.

So he stood on the platform above the river and waved and smiled to the cheering crowd, the wind biting into his dripping clothes, making him shiver with cold. Then the camera panned across to the wooden crate, showing the sides intact, the lid still securely attached, the ropes tightly knotted on the top, and down on the embankment and in living rooms across the country everyone was thinking the same thing: *How did he do that?*

Max was asked that very question a few minutes later, when he went into the makeshift studio the television company had set up at one end of the walkway. He just smiled in reply, but said nothing.

'It's a professional secret, I guess,' said Barry Sullivan, the veteran, silver-haired interviewer who'd been anchoring the television coverage. 'Like a magician refusing to divulge how he does his tricks.'

'Something like that,' Max said, wiping a trickle of water from his forehead.

'I have to say I'm baffled,' Barry admitted. 'The crate looks exactly the same as before, yet somehow you've managed to get out of it. And get out of it underwater. That is some feat, especially for a boy your age. How do you feel now?'

'Cold and wet,' Max replied, with a grin.

Barry laughed. 'I won't keep you long. You've risked your life to entertain us. We don't want you to die of pneumonia now. Did you enjoy yourself?'

Max nodded. 'Yes, a lot. And I hope everyone else did too.'

'You can be sure of that. It must give you a thrill, doing these kinds of dangerous stunts. Are you on a high?'

'I suppose I am,' Max said.

'*We* certainly are, and we just sat and watched you. Do you have anything to say to all your fans out there?'

'Just thanks for coming. Thanks for watching.'

'Can we expect more shows like this? More daring stunts from the Half-Pint Houdini?'

'I hope so.'

'Thank you, Max. It's been a real pleasure talking to you. Ladies and gentlemen, Max Cassidy, quite possibly the bravest – and maybe craziest – teenager in the country. Now let's go down to the embankment and get a few reactions from the spectators . . .'

Max got up from his chair and left the tiny studio. Consuela was standing close by, out of shot of the cameras. She wrapped a big towel around him and gave him a hug.

'You OK?'

'Yeah.'

'You were terrific. Did you have any problems?'

Max shook his head. 'It was just like in practice,' he said. 'Everything went exactly as we planned.'

He didn't tell her about dropping the nail when he was underwater. She worried enough about him already. He didn't want to make things worse.

'Let's get you out of those clothes, then,' Consuela said.

They turned to go and found their path blocked by the squat figure of Sheldon Mackenzie, the flamboyant show-business promoter who had organized this whole event. Mackenzie was a couple of centimetres shorter than Max, but very much wider. His stomach bulged beneath his bright pink shirt and emerald green waistcoat, hanging down over his trousers and wobbling like a water-filled balloon every time he moved. His face was pink and chubby, his neck completely hidden by the folds of his many chins, and jammed in the corner of his fleshy mouth was a cigar the size of a Swiss roll. The cigar was unlit – smoking was prohibited on the walkway – but he was sucking vigorously on the end like a baby with a dummy.

'That was great, kid,' Mackenzie said, removing the cigar from his mouth and waving it in the air. 'You're a star. You know that? With the right kind of management, you could be the biggest thing in show business since, well, since Houdini himself was performing. You could be bigger than him, in fact. Houdini had no TV, no syndication, no worldwide media or internet to promote him. We're living in a truly global age, kid, and you are perfectly positioned to exploit it.'

'Yes, thank you . . .' Max said, embarrassed by the praise.

'Have a think about your future. Then let's fix a meeting, have lunch, talk through the details. OK?'

Max nodded vaguely. He didn't want to think about his future right now. He just wanted to dry off and warm himself up. Squeezing past Mackenzie, he walked quickly to the south tower where two men in jeans and open-neck shirts were waiting for him. The taller of the two, who was called Rusty, had short-cropped red hair and a pale, gingery complexion. His companion, Zip, was darker and more compact, his bare arms rippling with muscles. Both men had quick, watchful eyes and an air of quiet confidence about them. Guys who knew how to take care of themselves. And Max.

They escorted him down a flight of stairs to the men's toilets that had been set aside for his use. Rusty checked inside the room first, then gave Max the all clear to enter, leaving him on his own while he rejoined Zip, who was standing guard outside.

Max stripped off his wet clothes and towelled himself dry. There was no shower in the toilets – he'd have one later when he got home – but there was a basin and soap. Max washed his face, removing the residue of the river water, then put on a set of clean, dry clothes.

Consuela was outside with Rusty and Zip when he finally emerged. She'd got changed too, swapping her sparkly show blouse for a less conspicuous black top.

The four of them continued on down the stairs to the exit from the south tower. A cheer went up from the waiting spectators as they came out onto the pavement. The bascules had been lowered, but the bridge was still closed to traffic, the road teeming with people held back by metal barriers and a squad of police officers.

Max walked past the crowds, waving and signing autographs, Rusty and Zip never more than a metre away, their eyes scanning the bridge for signs of danger. To the casual spectator, they looked like a couple of bodyguards hired to protect Max from over-enthusiastic fans. No one would have thought that, in fact, they were there to shield him from potential assassins.

At the bottom of the south approach, the police opened up a narrow corridor through the throng to allow Max and his companions to cross the road and disappear down a stairwell into the car park beneath an office block. The car park was deserted except for a tall, muscular man with dark hair and blue eyes, who was leaning lazily back on a sleek black Audi saloon. He smiled at Max, then Consuela, holding her gaze for a second, before pushing himself away from the car, holding up his hand and giving Max a high five.

'That was pretty good, Max. You're not bad at this escapology business, you know.'

'How much did you see?' Max asked.

Chris Moncrieffe gave a shrug. 'All the good stuff. I saw it on the screen by City Hall. That was some stunt. The crowd loved it. One minute shouting and screaming, then suddenly going deathly quiet when the crate sank into the river. I've never heard a crowd so silent. It was eerie. You certainly had us all worried. You were down for a hell of a long time. It was all I could do to stop myself diving into the water and hauling you out.'

'I was fine,' Max said phlegmatically. 'You didn't need to worry about me. It was all part of the show.'

Chris touched him lightly on the shoulder. 'I know. But we *do* worry about you, you know that.' He glanced at Rusty and Zip. 'Everything OK?'

Rusty nodded. 'No problem.'

'Let's go, then.'

Max and Consuela climbed into the back of the Audi, Zip and Rusty in the front, Zip taking the driver's seat. Chris went to the car in the adjoining bay, a small, blue Nissan that belonged to Consuela, and slid in behind the wheel. They left the car park in convoy, the Audi leading. Then, when they reached the main road, Chris dropped back a little, watching the Audi's rear from a discreet distance. Max was used to the precautions now, they'd done it so many times in the past few weeks. It was sometimes irritating, but he knew it was necessary. He was vulnerable in a car, out and about on the streets of London. Having two vehicles, one watching the other, was a sensible way of reducing the risks.

Rusty and Zip were old army friends of Chris's. They'd served together in the Paratroop Regiment for several years, then Rusty and Zip had resigned and set themselves up in business as security consultants – doing surveillance work, bodyguarding, sometimes undercover jobs. Chris had remained a soldier for longer, but when he, too, had left the army, he'd joined his former colleagues. He'd worked alongside them for a time before he grew disillusioned with his life and took a job in the Brazilian rainforest for an environmental charity that was monitoring illegal logging in the Amazon Basin.

It was there that he'd been abducted and taken to Shadow Island, the sinister fortress off the coast of Santo Domingo where Max and Consuela had been held prisoner by billionaire tycoon, Julius Clark, the man Max knew was responsible for the destruction of his family: the man responsible for his father's disappearance and his mother's arrest and imprisonment for his murder. Since their escape from the island together, Max and Chris had become good friends, their bond cemented by their later shared experiences in Britain and Sweden and Borneo, where Clark and his associates had tried to kill Max.

It was now almost three weeks since they'd returned from Borneo and Chris had enlisted the help of Rusty and Zip to protect Max. The three men made a good team. They were tough, experienced, completely reliable. Max felt safe with them around. He liked their self-assurance, their reassuring physical presence, the calm, professional way they went about their task. He knew he wasn't untouchable. That wasn't possible, particularly with an enemy as rich and powerful as Julius Clark. But he was as secure as he could be in the circumstances. If Clark tried to kill him again, he wasn't going to find it easy.

They drove west through Southwark, then crossed the Thames on Blackfriars Bridge and headed north through Finsbury and Islington. Zip drove fast, but safely, his eyes continually flicking to his rear-view mirror, checking to see where Chris was and who was behind them. Rusty, too, was vigilant, twisted sideways in his seat so he could scan the road ahead, monitor any vehicles overtaking them and keep an eye on Max with only a slight turn of his head.

When they reached Max's street, the two bodyguards became even more alert, examining every parked car, every pedestrian, every window for signs of anything unusual, anything suspicious. Zip reversed the Audi into the drive outside the house and kept the engine running while Rusty went inside to check all the rooms. Only when he reappeared at the front door and gave a thumbs up were Max and Consuela allowed out of the car and into their home.

Chris was already down in the basement. He'd parked the Nissan in the next street and climbed over the garden wall – his standard method of entry since the police had raided the house a couple of months earlier, searching for him on a trumped-up charge of terrorism. He was seated in front of a console, running through the CCTV footage that had been recorded during their absence. Rusty and Zip had installed tiny, almost invisible cameras in the hall, kitchen and upstairs landing, to watch the house when it was empty. They'd also fitted movement sensors and other sophisticated alarms to prevent anyone breaking in undetected.

'Anything?' Rusty enquired.

Chris shook his head, fast forwarding through the tapes, the images displayed on a screen that, when it wasn't in use, was concealed behind the doors of one of Max's trick cabinets – the specially-constructed props he used in his stage shows.

'Looks clear to me. You secured the exits?'

'Zip's doing that now,' Rusty replied.

'Consuela?'

'She's in the kitchen.'

'And Max?'

'He's gone upstairs to take a shower. Relax, Chris. Everything's fine.'

Chris nodded grimly. 'For the time being.'

Max lingered for a long while in the shower, washing away the dirt from the Thames and thinking about his parents, wishing that his dad could have been there to see the stunt, wondering whether his mum had managed to watch it from prison. Then he went to his bedroom and got dressed. The curtains were permanently drawn across the window to stop anyone seeing in – another of Rusty and Zip's precautions to keep Max safe. He appreciated their concern, didn't question their professional judgement, but he was starting to find all these security measures a bit oppressive.

He felt like a prisoner in his own home. He hadn't been to school for the past three weeks – it was too difficult to protect him there. Consuela had told the head teacher that he was ill and now, of course, they were into the summer holiday period. He hadn't seen any of his friends, hadn't been out anywhere except on essential business, and then only with Rusty and Zip watching carefully over him. When was it all going to end? When was he going to be able to get back to his normal life, his old life, before all this began.

He sat back on his bed, his pillow behind him, and thought again about everything that had happened to him since that fateful day a few months ago, when Luis Lopez-Vega had come to his dressing room after a show and told him his father was still alive. Everything had stemmed from that one meeting: Max later finding Lopez-Vega murdered, going to Santo Domingo to try to track down his dad, being imprisoned on Shadow Island where Julius Clark was conducting horrific scientific experiments on prisoners.

Max knew now what those experiments had been. Clark had been kidnapping his opponents from around the world – environmentalists, scientists, lawyers, anyone who stood in the way of his ruthless business activities. He'd brought them to Shadow Island and used a drug called Episuderon to brainwash them, to make them his faithful servants, before sending them back to their jobs and their countries as 'fifth columnists' – sympathizers in the enemy camp, who would supposedly still be fighting to protect the world, but in reality would be fighting to protect Julius Clark and his money-making interests.

Max's father, Alexander, had been one of those prisoners, but had somehow escaped and then vanished into thin air. Max had the names of five other prisoners too: James Abbott, Sergei Alekseev, Narang Anwar, Redmond Ashworth-Ames and Erik Blomkvist. He'd tracked down the last three, going to Sweden to find out more about Blomkvist and discovering the existence of a secret organization called the Cedar Alliance, a world-wide group of activists dedicated to protecting the Earth from overdevelopment by greedy businessmen like Clark. He'd found out also that his father was one of the leaders of the Alliance, but where was Alexander now? Where had he been and what had he been doing for the past two years?

Max had gone to Borneo to try to find some answers and had been captured by Clark, tied up and thrown into a river as crocodile food. But Max had used his escapology skills to get away and then found evidence that his dad had been to Borneo before him and had faked his own death with the help of an American doctor named Halstead.

Who was this Dr Halstead? Max knew that he'd left Borneo to take up a post in San Francisco, but so far he'd been unable to make contact with him. Halstead, it transpired, had not yet started work at San Francisco General Hospital and the hospital had refused to give Max his home address or phone number. It was deeply frustrating. Halstead was important, Max knew that. If he found him, he was convinced he'd find his father too.

He got up from the bed, went across to his desk and switched on the computer. Then he logged on to his Facebook page. Dozens of his friends had posted glowing comments about his stunt off Tower Bridge. 'Wow! Blew me away', 'Brilliant! Check it out on YouTube, everyone else is', 'You're out of your mind', were just a few of them. But it was the message from his best mate, Andy, that affected him most. 'When are you coming back to school? Everyone's missing you.'

Max read it and suppressed a sigh. He was missing his friends too – the daily routine of lessons, of kicking a football around in the playground at break. Even double maths was starting to seem an attractive option. He posted a reply, thanking all his friends for their support, then sent a separate private message to Andy, saying he hoped it wouldn't be long before he was back in touch properly, but he couldn't say exactly when. Andy would understand. He knew what Max was going through.

As he finished typing, his mobile rang. Max looked at the caller's name – Sheldon Mackenzie – and groaned. He didn't feel like talking to the promoter, but he knew he ought to. Mackenzie had put his all into organizing and publicizing the Tower Bridge event, had fought hard for months to get the authorities to agree to it in the first place. Max didn't want to be rude to him.

'Hi,' he said into the phone.

'Max, Sheldon here,' the promoter said in his loud, pushy voice. Max pictured him in his opulent office, a cigar in his mouth, his chins wobbling as he spoke.

'I had to tell you, kid,' Mackenzie went on. 'The phone's been red hot since the show. Everybody – and I mean *everybody* – wants to know you.'

'Really?' Max said, trying to sound more enthusiastic than he felt.

'We've had a terrific response from all round the world. The stunt's been shown in more than fifty countries and I've already had several promoters clamouring for a repeat performance on their local bridges. Sydney Harbour, the Brooklyn Bridge in New York, the Golden Gate in San Francisco, the Bosphorus Bridge in Turkey, the Rialto in Venice. They're offering you a lot of money to go there. We'll say no to the Rialto. The water in the Grand Canal is too shallow, and the pollution would probably kill you. You don't want to get typhoid and die – that wouldn't look good for an escapologist.'

'No,' Max agreed.

'If you're going to go, you want to go out in style. I think Sydney Harbour Bridge would be perfect. Australia's a nice place, great beaches. You could make a holiday out of it, kid, take that gorgeous assistant of yours. I'll come with you, keep her company, ha, ha, ha.'

Max's grip on the phone tightened. Did he really have to be having this conversation?

'You thought any more about what I said earlier?' Mackenzie continued. 'You've got real star quality. You're young, you're talented, you're good-looking. And you've got a fabulous newsworthy background.'

'Background?' Max said.

'You know, your family problems. Your mum in prison for killing your dad. People are fascinated by that.'

Max gritted his teeth and thought about hanging up. He was angry with the promoter. His mum and dad weren't some kind of publicity gimmick to be used to promote his career.

'You're fourteen now,' Mackenzie said. 'You could leave school in a few years, become a full-time performer, and be a millionaire in months. I guarantee you that.'

'Maybe I don't want to be a millionaire,' Max said quietly.

There was a silence on the line – and it took a lot to silence Sheldon Mackenzie. Then the promoter's voice came back, puzzled and incredulous. 'Why on earth would you *not* want to be a millionaire? Why else are you an escapologist, risking your life doing these stunts?'

'Look, can I get back to you on this,' Max said. 'Give me a bit more time to think about it.'

'Sure, but don't wait too long. You're only hot for a short time, then you go off the boil. People lose interest in you. Remember that.'

Max put down the phone and went back to his room, wondering why he wasn't more excited by Mackenzie's call. Promoters across the globe were interested in hiring him, in putting on one of his shows. That should have given him a buzz, but it didn't. It left him cold.

Was he just suffering from the aftereffects of his stunt on Tower Bridge? He was often like this following a show, when the adrenaline rush he got from performing subsided and left him with a feeling of anticlimax. Was it simply that, or was there some deeper explanation for his mood?

He thought about what Mackenzie had said – asking him why he was an escapologist. Why *was* he? What motivated him to do things that most people would have considered insane? It certainly wasn't money; wealth didn't interest him. In the early days, watching and learning from his father, he'd found it fun. It gave him the opportunity to be with his dad, to be *like* his dad. He still found it fun, still got a lot of enjoyment out of performing, but was it really what he wanted to do for the rest of his life?

He'd been on a high immediately after his escape from the crate in the river. He'd soaked up the cheers and the applause and let it fill some hollow space inside him. But he was down from that high now. He was back to reality – and the reality was that he didn't really know where he was going, or what he wanted to achieve. Except for two things, two things that drove him, that kept the fires burning in his core: to find his missing dad and to get his mum out of prison. Fulfil both those aims and maybe then he could think about the future.

They all ate together in the kitchen – a big pot of chilli and rice that Consuela had made. Rusty and Zip and Chris did most of the talking. They had that easy camaraderie of long-time friends, friends who'd been through a lot together. Telling stories about their army days, about places they'd visited, people they'd met. Max usually found it interesting, but tonight he was pre-occupied. They'd been living like this for three weeks. Sharing a house, sharing their meals, living on top of one another. How much longer could they keep it up? How much longer could they cope with the stress, the ever-present danger of an attack? Max was feeling the strain more and more. He knew Consuela was too, he could see it in her face. They were waiting for something to happen, waiting for a lead, and Max didn't like that. It was too passive. He wanted to *do* something. *Make* things happen.

They cleared away the dishes. Chris carried a pile of dirty plates to the sink and deposited them in the washing-up bowl. Consuela was standing next to him and Max saw her touch Chris's hand discreetly with her own, their fingers linking for a second before breaking apart. Maybe that was bothering him too. Chris and Consuela.

For the past two years, Consuela had dedicated herself to looking after Max. She'd put her personal life on hold for him. Max was grateful to her. He knew how much she'd sacrificed to put his needs first. But since Chris had appeared on the scene, things had started to change. Max had noticed how he and Consuela were spending more time together, how they looked at each other, those intimate smiles full of hidden meaning, and he was realizing that Consuela had found someone else, someone who might, in time, become more important to her than he was. He didn't resent that. He was delighted for Consuela. She deserved a good guy and Chris, beyond all doubt, was a good guy. But it was unsettling. It added an extra element of uncertainty to Max's already complicated life.

Rusty made a pot of coffee and got out a pack of cards for what was becoming a regular evening session of poker. Max was allowed to join in, although Consuela wouldn't allow betting with real money, only the paper money they'd extracted from the Monopoly set upstairs in Max's bedroom. He was getting quite good at it, though nothing like as good as Consuela who, much to the men's annoyance, nearly always won. If they'd been playing for real money, she'd have had the shirts off their backs by now.

They were on their third hand, Zip living up to his nickname by dealing out the cards with lightning speed, when Chris's mobile rang. He picked it up and listened. Everyone fell silent, sensing somehow that this was an important call.

'OK, thanks,' Chris said. 'We're on our way.'

He hung up and looked at the others.

'That was Lucas Fisher,' he said. 'He has something for us.'

Max looked around the table, feeling the under-current of anticipation. The waiting was over. They were on the move at last.

# THREE

This was when they had to be careful. The house was safe. The doors were reinforced with bolts and extra locks and protected by the alarm system that Rusty and Zip had installed. They could move freely around inside, secure in the knowledge that no one could see them. They could talk freely too – the electronic surveillance bugs that their enemies had once covertly hidden in the house had all been removed and Zip or Rusty did a daily sweep of the building to make sure that no one was listening in to their conversations. It was when they left the house that they really had to be on guard.

Chris was the first to go, heading out across the garden and over the wall to pick up the Nissan in the next street. Then the others went through the internal door into the garage. Zip, Max and Consuela got into the Audi while Rusty opened the garage doors and checked the road outside. Satisfied that there was nothing to worry about, Rusty waved to Zip. The Audi crept out onto the drive. Rusty closed, locked and set the alarm on the garage doors, then jumped into the front passenger seat, clipping on his seat belt as Zip gunned the engine and sped away along the street.

They didn't know for certain whether anyone was going to be following them, but they were taking no chances. Zip took a left, then a right, then another left, guiding the Audi expertly through the narrow corridor between parked cars. Rusty was twisted round in his seat, looking back through the rear window.

'We have a tail,' he said softly.

Zip glanced in his mirror. 'Which one?'

'Three cars back. The BMW. I recognize it.'

'OK, guys,' Zip said calmly. 'Hang onto your hats.'

He turned right at a sedate thirty miles an hour then, seeing the road ahead clear, floored the accelerator. The Audi hit sixty for a few seconds before Zip braked heavily, slewed round to the left and accelerated again. Max clung on tight to the door handle, bracing himself as the car twisted and turned through the labyrinth of streets. He could feel a tightness in his stomach, part nerves, part exhilaration at the cat-and-mouse manoeuvres they were going through to shake off the tail.

Zip was good, the best driver Max had ever seen. Not just the fastest, but the sharpest, the smoothest. He handled the car like a Formula One racer, caressing the wheel, hugging the curves, extracting every last bit of power from the engine. They'd been followed a few times before, but never had it been so important that they evade their pursuers. Tonight it was vital that no one discovered where they were going.

'You see him?' Zip asked, concentrating on over-taking a bus and rocketing across a junction just as the lights turned to red.

Rusty stared back up the road. 'I don't think so.'

'One more turn, just to be sure.'

Zip twisted the wheel to the left and the Audi shot up a tree-lined avenue, houses along one side, a row of shops on the other. The car slowed, then Zip did a U-turn and headed back the way they'd come for a couple of hundred metres, Rusty studying every vehicle going past on the opposite side.

'I think we're in the clear,' he said.

Zip took a left at the next crossroads and cut through a maze of residential streets before coming to a halt at the end of a deserted cul-de-sac. They waited for a few minutes, no one saying anything. No other vehicles turned into the cul-de-sac, or passed by the end. It seemed to Max that they'd done all they could to get rid of their tail and were now out of danger. But what made Rusty and Zip so good at their jobs was their caution, their thoroughness. They were always willing to go that extra distance to make absolutely sure they were safe.

So they all got out of the Audi and walked down an alley past a line of lock-up garages, emerging onto another quiet back street where – just as arranged – Chris was waiting in the Nissan.

Rusty joined Chris in the front of the car, Zip, Max and Consuela squeezed into the back, and they drove off, passing through streets and areas that were unfamiliar to Max until finally they turned into a yard at the rear of a workshop and got out.

The workshop was two storeys high, made of red brick with a tiled roof. It had the shabby, neglected look of an old industrial building – soot on the walls, rust on the metal window frames, weeds and grass spreading across the yard. But there was nothing old or neglected about the CCTV camera positioned above the door. That was a state-of-the-art piece of equipment. Chris pressed a buzzer on the wall and a man's voice crackled out through an intercom grille.

'Yes?'

'It's us,' Chris said, lifting his head to give the CCTV camera a clear view of his face.

'Come on up.'

The lock on the door clicked open and they went inside. Max noticed that the door was ten centimetres thick, reinforced with steel panels and with a complex lock that even he would have had trouble trying to pick.

They went up a flight of stairs to a second door, another CCTV camera watching their every move. The door swung open to reveal a skinny young man in a dirty white T-shirt, jeans and tatty trainers. He was only a few years older than Max and still had the gangly, boyish build and downy moustache of a teenager.

'Hi, you must be Max,' he said. 'Good to meet you at last. I'm Lucas Fisher. I saw your show today on the TV. Man, you were good. How the hell did you do that?'

Lucas backed away to let them enter. Chris closed the door and shot home the bolts at the top and bottom.

'How're you doing, Lucas?' he said. 'Let's see what you've got.'

They were in a long room running the full length of the building. At one end was a living area containing a bed, a table and a plastic chair. The bed was unmade, the floor beside it littered with discarded clothes, and on the table were several dirty plates, empty cans of lager and a stack of used take-away containers: Chinese, Indian, pizza – a lot of pizza boxes. The other end of the room was occupied by a desk and a computer terminal and printer. The place was stuffy and smelled of stale food and sweat.

Lucas walked over to the desk and sat down in front of the computer screen. His eyes were hollow and bloodshot. He looked as if he hadn't slept in days. 'Man, those were tricky files you gave me. Sorry it's taken me so long to crack them. They were just about the toughest codes I've ever had to deal with.'

Lucas Fisher was a computer specialist – a 'whizz-kid genius' was how Chris had described him to Max. He'd done work before for Zip and Rusty's security business, some of it legal, some of it decidedly illegal. For the past three weeks he'd been trying to break into the encrypted files that Max had brought back from Borneo on a memory stick – files that he'd copied from Julius Clark's computer.

'Take a look at this lot,' Lucas said. He clicked on an icon on the screen and pages of what looked like accounts appeared.

'What are they?' Chris asked.

'Hard to say,' Lucas replied. 'I've scanned through them. It's all gobbledegook to me. Company records, payments, sales figures, that kind of stuff. You'll need a financial expert to makes sense of them.'

'We can give them to Dan Kingston,' Max said. Kingston was a financial journalist on the *London News Chronicle* who had been helping Max in his fight against Julius Clark.

'You cracked them all?' Rusty asked.

Lucas shook his head. 'Just a few. But I thought you ought to see them straight away. I'm still working on the rest. This guy has got a hell of a security system. He must have a lot to hide.'

'He has,' Max said. 'Could you show us some more files?'

'Sure. But they're just as difficult to understand. For me, anyway, but then what do I know about money?'

He clicked on a couple more icons in turn. 'See, just meaningless numbers. This one too.' He clicked again. 'And this one. And this.'

He went quickly through the files he'd decrypted. Max caught the flash of numbers and columns of figures, then a glimpse of something else that triggered a response in his brain.

'Wait a second,' he said abruptly. 'Go back to that file.'

'Which one?' Lucas said.

'That one.' Max pointed to a file that was named EP01. It came up onto the screen.

'You understand any of that?' Lucas said.

Max was staring at a word at the top of the file – Episuderon, followed by a list of dates and what seemed to be invoices for payment.

'Episuderon?' Lucas said. 'Does that mean something to you?'

'It's a drug,' Max replied. He glanced at Consuela and Chris, who had moved closer to the computer to get a better look.

'A drug?' Lucas said with a frown. 'This guy's a drug dealer?'

'Not exactly,' Max said. He studied the words and figures on the screen, feeling a mounting sense of excitement. Episuderon – the drug Julius Clark had been using on Shadow Island to brainwash his opponents.

'What're we looking at here, Max?' Consuela asked.

'Orders and payments for Episuderon,' Max replied. 'Look at the dates. The last one is the end of June. That's *after* we destroyed Clark's laboratory on Shadow Island. He's still buying the stuff. Which means he's still using it, still brainwashing people.'

'But using it where?' Chris said.

Max touched the screen with his fingertip. 'You see the name and address of the supplier – Phobos Pharmaceuticals, Woodford Down Laboratories, Wiltshire. I think we should go there and check it out, don't you?'

Max went with Chris in the Nissan for the journey home. They knew there was no risk of them being followed this time, so Zip's expert driving wouldn't be needed. Max wanted to talk to Chris alone, discuss when they were going to head down to Wiltshire and what they would do when they got there. He was feeling exhilarated. This was the breakthrough they'd been waiting for. For the first time in three weeks he felt they were making progress, that they finally had a target to aim for.

Nearing home, they parked the car in a side street and walked the last quarter of a mile, scrambling over the garden wall and running across the lawn to the house. Chris unlocked the basement door and stepped inside. Max followed him, and was about to go past when Chris suddenly stuck out his arm to stop him.

'Wait a minute,' he said softly.

'What's the matter?'

Max could hear the warning note in Chris's voice, sense a tension in his body. He was staring at the keypad beside the door, the control panel for the alarm system.

'The alarm's off,' he said.

'The others must have got back before us,' Max said. 'They'll have turned it off upstairs.'

Chris had his head tilted to one side, listening hard. 'You hear anything?'

'No.'

'That's the problem. Wait here.'

'Chris—'

'Wait here.'

Chris padded quietly across the room and edged his

way cautiously up the stairs. His anxiety had infected Max now. The hairs on the back of his neck were prickling, his stomach beginning to tighten. He knew that something was wrong. He had an urge to follow Chris, to give him some support, but he made himself stay where he was. Chris could take care of himself, and do it better without Max tagging along behind.

Where were Consuela, Rusty and Zip? Not in the house, that was clear. The place was eerily silent. So why was the alarm off? Why was the house unprotected?

Then Max remembered the CCTV cameras. He darted across the basement, threw open the doors of the trick cabinet and switched on the monitor, rewinding the tapes from the three cameras. He checked the one in the hall first, fast-forwarding through the footage, one eye on the time code in the bottom corner of the screen. For a while there was nothing in the picture but an empty hall and a closed front door. Then the front door opened and a man came in. Max jabbed the 'play' button. The man was in his twenties, wearing a white T-shirt, jeans and, strangely for the summer, a pair of black leather gloves. He turned to the keypad immediately inside the door and swiftly levered off the front, taking another tool from the pouch around his waist and doing something with it on the keypad. Max couldn't see exactly what because the man's body was blocking the view, but he knew he was disabling the alarm.

'Chris!' Max yelled. '*Chris!*'

He kept watching the monitor. The man was moving away from the door now, heading down the hall. Max punched the button for the camera in the kitchen and fast-forwarded through the tape, searching for the right spot. There he was. Just entering the kitchen. The camera had a perfect shot of his face, his thin mouth and close-set, beady eyes. He seemed completely unaware that he was being caught on camera. He crossed the room and knelt down in front of the gas cooker. He pulled open the oven door and took an object out of his pouch. Max couldn't see clearly what it was, but he realized suddenly what the man was doing.

He spun round and raced across the basement and up the stairs. 'Chris! Chris, where are you?' he yelled. He burst into the kitchen, glancing across at the cooker, then sprinted down the hall. 'Chris!'

Chris leaned over the banisters on the first-floor landing. 'What is it?'

'We have to get out.'

'What's the—'

'Now!' Max was almost screaming. He gestured frantically with his arms. 'I've looked at the tapes. There was a man. We have to get out.'

Chris came hurtling down the stairs. 'What man?' he demanded urgently.

'In the kitchen. By the cooker.'

'The *cooker*? Jeez . . .'

Chris flung open the front door and tried to push Max through. But Max had thought of something, something important.

'The tapes . . .'

He dashed along the hall and back down the stairs into the basement. Chris came after him. The tape from the kitchen camera was still playing. Max ejected it and gripped it tight in his hand. Chris had the external door already open. He took Max's arm and hauled him out into the garden. Then they sped away across the lawn.

They were almost at the shrubbery when the bomb detonated. The force of the explosion knocked them off their feet, sent them tumbling into the bushes. Chris threw his arms around Max, shielding him with his body as debris flew out across the garden – bits of brick and mortar and plaster, all enveloped in a choking cloud of dust and smoke.

Max was winded by his fall, struggling to breathe. He whooped for air, then started coughing violently as he inhaled a mouthful of dust. Chris helped him to sit up.

'You all right?'

Max nodded, spitting out the dirt and wiping his

mouth with his hand. Then he looked back across the garden. For a moment he could see nothing but the thick cloud of dust, but then as it settled the house gradually began to emerge from the fog. The kitchen wall and part of the bedroom wall above it had gone completely. There was just a large, gaping hole in the house, a huge pile of bricks on the patio below and more scattered across the lawn.

Max took in the shattered remains of the kitchen – the fridge crushed like a tin can, the worktops and oven blown to smithereens, the ceiling obliterated, revealing the joists of the floor above. Flames were licking out through the opening, the fire spreading, feeding off the gas that must have been leaking from the broken pipe. The flames got bigger, fanned by the breeze until the back of the house was a raging inferno, clouds of smoke billowing out over the garden.

'We have to go. It's not safe here,' Chris said.

He picked up the tape that Max had dropped when he fell and slipped it away into his jacket pocket. Then he pulled Max to his feet. Their clothes were covered in dust, their faces smeared with dirt. Max's legs were shaking so much he could hardly walk. Chris helped him over the garden wall and down onto the street on the other side. Then he took out his mobile phone and punched in 999.

# FOUR

The fire brigade arrived first, three ordinary tenders and an engine with a long, extendable ladder that could reach the roof of the house. By then, Max and Chris had walked round the block to the front and sat down on a low wall seventy metres up the street. Chris had phoned Rusty to tell him what had happened and discovered that they were stuck in a traffic snarl-up caused by an accident near Bethnal Green. It would probably take them another fifteen minutes to get home.

The whole ground floor of the house was now ablaze, flames leaping from the windows, the sky thick with smoke. Max watched in a daze, feeling tired and numb all over. They'd got out just in time. A minute later and they'd have been caught in the explosion. The realization of just how close to death he'd been sent an icy shiver through him and he started to shake again, his whole body trembling, his insides suddenly freezing though it was a warm night.

Chris put his arm around him and pulled him close, trying to stop the spasms.

'What's the matter with me?' Max asked, his teeth chattering.

'You're in shock,' Chris replied. 'When the ambulance arrives, I'll get them to look at you.'

The firemen were swarming all over the street, connecting hoses to hydrants, getting the extendable ladder into position, making sure the neighbouring properties had been evacuated. Chris had already gone over and spoken to the officer in charge, told him that there was no one inside the burning house. He didn't want anyone risking their lives going in to look for the occupants.

It was a slick, practised operation, but even so it seemed to Max that it was an eternity before the firemen actually began to deal with the blaze, before the powerful jets of water were directed onto the flames, three hoses playing across the windows and roof, the fire sizzling, smoke belching from every orifice of the building.

*That's my home*, Max thought in deep anguish. *My family's home. Everything we own is in there. My parents' possessions, their furniture, my books, my music, all the equipment for my stage shows. The whole lot will have been destroyed.* He blinked away a tear and tried not to get upset. He and Chris were alive – that was all that mattered.

Three police cars had arrived shortly after the fire brigade. Uniformed officers had moved spectators away from the scene and cordoned off the area with blue and white tape. Now an ambulance was pulling in behind the police cars. A couple of paramedics got out and threw open the rear doors.

'Come on,' Chris said gently.

He pulled Max to his feet and led him over to the ambulance, giving the paramedics the story that they'd already agreed between them. Max had been alone in the house, but had fortunately just gone out into the garden when the explosion occurred. No mention of CCTV cameras or tapes, or the man planting the bomb in the cooker. No mention that Chris had also been present. Chris was a wanted man. At all costs, he had to stay out of the picture.

The paramedics made Max sit down in the back of the ambulance. They draped a blanket around his shoulders and probed him with questions. Did he feel any pain? Had he been injured or burned? Had any of the flying debris hit him? Then they cleaned the dirt off his face and examined the skin for cuts or bruises.

'How's your head?' one of the paramedics asked. 'Any aches?'

'No,' Max replied. He was feeling a bit better now. He wasn't so cold, his limbs were shaking less.

'I think you'll be all right,' the paramedic said. 'It's not clinical shock. No burns or blood loss. You've just had a pretty horrific experience. Take it easy for the next few hours, OK?' He frowned and peered more closely at him. 'Don't I recognize you? What's your name?'

'Max Cassidy.'

'I thought so. I saw you on the television, that Tower Bridge thing.' He glanced out of the ambulance at the burning house. 'My God, you'll never have a luckier escape than today.'

Max nodded in agreement. It had been a very close call. He wondered about the timing of the explosion. Why just then? He didn't believe the bomb had been planted simply to destroy the house. It had been put there to kill them. Which meant that whoever detonated it had known they were in the building. How? They must have been watching the garden and the rear of the house and seen them enter. That was disturbing. Max had thought the back way in was safe. Not that it mattered any more now. He wouldn't be going into the house any way for the foreseeable future. It would be uninhabitable for months.

He looked out through the doors. The fire seemed to be under control. The firemen were still hosing water over the house, but he could see no flames, just gusts of smoke and the gutted remains of his home behind them. He was stunned by how much damage had been done – maybe so much that the house would have to be demolished. The thought filled him with sadness. This was the only home he'd ever known. It wasn't just furniture and carpets the fire had incinerated, but a part of his life too. That made him angry. And the anger gave him energy, revived him.

He threw off the blanket, stood up and went to the doors of the ambulance.

'Hey, maybe you should rest a while longer,' one of the paramedics said.

'I'm OK now,' Max replied. 'Thanks for your help.'

He stepped down into the street. Chris was waiting for him, standing back a little from the ambulance where he wasn't so obvious. There were a lot of police officers around. They were preoccupied with the fire, but Chris still didn't want to draw any attention to himself.

'How are you, Max?' he asked.

'I'm fine.'

'You sure?'

'Yes.'

'The police are going to want to talk to you. You'll have to make a formal statement.'

'I know what to say.'

'If they come over, I'll have to disappear. But I won't

be far away. I'll be keeping an eye on you. You need me, just yell.'

At that moment, Max saw a police officer walking towards the ambulance and sensed Chris melting away into the crowd.

'You're Max Cassidy, aren't you?' the officer said, his eyes taking in the dust on Max's clothes. 'You were inside the house when the fire started?'

Max shook his head. 'I was in the garden.'

'Alone?'

'Yes.'

'What happened?'

'I don't know. There was some kind of explosion.'

The policeman took out his notebook. He studied Max with warm, sympathetic eyes. 'Have you been examined by a paramedic?'

'I'm OK.'

'Do you feel up to answering a few questions?'

'Yes.'

'Let's find somewhere more private. It's becoming a complete circus out here.'

He was only exaggerating slightly. In addition to the emergency services, the fire had attracted a large crowd of curious spectators – initially just the residents of the street, but their numbers had soon been swollen by people from the adjoining areas who had seen the smoke pluming up into the air, the flames lighting up the night sky. Press photographers and a television crew had followed, making the scene even more chaotic.

The policeman took Max to one of the police cars parked up the street and they sat in the front, Max answering the officer's questions as convincingly as he could without giving away what had really happened. When they'd finished, Max got back out of the car and walked away. He glanced along the street and stiffened. A black Mercedes, with tinted windows, was coming to a halt not ten metres away. The rear door opened and a plump, pink-faced man in a dark grey suit climbed out. He stared at the smouldering ruins of the house for a few seconds, then turned his head and saw Max. His face darkened, his mouth twisting into a grimace of distaste.

Max stared back at him. The last time he'd seen Rupert Penhall had been in Mount Pleasant lunatic asylum, where Penhall had imprisoned him, threatening to leave him there to rot if he didn't cooperate with him. Penhall was some kind of shadowy government official with close links to the security services and Julius Clark. He scared and intimidated Max, even more so now his house had been destroyed. He knew now without doubt that it must have been Penhall who had organized the bomb attack.

'Come home to a welcoming fire, eh, Max?' Penhall said with a sneer as he approached. 'You won't be going back in there for a long time. If ever.' He smiled gloatingly, as if the thought gave him great pleasure.

Max clenched his fists, his blood boiling. *Keep your cool*, he said to himself. *Don't let him see how upset you are.*

'Is that why you've come here?' he said. 'To enjoy watching my house burn? Did you hope I'd still be in there somewhere?'

'The gloves are off, Max. We mean serious business. But then, after your experiences in Borneo, you must have realized that by now.'

'You can't frighten me,' Max said, trying to keep his voice steady.

'Can't I?'

Penhall took another step towards him. Max held his ground. In one sense he was right: Penhall didn't scare him physically; he wasn't a big man and he was clearly overweight and unfit. But his power – the things he could make happen – was terrifying.

Penhall laughed. 'I don't like waging war on children, but you've left me no choice, Max. I gave you the chance to make peace once and you turned me down. Now you have to face the consequences of that decision.'

'So do you,' Max retorted. 'It works both ways. I'm

closing in on you and Julius Clark, and killing me will make no difference. There are others who know what you've been doing, who will continue the fight after I'm gone.'

'Others? You mean your friend Moncrieffe?' Penhall looked around the street. 'Where is he, by the way? Slunk away, leaving you to clear up the mess, I see. And what a mess it is. Where will you live now, Max? A hostel for the homeless? Are you going to start selling copies of the *Big Issue* on street corners?'

'You'll pay for what you did today,' Max said.

'Oh, *will* I?' Penhall fired back mockingly. 'And how will I do that?'

Max didn't reply.

Penhall's lip curled. 'You're all mouth, Max. A foolish little boy tilting at windmills. Incidentally, don't bother making allegations about bombs, because you'll just look like a crackpot. There'll be an investigation into this fire, of course. But the forensic evidence will show conclusively that it was caused by a leak from a faulty gas cooker.'

'How convenient,' Max said sourly. 'And the police and fire brigade are going to go along with that?'

'They'll do as they're told. Their political masters will make sure of that.'

Penhall turned and went back to the Mercedes, but

PAUL ADAM

paused before he got in, fixing Max with a chilling glare. 'You lead a charmed life at the moment, Max. I wonder how much longer you can keep it up.' He ducked into the back of the car and closed the door. The Mercedes reversed up the street, backed into an empty drive, then came out forward and purred away towards the main road.

Max watched it go. His legs had started shaking again and he felt slightly sick. He knew his life was in danger, but it was alarming to have it spelled out to him by a man who had both the power *and* the means to kill him.

He stumbled over to the wall of the nearest house and slumped down onto it, leaning forwards with his elbows on his knees and inhaling deeply to try to alleviate his feeling of nausea.

'Max! Max!'

He lifted his head and saw Consuela running along the pavement, Rusty and Zip following close behind. She came to a stop beside him, her eyes flickering across to the house.

'Oh, my God! It's a burned-out wreck! Max, are you all right?'

'I'm fine.'

'You're not hurt?'

'No.'

She sat down on the wall next to him and gave him a long, hard hug. Then she broke away and looked around, a sudden flash of panic crossing her face.

'Chris! Where's Chris?'

'Relax, I'm here,' a voice said behind them.

Consuela spun round and saw Chris just a few metres away. She stood up and threw her arms around him.

'I was just keeping out of the way of the police,' Chris explained.

Consuela glanced across at the house again. 'You were in there? And you survived? I don't believe it.'

'We got out just in time,' Max said.

He told her what had happened, from the moment he and Chris had come home to his confrontation with Rupert Penhall. Rusty and Zip moved in close to listen, automatically shielding Max and Consuela with their bodies.

At the end, Consuela gave a deep sigh and grasped Max's hands in her own. 'You're both safe, that's all that matters,' she said, her voice husky, tears in her eyes.

'But for how long?' Max said grimly.

'For as long as we're here,' Rusty said. 'No one's going to get near you while Zip and I are around.'

It was reassuring to hear, but Max knew it wasn't true. Rusty and Zip were terrific bodyguards, but even they couldn't protect him all the time. They hadn't protected him from the bomb. They probably couldn't shield him from an assassin's bullet. It was a cold, sobering thought.

'We have nowhere to live,' Consuela said despondently. 'Where do we go?'

Rusty and Zip exchanged glances.

'You can use my flat,' Rusty said. 'I don't live there much – I'm always away. We can go there now, if you're ready.'

Consuela nodded. 'Thank you. Just let me go and talk to the police and firemen for a minute. See how bad the damage is. There'll be paperwork to fill in, reports to make. I'll have to contact the insurance company.'

She walked away towards the cordoned-off area of the street. Max watched her talking to a senior police officer and a fireman. He wondered if there was anything salvageable left in the house, any of his belongings, perhaps some family photos. Maybe he'd be allowed into the ruins later to look around.

After ten minutes, Consuela returned and they walked away to the Audi parked at the far end of the street. Chris went off to fetch Consuela's Nissan, then followed them south towards the centre of London, Zip carrying out his usual evasive manoeuvres to shake off any tails before turning east. Twenty minutes later, they drove down into an underground car park beneath an apartment block in the Docklands and took the lift up to the fifth floor: a two-bedroom flat, minimally furnished and with the blank, sterile feel of a bachelor crash-pad – a place that was used only occasionally and that no one had bothered to make into a proper home.

Max sat down at the table in the living room. He was no longer feeling sick, but he had a hollow sensation in his stomach. He was thinking about his conversation with Penhall. The clear threat to his life had frightened him, but in some strange way it had also been a relief. Everything was out in the open now. Since his return to London from Borneo, Max had been continually on edge, waiting for another attack, wondering when it was going to come and what form it would take. Now it had finally happened and he had survived it, he was feeling less nervous. Penhall and Clark had shown their hands, shown what they were capable of, but had failed. That gave Max hope. They would try again, he knew that. He just had to keep one step ahead of them.

Chris put a hand on his shoulder. 'It's late, Max. You should get some rest. You and Consuela can have a bedroom each. The guys and I will sleep on the floor in here. You feeling OK?'

Max nodded. 'Just angry. Really angry. They've nearly

killed us, destroyed my home. Everything I possess was in that house.'

'They're only objects. They can be replaced.'

'Can they?' Max said doubtfully. They were more than just objects to him. Each one had had its own particular history, its own link with his life. Birthday presents from his mum and dad, Christmas gifts from Consuela, they all had something unique about them – they all encapsulated memories that were precious to him, memories that might now have been reduced to ashes. That was immensely distressing.

'You're alive,' Chris said. 'So am I. So are Consuela and Rusty and Zip. We could all have been inside the house when the bomb went off.'

Max looked at Chris, his anger firing him up, making him determined to get even. 'I want to hit back at them as soon as possible.'

'And you will.'

'Tomorrow. I want to go to that lab in Wiltshire tomorrow. Can we do that?'

'Yes, we can do that,' Chris said.

# FIVE

They went the following evening, after dark, just Max and Chris, leaving Rusty and Zip in the apartment guarding Consuela, who was also a potential target for their enemies. It was unlikely that anyone was on their tail, but Chris was taking nothing for granted. He drove away from the immediate area along the main road, then turned off into a housing estate and went slowly round the streets, watching his rear-view mirror all the time. Only when he was absolutely certain they weren't being followed did he go back out onto the main road and head west across London.

They took the M3 towards Southampton, branching off onto the A303 after Basingstoke. Max navigated, a road map open on his knees, a more detailed Ordnance Survey map of Wiltshire on the floor by his feet. They knew exactly where Phobos Pharmaceuticals was located – they'd looked up the address on the internet that morning. It was a few miles northeast of Salisbury, significantly, not all that far from Porton Down, the top-secret government chemical and biological warfare establishment where Max knew that Episuderon – a mind-altering drug originally invented by the Nazis – had been developed and tested by British scientists.

A couple of miles outside Andover, they turned off the A303 onto a smaller road and headed southwest across low, undulating countryside, passing through small villages whose streets were deserted at this time of night, the houses and shops in darkness. After twenty minutes, they entered a region that on Max's map was marked in bold red capitals: DANGER AREA. Chris had told him that indicated Ministry of Defence land – firing ranges and other facilities for the army who had a lot of bases in this part of the country. There were no villages here, only the occasional isolated farm. Walkers and other visitors were warned to keep away for their own safety.

'How far now?' Chris asked.

'Next left,' Max replied, checking the map in the dim light from the dashboard. 'Then it's about a mile after that.'

Chris slowed and turned off along a narrow country lane, with a hedge along one side, open downland on the other. There was no other traffic, no lights showing anywhere. They passed a low wire fence, a white board with some words written on it: MINISTRY OF DEFENCE PROPERTY. KEEP OUT. Max felt a prickle on the back of his neck. He didn't like this area. There was something creepy about it, something sinister.

They crested a rise in the road and suddenly, in the distance, they saw the glow of lights. A quarter of a mile ahead of them was a building beside the road: an ugly, single-storey, flat-roofed concrete box inside a fenced compound that was illuminated by floodlights.

'That must be it,' Max said.

He glanced sideways as they drove past the building, saw a sign reading PHOBOS PHARMACEUTICALS. WOODFORD DOWN LABORATORIES, a barrier across the entrance and a gatehouse beside it in which a uniformed security guard was sitting.

Chris didn't slow, just kept going for a further mile until they were out of sight of the building, then he turned off onto a rough track that ran through fields to a patch of woodland. He parked under the trees and cut the engine and headlights. They'd found this spot on the map before they left London, and worked out in advance how they were going to get near the Phobos Pharmaceuticals site.

'You ready?' Chris asked.

Max nodded.

'Let's take a closer look, then.'

They got out of the car and plunged into the woods. Chris was carrying a pair of heavy-duty bolt-cutters and a torch, Max had one of his professional lock-picks in the pocket of his jeans. They didn't use the torch – it would destroy their night vision and probably be visible from the Phobos laboratory. They didn't want anyone to see them approaching.

At the far side of the wood, they emerged onto open land, the terrain rough and uncultivated, covered with coarse grass, weeds and thickets of bramble and gorse. The lab was half a mile away, a shining beacon on the horizon. They walked in single file in silence, Chris leading the way. Max was nervous, uncertain of what they were going to find.

Fifty metres from the laboratory, Chris dropped to the ground and snaked forwards on his knees and elbows. Max did the same, drawing alongside him on the slope of a low mound overlooking the site. They peered cautiously over the top of the mound. Below them was a wide, deep ditch and, beyond that, the perimeter fence of the lab. Inside the fence was a tarmac yard about twenty metres wide, then the laboratory itself. Both the building and the yard were bathed in bright light.

Chris murmured an obscenity under his breath and slid back a little down the slope. 'I don't like the look of this,' he said softly.

'Why, what's the matter?' Max asked.

'Did you see the fence? Four metres high, steel mesh, razor wire along the top.'

'We've got the bolt-cutters. They'll cut through it, won't they?'

'They'll cut through it all right. That's not the problem. The problem is the thin alarm wire running through the fence about a metre or so above the ground. You notice it? I've seen them before. They're touch-sensitive. The moment we put any pressure on the fence, the wire will pick up the vibrations and set off an alarm.'

'Can't we cut through that too?'

Chris shook his head. 'Same problem. Cut the wire and the alarm will automatically go off.'

'So what're you saying? We can't get through the fence?'

'Not without being detected immediately. And even if we did get through, we'd be easily spotted. There are CCTV cameras all over the outside of the building, no doubt covering every inch of the yard.'

Max was silent for a moment. This was a depressing discovery, something they hadn't anticipated, but he wasn't going to let it defeat them. 'There must be another way in. What about the main gate? Could we get through there?'

'How?'

'I don't know. Could you drive up and talk to the guard, pretend you're lost and need directions? Keep him busy while I sneak through behind his back.'

'I can't see that working,' Chris said sceptically. 'And you'd still have to get across the yard without being picked up by the cameras.'

'We can't just give up,' Max said. 'We've come all this way.'

'We weren't expecting this: security guards, CCTV cameras, floodlights, alarm wires. It's better protected than we thought.'

'Let's check all round the site,' Max suggested. 'See if there are any weak spots.'

Chris gave a nod. 'OK. But keep low. The cameras seem to be covering the yard, but they might be sensitive enough to detect movement outside the fence too.'

They slithered over the mound and down into the ditch, which was deep enough to hide them from view, provided they didn't stand up. Slowly and carefully, they began to work their way around the perimeter of the lab, crawling some of it, doing the rest flat on their bellies. Max was glad it was summer and dry. After rain, the ditch would probably be swimming with water.

At intervals, they edged up the far side of the ditch to survey the compound. It was brilliantly lit all the way round – no dark spots where the floodlights failed to penetrate – with CCTV cameras on every side. The fence, too, didn't change – same height, same razor wire on the top, same alarm filament running through the mesh.

On reaching the rear of the site, there was a brief glimmer of hope when they saw the opening of a land drain in the side of the ditch, a pipe coming out from under the fence. Chris switched on his torch, shielding the beam with his hand, and shone it into the opening. But it was hopeless. The pipe inside was barely thirty centimetres in diameter. Even Max, lithe and whippy though he was, couldn't have squeezed through it.

Twenty minutes later, they'd looped round to the other side of the compound, to within ten metres of the entrance. They had a good view of the security guard in the gatehouse. He was in his twenties, his hair cropped close to the scalp, and was wearing a dark blue uniform with a white logo above the left breast pocket. He was sitting at a desk, reading the newspaper. As they watched, he stood up and stretched, taking a couple of paces around the cramped little cubicle. Max sensed Chris stiffen next to him and turned his head.

'What's up?'

'The guard,' Chris whispered. 'You see his belt, the holster? He's carrying a side arm.'

'A gun, you mean?'

'Let's get back to the car.' Chris twisted round and began to crawl back the way they'd come.

Max went after him, trying to get him to stop. 'Chris . . . what's the matter? Chris . . .'

Chris came to a halt and waited for Max to catch up.

'What's the rush?' Max said. 'What's happened?'

'I didn't like this place the moment I saw the fence, the cameras,' Chris replied. 'I like it even less now I've seen the guard.'

'He's just an ordinary security guard, isn't he?'

'Ordinary security guards don't carry weapons. They carry torches and phones, but not guns. But then this isn't an ordinary laboratory.'

'What do you mean?'

'It looks like a private business on the surface. With the name, Phobos Pharmaceuticals, it could be just a small drugs company, making a few products to sell over the counter in chemist's shops. But companies like that don't employ armed guards – it's against the law. Only military personnel and certain police officers are allowed to carry guns in this country, Max. This is a government laboratory and that guy over there isn't a private security guard, he's a soldier.'

'A soldier? Are you sure?'

'I've seen a few in my time. Look at his haircut. You

think a civilian would pay for a haircut as bad as that?'

'What're you saying? The British government is making Episuderon here?'

'That's how it looks to me. And there's no way we're going to get inside. We're not even going to try. Not unless we want to get shot. 'Chris crawled away along the ditch.

Max hurried after him. 'Chris . . . wait a second. Just stop, will you?'

Chris paused.

'Let's think for a moment,' Max said. 'There must be a way to get inside.'

'I'm sorry, Max, there isn't. We can't get through the fence, we can't get under it. We can't get past the guard, or the CCTV cameras. That doesn't leave many other options.'

Max gazed away through the darkness. Not at the laboratory, but at something out on the downland, something he'd noticed as they circumnavigated the site. 'We can't go through the fence, or under it,' he said thoughtfully. 'But what about over it?'

'Over it?' Chris said. 'I've already told you, it's got a touch-sensitive alarm wire. You lay a finger on it and bells will start ringing.'

'Over it, but without touching it.'

Chris stared at him. 'What're you talking about? The

fence is four metres high. Are you going to fly over it?'

'Something like that.'

Chris kept staring at him. He knew Max well by now. He knew how ingenious, how determined he was. It never paid to dismiss his ideas out of hand. 'Go on,' he said quietly.

Max gestured at the open countryside behind the laboratory compound. 'You see out there? The pylon?'

Chris turned to look. Silhouetted against the horizon, about sixty or seventy metres away, was the skeletal outline of a tall electricity pylon. From one of the arms of the metal tower a cable ran across to a transformer on the roof of the Phobos Pharmaceuticals building.

'I see it,' he said.

'That cable. It's three or four metres above the fence, and also out of sight of the CCTV cameras. They're all angled down to cover the yard. They can't see anything above the roof of the lab.'

'Max, you're not proposing to somehow use that cable, are you?'

'It's an idea.'

'It's a high-voltage power line. You'd kill yourself if you even touched it.'

'Only if I was earthed,' Max said.

'*What?*'

'We did it in science lessons at school. It's the electricity running to earth that kills you. If I climb the pylon and put my hand on the cable, you're right, I'd be killed instantly. But if I hang onto the cable with my body dangling in space, I'll be OK. That's why birds can sit on electricity wires. The current goes past them, but it doesn't fry them because they're not earthed.'

'You're crazy. Come on, let's get back to the car.'

Max didn't move.

'Max . . .'

'You go. I'm not coming with you,' Max said.

'Look, this is stupid,' Chris said. 'You're not going near that cable.'

'Yes, I am. They're making Episuderon in that lab – the drug Julius Clark gave my dad. It brainwashes people, kills them sometimes. I need to know what Clark is doing with the Episuderon, where it's going.'

'It's a suicidal idea. I can't possibly allow you to do it. It's way too risky.'

'I take risks all the time in my show. The key is knowing which risks are controllable, and which aren't. Knowing how to eliminate the real dangers so that what's left is manageable.'

'No, Max,' Chris said firmly. 'I'm not even going to discuss this further.'

'OK, see you later.'

'You're coming with me.'

'No, I'm not.'

'You want me to pick you up and throw you into the car?'

'I'd like to see you try.'

Stalemate. There was a silence. Chris glared hard at Max. Max glared back, not flinching, stubborn as could be.

'Let me get this straight,' Chris said eventually, knowing that he'd lost the argument simply by continuing the discussion. 'You're going to hang off the cable and go hand over hand along it until you reach the roof of the lab? It's – what – a hundred metres long? You'd fall off well before you got to the end.'

'I'm not going hand over hand,' Max replied. 'Look at the angle of the cable. It slopes down to the roof. I'm just going to slide down it. I'll need to borrow your leather jacket.'

'For what?'

'Insulation.'

Chris looked across at the pylon again, then back at Max. 'You think it'll work?'

'Yes,' Max said confidently.

'Then *I'll* do it.'

'You're too heavy. The cable would break under your weight. It has to be me.'

Chris shook his head. 'I can't let you do it. You're just a kid.'

'I'm not "just a kid," Max snapped back angrily. 'I'm a professional escapologist. I can *do* it, Chris, trust me.'

'I'm here to look after you, Max. What if something happened to you? I'd never forgive myself.'

'I know you're only thinking about my safety and I appreciate that. But I'm going ahead anyway. You don't have to stay. I'll make my own way home.'

Chris sighed. He knew he'd been outmanoeuvred. He didn't want a fight. Despite his earlier threat, he had no intention of trying to use force to drag Max back to the car. He couldn't do that to him, and it probably wouldn't work, in any case. Max was a strong, determined teenager. Overpowering him wouldn't be easy, certainly not without hurting him – and the last thing Chris wanted was to hurt him. He had no choice really. He had to help him.

'We're wasting time,' Max said. 'What do you say?'

'You're the craziest, most pig-headed person I've ever come across. If you kill yourself, don't blame me.' Chris slipped off his leather jacket and tossed it to Max. 'So let's do it before I change my mind.'

They scrambled out of the ditch and ran across to the pylon. It towered over them like a six-armed, fleshless metal giant. Max tied the leather jacket around his waist, his pulse racing. Going in without Chris hadn't been part of their plan, but there was no alternative now.

'I'll call you on my mobile when I get inside.'

'You take care, Max,' Chris said, his anxiety clear from both his face and voice.

'I will.'

'Here, you'll need this.' Chris held out the torch and Max stowed it safely away in his jacket pocket.

There was a large metal sign fastened to the base of the pylon. DANGER. HIGH VOLTAGE. KEEP OFF, it read. Max glanced at it and immediately put the warning out of his head. If he gave too much thought to what he was about to do, he knew he'd never go ahead. Chris was right: this was a crazy plan, though not suicidal. Max wasn't stupid enough to do anything that would result in certain death, but he had a more reckless approach to danger than most people. He was used to assessing risk, weighing up hazards. The plan was a gamble. There was a chance that he would kill or seriously injure himself. But there was also a chance that he would get inside the lab and find out something that would help in his search for his missing father. On balance, Max decided that success was more likely than failure. It was a hazardous undertaking, but the potential benefits outweighed the risks.

There was no ladder up the pylon, but the framework of steel girders and cross-struts was as good as one to someone as agile as Max. He climbed from one strut to the next, reaching up with his hands, then swinging his legs up behind him until he reached the lowest pair of the pylon's six arms. This was as high as he needed to go. The cable supplying electricity to the Phobos Pharmaceuticals laboratory branched off the main power line at this point. Max looked down. He could just see the shadowy figure of Chris twenty metres below him, his upturned face paler than the rest of his body, his expression impossible to make out in the darkness.

Max turned his gaze to the lab, a hundred metres or so away across the rough countryside. The power cable from the pylon sloped down at a fairly gentle angle, swooping over the perimeter fence and yard to the transformer on the flat roof of the building. It reminded him of the zip wire he'd gone down a few times during a school trip to an outdoor pursuits centre in Year Eight, the main difference being that this particular wire had thousands of volts of electricity pulsing through it.

He untied the leather jacket from his waist and, gripping it in his right hand, edged slowly out along a horizontal girder, his left hand hanging on tight to the cross strut by his shoulder. Nearing the end of the girder, he stopped. The power cable was a metre and a half above him. Max could hear a low hum, feel the electric field radiating out around him, making his skin tingle, his hair prickle.

He had to be very careful indeed here. He was still touching the pylon. If he got too close to the cable and accidentally completed the electric circuit to the earth, he was toast – literally. His whole body would be incinerated, burned to a blackened crisp. He hooked his left arm around the cross strut to secure his position and manipulated the leather jacket so that he was holding it by the end of one sleeve, the rest of it dangling down into space. Then he started to swing the jacket to and fro in an arc, gradually building up momentum before whipping it up in a circle over his head and letting go. The jacket flew through the air and hooked over the cable, the sleeves hanging down on either side. It slid a few centimetres down the wire, then stopped. Max heaved a sigh of relief. The jacket was just where he wanted it.

Now for the really dangerous bit. One slip and he would either plummet to his death, or electrocute himself. He didn't dwell on the thought, but adjusted his feet on the girder, shuffling out to the very end. There was nothing between him and the ground now. He didn't look down. The leather jacket was diagonally above him, the sleeves dangling half a metre away, almost level with the top of his head.

Max said a silent prayer, took a deep breath and threw himself outwards and upwards, bending his knees and lifting his feet to make absolutely sure he was clear of the pylon before his hands touched the jacket. His fingers found the sleeves and he snapped them shut around the leather, gripping tight as the jacket began to glide away down the cable. He swung his legs and felt the momentum increase, the jacket sliding easily over the smooth metal wire, getting faster and faster, hurtling down towards the ground at a terrifying speed.

It might have been fun, if the stakes hadn't been so high, the penalty for failure so potentially fatal. The wind gusted into his face, clawing at his hair, stinging his cheeks like sharp needles. He screwed his eyes shut to protect them and counted the seconds, estimating how much further he had to go. He snatched a quick glance down. He was whizzing high over the ditch around the compound, then he was over the fence and speeding across the yard, the ground just a blur beneath him. The building rushed up to meet him and he let go of the jacket instinctively, dropping three metres and rolling over as he hit the flat concrete surface of the roof.

Winded, and bruised, he lay on his side for a few seconds until he could regain his breath, listening hard throughout for any sound of an alarm, any indication that his arrival had been spotted. But he heard nothing.

He pulled himself up into a crouch and looked around, panting a little, rubbing his hip where it had struck the roof. The transformer was right in front of his nose – a big metal box with coils and wires on the top, an on-off lever on the side and a protective cage all around it. Chris's leather jacket was still dangling from the power line. Max left it where it was – it was too dangerous to risk touching it. He stood up and padded across to the raised stairwell behind the transformer. The access door was locked, but Max took out his L-shaped pick and had it open in a few seconds. He listened again for any sound of an alarm, but the building was silent. Pulling out his mobile, he punched in the preset number for Chris's phone.

'I'm going inside,' he said softly when Chris answered.

Then he put the phone away in his pocket and went cautiously down the stairs.

# SIX

The inside of the building was in darkness, but there was enough light coming in from outside for Max to see what he was doing. At the foot of the stairs was a long corridor, with doors along one side and windows on the other looking out over the floodlit yard. He paused in the shadows, studying the corridor carefully. He could see no CCTV cameras, no light trickling out beneath the doors. It was the middle of the night, but it was always possible that someone might be working – someone apart from the security guards, that is.

How many guards were there? Max had seen only the one in the gatehouse, but he knew that there had to be more. This was a high-security site. It had the fence and the cameras to protect its exterior, but there'd surely be guards inside the premises too. Where were they? he wondered. Patrolling the building? Making regular rounds of all the corridors and rooms? He had to be vigilant, listen out for any signs of activity.

He had no idea of the layout of the place. There'd be laboratories and other facilities for the production of

Episuderon and maybe other drugs too, but none of that interested Max. He wanted to know where the Episuderon was going after it left the site. And that meant he needed to find the management offices. To find the company records – invoices, billing addresses, shipping details, that kind of thing.

He moved off along the corridor, hugging the wall to keep away from the windows. If the yard outside was also patrolled by guards – and he was sure it would be – he didn't want to be caught unawares. He stopped by the first door. It was solid wood – no sign on it to indicate what the room beyond contained. He tried the handle. The door was locked. Taking the pick from his pocket, he crouched down and went to work, slipping the implement into the keyhole and clicking back the tumblers one by one.

It wasn't a difficult lock. Ten seconds later and he was easing open the door and slipping inside. He was in some kind of laboratory – a small, rectangular room with steel-topped benches in the middle and bits of scientific apparatus on worktops around the edges. The far wall was mostly glass, a series of windows over-looking a courtyard in the centre of the building. It was dimmer here than in the corridor, but the compound flood-lamps were so powerful that some of their diffused light spread out across the roof and down into the courtyard. Max saw paving stones, a few shrubs and more windows on the other side, with what looked like offices behind them. He could just make out filing cabinets, desks with computer terminals on top of them. That was where he needed to be.

He went back out into the corridor and retraced his steps, going past the bottom of the staircase to the roof and continuing on to where the corridor made a ninety-degree turn to the left. He put an eye out warily round the corner. The corridor was deserted. He ran lightly along it, his trainers making hardly any noise on the lino floor, and rounded another corner at the far end. There were doors on both sides here, white plastic signs screwed to the wood: CLEANING STORE, MEDICAL ROOM, CHIEF SCIENTIFIC OFFICER, LABORATORY ADMINISTRATOR. Max went slowly along the corridor and stopped by a door marked 'Sales Manager'. He unlocked it with his pick and pushed it open.

The office inside was small and cramped – just a few metres square and crowded with furniture: a desk, a chair, a cupboard and a row of five tall, grey filing cabinets. Max used his pick to unlock the first cabinet and pulled out a few files at random, to see how the filing system worked. He opened the cardboard folders on the desk and took the torch from his pocket, cupping his hand around the end to narrow the beam and stop the light spreading too far. The files were arranged in alphabetical order according to the names of the customers, each one containing details of the drugs ordered, how and when they were supplied and when payment was made. It was clear that Phobos Pharmaceuticals manufactured a range of different drugs. Max studied the names, but found no mention of Episuderon.

He put the files back in the first cabinet and turned his attention to the last one in the row. Julius Clark was rumoured to own dozens, perhaps hundreds, of companies around the world, but his main corporation was called Rescomin International. Max searched through the 'R' section of the cabinet. There was no file for Rescomin.

Puzzled and frustrated, he sat down in the swivel chair behind the desk to think for a moment. Clark must be buying the Episuderon through one of his other companies. That complicated matters. Max didn't know the names of any of those companies and without a name he had only one course of action open to him. He would have to go through every file in the office and hope he found a customer who'd bought Episuderon. Would there be more than one? Max knew that Julius Clark was buying it, but it was possible there were other customers too.

He gazed at the filing cabinets. It would take him hours to go through every folder – and he didn't have hours. If a security guard walked around the building and happened to glance up, he was bound to see Chris's leather jacket draped over the power line and raise the alarm. Max couldn't afford to linger. He had to complete his task and get out fast.

His eyes strayed across to the cupboard in the corner of the office. It was made of metal, and something about its lock suddenly drew Max's attention. He got up from the chair and went to take a closer look. He knew a lot about locks: he'd spent years studying them, practising how to pick them. The filing cabinet locks were cheap, basic models. A beginner could probably manage to open them with little more than a paper clip. But this cupboard was different. Its lock was big and heavy, the kind of lock Max would have expected to find on a safe or a strongbox. Interesting. Why put a lock like that on an office cupboard? Unless you had something important, or valuable to protect.

Kneeling down on the floor, he slipped his pick into the keyhole of the cupboard. It was a tricky job, and he had to borrow a thin, metal paper knife from the desk to help him manipulate the tumblers, but in a little under three minutes he had the lock open.

There were various files on the shelves inside

the cupboard, one of them labelled RESCOMIN INTERNATIONAL. Max took the file to the desk and examined it in the light of his torch. The papers went back three years, documenting – Max counted them all – thirty-three separate purchases of Episuderon. He felt a surge of excitement. He'd found what he was looking for. On each occasion, the order was the same – three hundred five-millilitre ampoules of the drug – but the price had gone up over the course of the three years. Max stared at the figures on the invoices, wondering if the decimal points were in the wrong place. But there was no mistake. The last consignment, dated just a week earlier, had cost Rescomin a cool hundred thousand pounds. That was one very expensive drug.

The ampoules had all been despatched by air, using a freight service at Heathrow Airport, and sent to San Francisco. Max memorized the address: *Rescomin Tower, Eldorado Plaza, California Street, San Francisco, USA*, and photographed the invoices with his phone. Then he replaced the file, closed and locked the cupboard and went to the door. He peered out cautiously. The corridor was dark and deserted. Max stepped out and began to walk quickly back the way he'd come.

He'd gone only ten metres when the overhead lights suddenly snapped on. He stopped dead in surprise. A security guard was standing at the end of the corridor, his arms stretched out in front of him, both hands together. Max realized with a jolt of alarm that the man was pointing a pistol straight at him. He looked around, wondering recklessly whether he could make a run for it, but a second guard was advancing towards him from the opposite end of the corridor. He, too, was aiming a pistol at him.

'Lie down on the floor and put your hands behind you,' the first guard ordered.

Max did as he was told. His mouth had gone dry, his heart palpitating. He heard the guards' footsteps drawing nearer, the rattle of something metallic. Then he felt the steel cuffs being clipped round his wrists, hands grasping him by the arms and hauling him roughly to his feet.

He was escorted round to the front of the building, across the wide entrance foyer and into a small room behind the main reception desk that seemed to be part guard room, part office, part kitchen. In the centre there was a battered metal desk with a solid front, and a sink and cooker against one wall. Next to the sink were a frying pan and a couple of dirty plates smeared with tomato ketchup. On a shelf above was an open plastic bag from which sesame seed burger buns were spilling.

The guards must have been cooking themselves a meal. The place reeked of fried onions and meat.

But what shocked Max was the bank of three television screens on the wall, showing CCTV pictures from around the site, the images changing every few seconds according to which camera was recording. Max saw a picture of the internal corridor he'd walked along and cursed himself for his stupidity. The cameras must have been cunningly hidden for him not to have noticed them. He realized that the guards had probably been watching him from the moment he'd entered the building, no doubt waiting to see what he was up to before they moved in to seize him. Did they know about Chris? Had they caught him too?

The two men led him to a metal chair behind the desk and forced him to sit down. His hands were released, but only to bring them round to the front where they were manacled to the arms of the chair with two pairs of cuffs. One of the guards searched his clothes, finding his mobile and torch, but not his lock-pick, which he'd managed to slip out of his pocket and up the sleeve of his shirt while he was lowering himself to the floor in the corridor.

The guards were both young men, in their early twenties, with the same military-style haircuts as the guard at the main entrance – the crude crop-cuts that seemed to take away the individual characteristics of their faces so that they looked almost identical. One of them gazed coolly at Max. He had pale blue eyes and the stubble on his scalp had a gingery tint to it.

'What's your name?' he demanded curtly.

Max toyed with the idea of saying nothing, but decided to put on a show of cooperation instead. These men were armed. He didn't want to antagonize them. 'Jack Singleton,' he replied, giving the name of one of his classmates at school.

Would they recognize him? he wondered. His Tower Bridge stunt had been shown on national television and his photo had been in all the papers, but he knew that to adults a lot of teenagers looked alike. Why would they link a kid caught breaking into a pharmaceuticals lab in Wiltshire with an escapologist in London?

'How old are you?' the second guard asked.

'Fourteen.'

'Where d'you live?'

'Salisbury,' Max said glibly.

'Where in Salisbury?'

Max made up an address. 'Twenty-four London Road.'

That sounded plausible. There was a London Road in half the towns of England and he could tell from their accents that neither of these two young men was local.

They probably wouldn't know much about street names in Salisbury.

'This is private property. What're you doing here?' the first guard said.

'Just taking a look around.'

'A look around? For what? To steal something?'

'I haven't stolen anything. You can see that. You searched me.'

The two guards exchanged glances.

'Maybe he's a junkie looking for drugs,' the first one said. 'We've had them before.'

'He doesn't look like a junkie.'

They turned back to Max.

'How did you get in?'

'There was a hole in the fence,' Max replied without hesitation.

'Yeah? Where?'

'At the back, over there.' Max inclined his head. 'I haven't done anything. I haven't damaged anything, or stolen anything. I was just curious to see what this place was, that's all.'

They didn't believe him, Max knew that. He didn't expect them to. He was buying time, sowing a few seeds of confusion in their minds so they weren't sure what to make of him. And he was succeeding. He could see the bemusement in their faces. They were very young soldiers, probably only privates, he guessed, and he wanted them to do what all junior soldiers did in circumstances like this – go away and contact their superior officer for instructions. If he could get them out of the room for a few minutes, he had a chance – a slim chance – of escaping.

The two men glanced at each other again. Then the one with gingery hair nodded at the door.

'Let's go outside.'

They went out of the room, locking the door behind them. Max didn't wait for even a second. He bent forward and got his teeth on the cuff of his right sleeve, pulling back the jacket and shirt to expose the lock-pick he'd secreted there. He didn't have much time, but he had to stay calm, try to control his nerves. He'd been lucky. Maybe the guards hadn't seen him picking the locks on the two internal doors on the CCTV monitors. If they had, they would surely have wondered how he'd done it and searched him more thoroughly. Or maybe they just weren't thinking too clearly, or weren't too bright.

He gripped the pick between his teeth and inserted the end into the lock on the cuff around his right wrist. It wasn't the first time he'd used his teeth to manipulate a pick. One of his regular stage tricks required the skill, so he had had plenty of practice. Nevertheless, it wasn't easy, particularly when time was against him.

How long did he have? The guards would be discussing what to do next, ringing someone with greater
authority for orders. But who would they ring? Who
was ultimately in charge of this laboratory, and what
would they decide to do with him? Hand him over to
the local police to deal with? That was the best-case
scenario from Max's point of view. And the worst case?
If word somehow got back to Max's enemies in the
British government and through them to Julius Clark,
he was in big trouble. A teenage boy found inside the
Episuderon laboratory. Clark would know immediately
that it was Max. Then it wouldn't be the police for him,
but a bullet in the head and an unmarked grave in some
faraway wood.

He felt the tip of the pick catch on the tumbler inside
the lock and pulled back hard with his teeth. The cuff
clicked open. Extricating his hand, he took the pick
from his teeth and attacked the cuff around his left
wrist. That was more straightforward now he could use
his fingers. It took him less than five seconds to get the
cuff off. Both pairs of manacles were now dangling
loose from the arms of the chair.

Max grabbed his torch and phone from the desk and
stuffed them back in his pockets. He went to the door
and put his eye to the keyhole. He could just see the two

men outside in the foyer, hear them talking quietly to each other. There was no way out here, but there were two more doors in the room. The first, on the left wall, he discovered, was unlocked but gave access only to a store cupboard. The second, on the opposite wall, was locked. Max opened it with his pick and stepped through.

The first thing he noticed was the smell. Not the acrid odour of fried food that permeated the guard room, but something riper and more pungent – more animal, Max thought. Then he heard a rustle of feet and froze. He snapped on his torch and directed it around the room. He was in a long, narrow laboratory crammed full of stainless steel benches. On top of the benches were cages containing animals – mice, rats, rabbits, guinea pigs. They fidgeted nervously as the torch beam hit them, their eyes glowing brightly in the light.

Max moved deeper into the room. There must have been hundreds of animals there, all presumably used for testing drugs. It was disconcerting, hearing the frightened creatures shuffling around their cages, hiding in corners or in their bedding, all the while that sour, animal stench getting stronger.

Max shut out the sounds and smell and concentrated on exploring the lab. There were no windows, not even any skylights, and only two doors – the one he'd come through and a second a few metres away on the side wall that Max knew, from its position, would open onto the foyer. Could he get out that way? Not a chance. He'd never manage to creep unseen past the two security men. He could hear them faintly through the door. One of them was on the phone, talking to someone more senior now. Max could tell from the deferential tone of his voice, the 'Yes, sir, no, sir' he kept repeating.

He was running out of time. He was free of his handcuffs, but what use was that if he was trapped in these two rooms? Could he fight the guards, somehow overpower them and make his escape? That was just wishful thinking. Max was young and strong, but not strong enough to deal with two trained soldiers. What about releasing the animals, causing a diversion to distract the guards so he could slip away? He liked the idea, but couldn't see it working, couldn't see a way around his fundamental problem – how did he get into the foyer and then out of the building without being caught again?

His torch beam passed over a plump black and white guinea pig and alighted on a big metal cylinder which had N2O stencilled on the side. N2O? Some faint, deep-seated memory from his science lessons began to stir in his head. This was the second time that night he'd remembered something from science classes. Maybe school wasn't such a waste of time, after all. He knew that chemical formula. It was nitrous oxide – laughing gas – an anaesthetic used in medicine and no doubt used here to knock out the animals for experiments. An anaesthetic? He couldn't use force to beat the guards, but maybe he could use his brains.

Lifting the cylinder up – it was so heavy he had to wrap his arms around it and brace it against his chest – he went back into the guard room and lowered it to the floor under the desk where it couldn't be seen from the front. Then he quickly closed the lab door and sat back down in the chair, slipping his wrists into the open handcuffs so that it appeared as if he was still firmly manacled to the arms.

He was only just in time. Just a few seconds later, the security men returned, closing the door behind them. Under the desk, Max used his feet to turn the valve on the cylinder, twisting it round until it was fully open. Then he inhaled deeply, filling his lungs, and held his breath.

'You're in big trouble,' the first soldier said. 'We've done some checking. There's no Singleton family living at number twenty-four London Road, Salisbury. What do you have to say about that?'

Max said nothing. He could feel the nitrous oxide seeping out into the room, drifting up past his face, and was relieved that it made no sound. The valve on the cylinder was so wide open that the gas was escaping without any tell-tale hissing noise. Would the security men smell it? Nitrous oxide wasn't odourless – Max, like most of his class, had tried a sniff of it during science lessons – but nor did it have a strong scent. Max was banking on the overpowering reek of fried onions and burgers to cover the presence of the gas.

'You lost your tongue?' the guard snapped. 'You're lying to us. You're not called Jack Singleton. What's your real name?'

Max didn't reply. He was counting the seconds. How long did it take for nitrous oxide to work? Half a minute? A minute? The security men were so far showing no signs of succumbing to it.

'Let me give you a bit of advice, kid,' the guard said. 'Our boss is on his way here to see you and, believe me, he's not going to be anything like as nice as us.'

He paused, wrinkling his nose and blinking. *It's working*, Max thought. *He's breathing the gas in, but doesn't realize it.*

'He's going to want some answers from you,' the guard went on. 'And he won't care how he gets them. You understand me? You're a burglar, a criminal. You've committed a serious offence. Now what's your real name?' The man glanced across at his colleague, who was looking pale and slightly unsteady on his feet. 'You OK?'

'I think so.' The second soldier sat down heavily on the corner of the desk. He seemed to be having difficulty breathing.

'You sure?'

'I don't know. I feel funny. A bit sick.'

He took a couple of deep breaths, but that seemed to make him worse. Max watched him intently. Two minutes had passed. He was starting to feel uncomfortable himself now. He couldn't hold his breath for much longer.

'Sick?' the first guard said. 'I know what—' He broke off and started to sway from side to side, as if he were feeling dizzy.

*Just hold on*, Max said to himself. *Just a few seconds longer.*

'The room . . .' the second guard said. 'You feel it going round and round? What the—'

His eyes rolled up into their sockets and he suddenly toppled over sideways and fell to the floor with a crash. A few moments later, his colleague also collapsed, tumbling over unconscious in a heap by the desk.

Max whipped his hands out of the cuffs and bent down to shut off the valve on the cylinder. His lungs were bursting, his chest in agony. He ran to the door and flung it open, throwing himself out into the foyer and sucking in great gasping mouthfuls of air.

He was still panting when he made himself get moving. He didn't know how long the guards would remain unconscious, but it might only be a matter of minutes. He ran across the foyer and along the corridor, taking out his mobile and speed dialling Chris's number.

'Max?' Chris said anxiously. 'Where are you?'

'I'm coming out the back way,' Max replied. 'Can you cut a hole in the fence?'

'What about the alarm?'

'Wait for the power to go off.'

Max reached the stairs and ran up them two at a time, bursting out onto the roof. The cage surrounding the electricity transformer was fastened shut with a padlock, but he had no trouble undoing it with his pick. He depressed the shutdown lever that he'd noticed earlier and all the compound floodlights cut out abruptly.

Max went to the edge of the roof and lowered himself over the side, hanging by his arms and dropping nimbly to the ground. He didn't care about the CCTV cameras or alarms now – they couldn't function without electricity.

He sprinted across the yard and saw Chris waving to

him from outside the perimeter fence. He'd already cut a metre-square hole in the wire mesh with his bolt-cutters. Max scrambled through.

'You OK?' Chris asked. Max nodded. 'What happened? You find anything?'

'Not now,' Max said urgently. 'I knocked the guards out. They might be waking up.'

Chris gaped at him. '*Knocked them out?*'

'I'll tell you later.'

Max slithered down into the ditch, clambered up the other side and raced away across the downland. Chris ran after him. It was a good mile to the car over difficult terrain, but they did it in under ten minutes. Three minutes after that they'd negotiated the farm track and were back out on the main road, speeding away from the laboratories.

They were entering the outskirts of Salisbury, almost no other vehicles on the road, when they heard the sound of sirens coming towards them. Chris reacted with lightning speed, braking hard and veering off into the driveway outside the nearest house.

'Get down!' he ordered.

Max doubled up and ducked down, snatching a quick look through the side window to see two police cars hurtling past, their roof-lights flashing, sirens blaring.

They waited a while, to make sure no other police cars appeared, then reversed back out of the drive and headed away along the road.

Chris glanced at Max. 'OK, let's hear what you have to say. I get the feeling it's going to be good.'

# SEVEN

Dawn was breaking when they got back to London. They left the car in the underground car park and went up to the apartment. Rusty was waiting for them – Max had called him on his mobile as they drove up from Wiltshire to let him know they were on their way. Consuela was still in bed, Zip curled up in a sleeping bag on the living-room floor. Rusty made coffee for Chris and himself while Max had an early breakfast of toast and marmalade, then went into his bedroom.

He was worn out, but tense. The two-hour drive home had relaxed him a little, taken his mind off what had happened at Woodford Down, but now he was alone in his room, vivid memories of the previous few hours returned to disturb him. He saw himself climbing the pylon again, whizzing down the power line and wondered what madness had possessed him, driven him to take such a foolhardy risk. He knew the answer to that, of course – the search for his missing father. And the risk had been worth it in the end. He'd found out where the Episuderon was going. He wrote down the address on a piece of paper before he got into bed and gazed at it for a moment.

San Francisco. Dr Halstead, the man who'd helped his father in Borneo, was also in San Francisco. Was that a coincidence? Max didn't think so. Nothing in all the traumatic events of the past few months was co-incidental. Everything was linked, everything had a reason, a logical explanation. Max just had to join those links together and he'd find his father.

He struggled to get to sleep. Woodford Down kept preying on his mind. He still couldn't believe he'd been so stupid as to miss the CCTV cameras. His image had now been captured on tape, so it wouldn't take very much investigation for him to be identified. A couple of phone calls, his picture sent round the right govern-ment circles and Rupert Penhall would quickly get to hear about it. Even without Penhall's intervention, Max knew he'd be identified sooner rather than later. He'd been on television only recently – his face was familiar to a lot of people. How long would it be, he wondered, before the police – or the security services – came knocking on his door?

In time, he drifted off and slept heavily until noon. When he got up and went out into the living room he found Consuela and the three men having lunch. Chris had obviously told them all about Woodford Down for the first thing Consuela said to him was, 'Max, are you all right? What were you thinking of, risking your life like that?'

Max shrugged. 'I'm fine,' he said indifferently.

He went into the small kitchenette and cut himself a couple of slices of bread, then took some Cheddar from the fridge and began to make himself a sandwich, hoping to deflect Consuela. But she wasn't going to be put off.

'Max, I'm talking to you. You could have killed yourself.'

'I knew what I was doing. It's all over and done with now.'

He didn't want to think about last night. He was worried that if he dwelt on it too much, he would lose his nerve, not have the courage to do something similar again in the future. He couldn't afford to let that happen. He had an inkling – no, it was more than an inkling. He *knew* that before all this was over he would have to face many more dangers and he had to have the guts to overcome them.

'See, I told you he was OK,' Chris said. 'He's a very tough kid.'

Consuela's mouth tightened angrily. 'You still shouldn't have let him do it. You should have taken better care of him.'

Max brought his sandwich to the table and looked around at the others. There was an atmosphere in the flat, a tension in the air, particularly between Chris and Consuela. Max could tell they'd been arguing, that Chris had been on the receiving end of some heavy criticism.

'It wasn't Chris's fault,' he said to Consuela, trying to patch up their quarrel. He couldn't bear to see them fall out over him. 'It was all my fault. Blame me, not Chris. He tried to stop me, but I wouldn't listen. OK?'

He touched Consuela gently on the arm. 'OK?' he repeated.

'Yes, all right,' she replied eventually. She flashed a glance at Chris. 'But next time, I'm coming too. Is that understood? *Someone* has to look after you.'

She got up from the table, went over to the sink and began to wash up her coffee cup and plate, scrubbing the china so forcefully that it was a wonder it didn't break.

Max and Chris exchanged looks, then Chris pointed an accusing finger at him. 'You owe me a new leather jacket,' he said lightly, defusing some of the friction in the room.

Max smiled. 'I know. I'll get you a decent one this time. Something more fashionable.'

'Hey, careful. I liked that jacket. I got it in a market in Marrakesh.'

'Yeah? How much did you pay for it?'

'I don't remember. The equivalent of about a tenner, I think.'

'You could tell,' Max said. He grinned at him and chewed some of his sandwich.

Consuela came back to the table and sat down beside him. She seemed to have calmed down a little. 'Chris has told us what you found out,' she said. 'About the laboratory being protected by soldiers disguised as civilian security guards. He reckons it's a government establishment.'

'I think he's right,' Max said. 'Maybe an offshoot of the germ warfare place at Porton Down, which is only a few miles away from it.'

'So the British government is making Episuderon and selling it to Julius Clark. They know about his brainwashing programme?'

'They either know, or suspect and are turning a blind eye,' Max replied. 'That's what Episuderon is for, after all. And Clark is buying such large quantities of the drug that it must be obvious he's up to something dodgy.'

'And the drug is going to San Francisco?'

'That's right.'

She turned to look at him. 'Where the mysterious Dr Halstead is.'

'Exactly. And where my dad probably is too.'

Consuela frowned. 'You don't know that, Max.'

'No, but it makes sense. Halstead was with my dad in Borneo. I think he's still with him, hiding him in San Francisco.'

'You think Clark is brainwashing people in San Francisco?'

'I don't know. But that's where the Episuderon is going. And it's where we should be going too.'

There was a silence while Consuela absorbed this. Max was expecting her to argue with him, to be cautious, protective of him, but she merely gave a pensive nod, as if she'd already accepted the need to go to America. Maybe they'd been discussing that very subject while he'd been asleep.

'When?' she asked.

'As soon as we can,' Max replied. 'But we'll need a cover, a different reason for going. If Clark suspects we know about the Episuderon, he'll take steps to hide his tracks.'

'Cover?' Chris said. 'What do you mean?'

'I've been thinking about this since Sheldon Mackenzie phoned me the other day. That stunt I did off Tower Bridge, Mackenzie has had approaches from all around the world, people wanting me to do it off their local bridges – including the Golden Gate, in San Francisco.'

Chris glanced around at the others. 'That's not a bad idea. What do you think, Consuela? You'll have to be there, helping Max.' He paused. 'And taking care of him,' he added with a smile.

Consuela eyed him narrowly, suspecting he was being sarcastic, but it was obvious he was only trying to make it up with her, to put their argument behind them. She gazed at him for a time, then gave a nod of approval to Max. 'Why don't you give Mackenzie a call?'

The promoter was delighted to hear from him, even more so when Max explained that he wanted to repeat his trick off the Golden Gate Bridge.

'Good choice, kid,' Mackenzie said. 'There'll be a massive audience in America. Network coverage, huge syndication opportunities. Leave it with me and I'll get back to you later.'

Max rang off. 'He's taking care of it,' he said.

He wolfed down the remainder of his cheese sandwich and turned to Chris. 'You got any plans for this afternoon?'

Chris shook his head. 'No, why?'

'I want to go and see Dan Kingston.'

\*    \*    \*

Max had first met Dan Kingston only a few weeks earlier, after he'd read an article Kingston had written about Julius Clark. He liked and trusted the journalist, who was conducting an ongoing investigation into Clark's shadowy business empire.

'It's good to see you again, Max,' Kingston said, shaking hands in the foyer of the *London News Chronicle*'s offices. He was a small, slightly built man with shrewd, intelligent eyes behind his wire-rimmed spectacles.

'You too,' Max replied.

'Come upstairs.'

Kingston took them up to the second floor in the lift and then across the open-plan newsroom to a small office where they could talk in private. He got Chris and himself coffees and Max a Coke from the vending machine in the newsroom, then came back and settled himself down behind the desk. He'd taken off his suit jacket and hung it carefully on the back of his chair.

Max handed him a slim 8GB memory stick containing the computer files that Lucas Fisher had decrypted, and explained what it was.

Kingston stared at him incredulously.

'You've got hold of Clark's files? How?'

Max told him about what had happened to him at Clark's palm-oil processing plant in Borneo, how the billionaire tycoon had tried to kill him, how he'd escaped and managed to copy the files.

Kingston listened attentively, then shook his head in disbelief. 'That's one hell of a story,' he said. 'You're not an ordinary teenager, are you, Max? How did you survive all that?'

Max shrugged. He didn't want to talk about the past, he wanted to move on to the future. 'The files were encrypted,' he said. 'But we got an expert to break the codes. There's all sorts of financial stuff in there, stuff we don't understand, but I'm sure you will.'

'What kind of financial stuff?'

'I don't know. I haven't looked too closely at it – it's all mumbo jumbo to me. But company records, accounts, that kind of detailed information.'

The journalist pursed his lips and let out a soft, low whistle. 'That could be gold dust. You know how secretive Clark is, how he hides his business activities behind a complex wall of offshore trusts and shell corporations. If we can break through that wall, we might be able to get an accurate picture of exactly what he's up to.'

'There's more where that came from too,' Chris said. 'Our computer expert is still trying to decrypt some of the files. We'll let you have the rest when he finally cracks them.'

'When? Or if?' Kingston asked sceptically.

'There's no "if" about it,' Chris replied. 'This guy is good, really good. He'll break the codes all right.'

The journalist gave a nod and put the memory stick in his pocket. His eyes were gleaming with excitement.

'This is terrific stuff, Max. Just what I've been trying to find for months. I'll take a close look at it, add the information to all the rest I've been compiling.'

Max drank some of his Coke. 'What do you know about Clark's activities in San Francisco?' he asked.

'San Francisco?'

'Rescomin Tower, Eldorado Plaza.'

'That's the headquarters of Rescomin, his main company.'

'The brainwashing drug, Episuderon – I told you about it when we met before,' Max went on. 'Clark is flying it out from the UK to that address in San Francisco. Could he be brainwashing people there?'

Kingston gave the question some thought, then shook his head. 'I doubt it. Not in a big, densely populated city like San Francisco. And particularly not in his corporate headquarters. There must be several hundred employees working in that building. He'd never risk running his brainwashing programme from there – he'd go for somewhere more remote, where he could do it undetected.'

'Like he did on Shadow Island,' Chris said.

'Precisely. An isolated site, preferably in a country where the government won't interfere with him. Do you think he's still using Shadow Island?'

'I can't see it,' Chris said. 'We burned the place to the ground. It would take him months to rebuild it.'

'And he's using the Episuderon now,' Max added. 'A new batch was sent to San Francisco only last week.'

'So, if not Shadow Island, where then?' Kingston said pensively. 'Let me show you something I've been putting together.'

He opened a folder on the desk and pulled out a large map of the world, turning it round so that Max and Chris were looking at it the right way up. Max noticed that the map was covered with shiny red and green stars.

'I've been marking all of Julius Clark's business interests around the globe,' Kingston explained. 'Or, at least, the business interests I know about. I'm sure there are many more I'm not aware of. The green stars mark the location of his offices, the red stars his industrial operations.' He pointed to Brazil. 'This green star shows his South American headquarters in Rio de Janeiro. These red stars across the country indicate where his companies are engaged in logging and rainforest destruction. Rescomin has been clearing vast areas of tropical rainforest, then planting the cleared land with soy to make cattle-feed for the American and European beef markets – a very controversial practice, as are nearly all his business activities.'

The journalist moved his finger across the Pacific Ocean to Borneo. 'You know all about his palm oil business in Borneo, of course. The stripping of the rainforest there to make biofuels, a substitute for petroleum. But he hasn't given up on the traditional oil business, far from it. His companies are drilling here in the Middle East; in Iraq and Saudi Arabia. They are here in central Russia, drilling for both oil and gas. They are up here in Alaska and they are here in Nigeria.'

'What's this one here?' Max asked, indicating a red star on a peninsula on the northeast coast of Russia.

"That's Kamchatka,' Kingston answered. 'Rescomin has a platinum mine there, at a place called Zaliv Myertvetsa. Clark's mineral interests are huge. He controls copper mines in Australia and Chile; gold mines in South Africa; zinc and tin mines in Peru, Bolivia, China, Canada, Mexico, the USA – the list goes on and on. And that's just his mining and extraction companies. He has others which are involved in processing the minerals and metals and still others in the manufacturing business. If you want a man who epitomizes the term "global economy", it's Julius Clark.'

Max stared at the map. There were dozens of red and green stars scattered across every continent, bar Antarctica – and that was only left out because no one was allowed to mine or drill commercially there.

'There are so many places to choose from,' he said with a sigh of frustration. 'And a lot of them are isolated. Forests, jungle, deserts, arctic tundra – all of them suitable for holding people captive and brainwashing them.'

'But which place is Clark using?' Chris said.

Max turned to look at him. 'That's what we've got to find out.'

# EIGHT

Max found it strange, and uncomfortably claustrophobic, sharing this small, unfamiliar Docklands apartment with four other people, three of them big men who took up a great deal of room. He was used to his own space, his own bed, all his possessions around him – his CD player, his computer, his games console. He didn't know how much of that was gone for good now. Consuela had been in touch with the fire brigade who'd told her that the damage to their house wasn't as bad as they'd first feared. The ground floor had been gutted, but the basement and the first floor had escaped the worst ravages of the fire. It was likely that a lot of the contents would have survived, though Max and Consuela wouldn't be allowed in to check until the building had been declared safe.

The thought that some of his belongings, including maybe his escapology equipment, were still intact cheered Max up a lot, but it didn't get round the fact that he had no clothes other than the ones he'd been wearing for the past couple of days. Consuela was in the same position, so next morning they went to a shopping centre in the East End and bought themselves a few new outfits. Then they drove to a café near Victoria Station where Max had arranged to meet a police officer from Scotland Yard.

They got to the café early. Max and Consuela sat at one table, while Chris, Rusty and Zip took another near the door, where they had a good view of the street outside. Detective Sergeant Kevin Richardson came in ten minutes later. The detective looked uncannily like his late father, DCS John Richardson, Max thought: the same height and heavy build, even the same toothbrush moustache – though Kevin's was jet black while his father's had been tinged with grey.

Richardson sat down at the table opposite Max and studied him intently. Max gazed back, making his own assessment of the detective. He liked what he saw. Richardson had an open, honest face – again like his father – and trustworthy eyes.

'Would you like something to drink?' Consuela asked.

Richardson shook his head. 'No, thanks, let's get straight down to business, shall we? What's this all about? Your phone call was very mysterious. Something important about my father, you said.'

Max took a moment to get his thoughts together.

Kevin Richardson's father, John, had also been a police officer – a detective chief superintendent and head of the Metropolitan Police's Criminal Investigation Department. He'd helped Max try to find out more about Rupert Penhall, then been killed by a lorry while crossing a busy main road near his home in west London. Max didn't believe his death had been an accident.

'You know I knew your father?' Max said.

'Yes. He assisted you with one of your shows, didn't he?' Richardson replied. 'That one in Hyde Park. I wanted to come and see it, but I was on duty that night.'

'He helped me shortly after that too,' Max went on. 'When I was having trouble with a man called Rupert Penhall. He's some kind of high-up government official, something to do with MI5, I think. Your dad tried to find out who Penhall was, what he was up to, but he was warned off by his boss.'

'The commissioner, you mean?'

'That's right. He threatened to sack your dad if he kept asking questions.'

Richardson's eyes opened wide. 'Did he indeed! You're sure about this?'

'Your dad told me himself. He wasn't put off, though. He said he was going to carry on regardless.'

The detective smiled. 'That sounds like my father.'

'I think it cost him his life.'

Richardson frowned at Max, his face puzzled, uncertain. 'What are you talking about?'

'I think he was murdered,' Max said.

'*Murdered?* You have some evidence to back that up?'

'No real evidence. But it was too much of a coincidence. He starts asking questions about Penhall, then gets knocked down by a lorry. I think he was pushed in front of it.'

The detective sat back heavily and stared at Max. The colour had drained from his face. He was clearly shocked. 'That's a very serious allegation to make,' he said.

'I think it's true,' Max replied. 'They've tried to kill me too.'

'*What?*' Richardson was gaping at him now. 'Look, you're losing me here. I think you'd better tell me the whole story.'

Max did. He told him everything that had happened over the past few months – from his trip to Shadow Island, through his adventures in Sweden and Borneo, to the bomb explosion in his house. Richardson said nothing as Max came to the end of his tale. He seemed to be dazed by the revelations. Finally, he said, 'I think maybe I do need a drink.' He got up from the table and walked over to the counter.

Consuela followed him with her eyes. 'Do you think he's going to help us?'

Max nodded. 'Penhall and Clark had his father murdered. He's going to want them punished for that.'

'But, realistically, can he do anything?'

'He's a police officer. He can do things that we can't. He has colleagues who can help him. Maybe together they can deal with Penhall and Clark.'

'His father was murdered, Max. What if all we're doing is putting him in danger too?'

'He knows that. It's his choice. But he's forewarned now. He'll be much more careful than his dad was.'

Richardson came back to the table with a cappuccino. He took a sip and wiped the froth off his moustache with the edge of his forefinger.

'That's an unbelievable story,' he said. 'But I believe you. Why would you make something like that up? What I want to know is why you've come to me now? Why didn't you tell me just after my dad died?'

'Because, as I said, I had no evidence that your dad's death wasn't an accident,' Max replied. 'Never mind proof. You'd have thought I was crazy. But I do have evidence relating to the bomb in our house. That's why I asked to meet you. To see if you could help us.'

Max glanced around the café. Chris, Rusty and Zip were slouched in their seats, drinking coffee and eating

Danish pastries. They appeared relaxed, half asleep, but Max knew that was a carefully cultivated illusion. Rusty and Zip's eyes never left the street outside, watching every pedestrian, every car that passed by. And Chris was monitoring the inside of the café with equal vigilance.

Max took a DVD out of the carrier bag on his lap, a copy that Lucas Fisher had made of the CCTV tape Max had saved from the fire. He handed it to the detective.

'We've got CCTV cameras in the house. Or we *had* before the fire. Some friends installed them to protect me and Consuela.'

'The friends at the table by the door?' Richardson said.

Max was surprised. 'How did you know?'

'I'm a copper. I keep my eyes open. I've seen the way they've been checking out the customers, watching over you.'

'The cameras were recording when a man broke into the house and planted the bomb in the kitchen. He wasn't aware of them and didn't cover his face. This DVD shows it all: what he looks like, what he did. Maybe you can use it to identify him.'

The detective slipped the disc into his jacket pocket. 'This is the original?'

'A copy. The original is in a safe place.'

'It survived the fire?'

'I grabbed it before I got out of the house.'

Richardson gave a nod of respect. 'That was very quick thinking, considering the pressure you must have been under. You know, Max, I'm beginning to see why these guys haven't managed to bump you off yet.'

Max smiled ruefully. 'Don't speak too soon.'

They were back in Rusty's apartment an hour later when Max's mobile rang.

He didn't respond immediately. Only a few people had his number, all of them friends or acquaintances he could trust. But he was wary of talking on the phone. You never knew who might be listening in. Finally, the insistent ring-tone got too much for him. He pulled out the phone, saw the caller's name, and answered.

'Sheldon, hi,' he said.

'Hi, kid,' Mackenzie said. 'San Francisco. It's all fixed.'

Max sat up, suddenly energized by the news. 'That was quick.'

'You have to strike while the iron's hot. Your Tower Bridge stunt was big news in America, got huge ratings. The promoter over there, a guy named Herb Feinstein, is desperate to get you. So are the mayor of San Francisco – he's running for re-election in a few months time and thinks it will help his chances – and the tourist board. They've pulled out all the stops and are going to close the northbound carriageway of the Golden Gate Bridge for you next Sunday night.'

'They want me to do it at night?' Max said, a little uncertainly.

'It has to be night, when there's less traffic using the bridge. It'll be terrific, kid, even better than Tower Bridge. Think of the atmosphere. The bridge and the bay in darkness, your wooden crate floodlit as it's lowered down into the water. It's going to be a big event. I'll let you know your full timetable when I get the details from Feinstein, OK?'

'Yes, yes, I suppose so,' Max said, taken aback by how rapidly it had all been arranged.

'I'll sort out air tickets for you and Consuela. You get your equipment together and we'll get it flown out as soon as possible. I'm really excited, kid. I told you that you were going to have a big international career. This is just the start. I'll keep you posted. Oh, and Max – it's a big fee, you know.' He named a figure that Max could barely believe and then breezily finished with, 'Bye for now.'

The promoter hung up. Max stared at his phone for a time. Talking to Sheldon Mackenzie always left him feeling slightly breathless, but there was something infectious about the promoter's electrifying enthusiasm.

Max was excited too, now. Not just about performing in the United States, but about going to San Francisco – about getting away from Britain and Rupert Penhall and, most importantly, embarking on the next stage of his search for his father.

# NINE

The following couple of days were very busy for Max and Consuela, ordering all the equipment they needed for the stunt off the Golden Gate Bridge, then arranging for it to be flown to San Francisco. When all that was completed, there was one other important thing that Max had to do before he left the country: visit his mother in prison.

Rusty and Zip weren't keen on the idea. The flat was a safe haven; no one knew they were holed up there. So long as they stayed put they weren't in any danger. Even going out to the local shops or to places they'd never visited before – like the café in Victoria – were relatively risk-free. It was highly unlikely that Penhall's men would pick them up by chance in a city as big as London. But Levington prison, where Max's mum was being held, was more of a problem. Max went there regularly – and Penhall would know that. All he had to do was put a team of watchers near the prison and wait for Max to show up.

Max was aware of the danger, but considered it a risk

worth taking. He wanted to see his mother before he went to America. And just as importantly, he knew his mother would want to see him. Locked away in a small cell, with a further eighteen years of prison ahead of her, Max's visits were a lifeline for Helen Cassidy. They were just about the only thing that kept her going. For her sake, if nothing else, Max insisted on going to see her. He didn't know how long it would be before he got the opportunity again. In theory, he was going to San Francisco for only a few days, but Max had a premonition that it might be longer. Or that he might not come back at all. That wasn't something he wanted to consider, but in a dark corner of his brain was festering the fear that, if something went wrong, this might well be the last time he saw his mother.

Zip drove the Audi as usual, Rusty in the passenger seat next to him, Max and Consuela in the back. Chris followed behind in the Nissan. They went north through Leyton and Wanstead, then took the M11, turning off near Saffron Walden and heading east across Suffolk.

Levington prison was in the middle of open country-side, a grim concrete complex surrounded by a high wall and a fence topped with razor wire. Zip drove into the car park outside the perimeter of the prison and went slowly around it, checking every car for anything suspicious, particularly anyone who looked like part of a surveillance team. But the cars were all empty, the occupants presumably inside the prison visiting friends or relatives.

Max and Consuela went in alone and sat at the small table in the visiting room until Helen was brought out from her cell by a prison officer. Max gave her a long hug, then Helen embraced Consuela.

'It's good to see you both,' she said, sitting down at the table with them. She smiled at Max. 'I saw your Tower Bridge stunt on the television. You were brilliant. I was so proud of you. The other women thought it was terrific too. They said I should get you to break us all out of here – a mass escape.'

She chuckled. Max felt a warm glow inside him. That was the first time in all his visits that he'd heard his mother laugh. Her spirits seemed to be higher than usual today. She was looking better too. Her face was less gaunt. There was some colour in her cheeks, her eyes had lost some of their habitual sadness.

'I don't need to break you out, Mum,' Max said. 'Though I've often thought about it. I'm going to get you out legally, just as soon as I've found Dad.'

Helen took his hand and squeezed it. 'Have you managed to track down this elusive Dr Halstead yet?'

Max shook his head. 'But I'm going to San Francisco to try and find him. I'm repeating my

Tower Bridge stunt off the Golden Gate Bridge.'

Helen gazed at him with concern. 'That's a very high bridge, Max. And the currents beneath it are notoriously dangerous. Are you sure that's a good idea?'

'It's all arranged. I know what I'm doing, Mum. You don't have to worry about me.'

'Yes, I do,' Helen replied. 'I'm your mum. I worry about you all the time.'

'He'll be fine,' Consuela said to Helen. 'I'll be with him. I'll make sure he's careful.'

Helen smiled at her. 'I know you will. I know how well you're looking after him. I'm really grateful for everything you do, Consuela.'

'You'll be back home looking after him again very soon,' Consuela said.

'Will I?' Helen's face clouded for a moment. 'I hope so. But I can't see when.'

'It won't be long,' Max said, trying to sound upbeat. He was always selective about what he told his mother, leaving out things that he knew would upset her. He'd visited her a couple of times since his return from Borneo, but he'd not mentioned Julius Clark's attempts to kill him. That would have distressed her so much that her already fragile health would have been undermined. But he'd told her that he'd found evidence his father had been in Borneo just before him. That had lifted her spirits enormously. What better news could there be than finding out for certain that her husband was alive?

'Just hang on a bit longer,' Max said. 'I'm going to find Dad in San Francisco and then get you out of here. I can feel it in my guts.'

He glanced at Consuela and she gave a discreet nod. They'd discussed this in the car on the way up to Suffolk. Helen couldn't be protected from everything bad. It would be a shock to her, but she had to be told about the fire. She was still the owner of the house and the insurance company wouldn't process any claim without her consent.

'Helen,' Consuela said softly, 'I want you to prepare yourself for some bad news.'

'Bad news?' Helen gave her an anxious look. 'What do you mean? Tell me.'

Max gripped her hands in his own. 'It's about the house, Mum.'

'The house?'

'There was a fire,' Consuela said. 'The house was badly damaged.'

She described what had happened, omitting any mention of a bomb or CCTV cameras, and Helen turned pale, pulling her hands away from Max and covering her mouth.

'Oh, my God!' she exclaimed. 'You were inside it at the time?'

'Fortunately not. The house was empty.'

'But what caused it?'

'We don't know. It may have been a gas leak,' Max said.

'And the contents? Was anything saved?'

'We don't know for certain yet. But the kitchen, sitting room and dining room were gutted. The other rooms weren't so badly damaged. It's possible we can salvage some of the contents.'

Helen's face crumpled and her eyes filled with tears. Max watched her, feeling his own eyes moisten. He knew how much the house meant to her. She and his dad had moved into it shortly after they were married. Her memories of it would be as vivid and happy as his, the loss just as painful.

'I'm sorry, Mum,' Max said.

The tears started to pour down his mother's cheeks. There was no sound – no sobs or sniffs. Helen was holding them in, trying not to draw attention to herself in the crowded visiting room. Max stood up and went round to the other side of the table, bending down and putting his arms around his mum's shoulders to comfort her. Heads turned, people were starting to notice and whisper among themselves, but Max didn't care. He just wanted to make his mum feel better.

'We can repair the house,' he said. 'Make it the way it was. It's just a few bits of furniture and carpet that have been lost. Nothing really important.'

An officious prison officer came striding across the room and told Max to sit back down. They were creating a disturbance. Max glared at the woman, but returned to his seat. Consuela handed Helen some tissues and she wiped her eyes.

'One minute!' the prison officer called out, and the visitors began to make their farewells.

'We had to tell you,' Max said to his mother. 'But don't let it get you down. There are plenty of things to be up about.'

'Are there?' Helen said bleakly.

'No one was killed or injured in the fire. We know Dad's alive. I'm going to San Francisco to look for him. Think about that while I'm gone. The next time I visit you, it will be to get you out.'

Helen smiled at him through her tears. 'If anyone can do that, it's you, Max. Good luck, and look after yourself.'

'I will.'

Max stood up again and went round the table. Helen got to her feet and they hugged each other tightly, clinging on desperately until the prison officer broke them apart and led Helen back to the cells.

\* \* \*

For a very wealthy man, Julius Clark was remarkably uninterested in money. He had long ago lost track of how much he was worth. The financial press estimated his personal fortune at somewhere between ten and twenty billion US dollars, depending on which journalist was writing the article, but Clark himself couldn't have put an exact figure on it. He simply didn't know – and didn't care – how much money he had. After the first few hundred million, what did it really matter?

He possessed all the traditional trappings of a billionaire – a private jet, a massive yacht, luxurious houses scattered all over the globe – but he took no real pleasure in any of them. To him, they were just places in which to do business. It was business, and the power that came with it, that really interested him. It was doing deals that he enjoyed – like a market trader buying and selling, only on a vastly bigger scale. Finding new oil deposits to extract, new mineral sources to mine, new land to acquire and exploit. That was what motivated him, what drove his insatiable ambition.

His office in the City of London, just down the road from the Bank of England, was pretty much the same as all his offices around the world. It had a desk and swivel chair, a computer and a phone and little more.

What else did he need? Yes, there was some expensive art on the walls and a thick carpet on the floor, but Clark barely noticed them. They'd been installed by an interior designer, hired to create an environment that would impress others, that would emphasize to them what a formidably successful businessman he was. Clark knew that counted for a lot in the international circles in which he moved. Politicians, in particular, loved to wallow in other people's wealth. They liked being entertained on his yacht and at his beachfront house in the Bahamas, they liked eating his caviar and drinking his champagne. And that suited Clark just fine. He needed politicians to approve his business ventures, to allow him to drill and quarry and chop down trees wherever he fancied. And he needed other people lower down in government – corrupt public servants – to help him, to do his bidding.

People like Rupert Penhall.

Penhall was impressed by Clark's wealth. He noticed his money and cared about it, even though Clark himself didn't. He was overawed by the tycoon – and frightened of him, too.

The billionaire's eyes were fixed on him now – pale blue eyes that were as cold and hostile as the polar icecaps. Penhall found them unsettling. They seemed to bore into him, seeking out his weaknesses and then exploiting them.

'You missed a perfect opportunity, Rupert,' Clark said witheringly. 'You could have killed both Max Cassidy and Chris Moncrieffe, but you failed.'

Penhall squirmed uncomfortably in his chair and looked away. Through the windows, he could see the famous glass-walled Gherkin office block and, further down the Thames, the towers of Canary Wharf. At another time, he might have enjoyed the view, but not today. He was too nervous, too aware of Clark's simmering anger.

'Yes, I'm sorry about that,' he said feebly.

'*Sorry?* Is that all you can say?'

Penhall held out his arms in a helpless gesture. 'It was a mistake, I admit that. We wanted to make sure of getting them both, but we waited a fraction too long. It gave them time to get out.'

'They knew about the bomb?'

'I don't know. Of course, if you'd dealt with them in Borneo, then—'

Penhall saw Clark's mouth tighten and stopped himself in mid sentence, realizing that it was a mistake to remind the billionaire that Max had escaped assassination before, when Clark had had him at his mercy.

'We're not talking about Borneo,' Clark said angrily.

'We're talking about London. Have you found them yet?'

'No. They've gone to ground somewhere. But it won't be for long. Max and Consuela Navarra are booked on a flight to San Francisco on Friday.'

Clark raised an eyebrow. 'For what purpose?'

'Max is doing a stunt off the Golden Gate Bridge. The same one he did in London, off Tower Bridge.'

'Is he now? The one when he's nailed inside a wooden crate and lowered into the water?'

'I believe so, yes. We can pick them up at Heathrow airport on some pretext, then deal with them.'

Clark turned his head to stare at one of the paintings on the office wall – a Jackson Pollock that was just random splashes of paint on a huge canvas, but had cost him several million pounds. The light reflected off the lenses of his spectacles, so Penhall couldn't see his eyes. Clark thought for a time, then turned back.

'No, don't do that,' he said softly. 'Let them go. I have people in San Francisco who can take care of them.'

'You have something in mind?'

'Max is an escapologist. He's performing a very dangerous stunt.' Clark's mouth twisted into a menacing smile. His eyes glinted like sunlight on frost. 'And when you do dangerous things, accidents can happen.'

# TEN

The Boeing 747 flew across San Francisco Bay from the northeast, then looped out briefly over the Pacific Ocean. From his window seat in the first-class cabin, Max got his first glimpse of the city. It was a sunny, cloudless day and he had a clear view of the downtown area, the dense urban sprawl broken up by patches of green parkland. He could see that San Francisco was built on a peninsula, like a long thumb, the ocean on one side, the bay on the other. To the north, spanning the entrance to the bay, was the red-orange framework of the Golden Gate Bridge. The plane was low enough for Max to be able to make out the tiny vehicles moving across the bridge. Then the 747 banked and came round in a long curve to approach the airport over the glistening waters of the bay. The wheels touched down and the whole plane juddered as the pilot applied the brakes.

Max closed his eyes, savouring the moment. Inside the protective shell of the jet he had felt safe for a few hours. He'd spent time planning what he was going to do in the city, but also watched a couple of films, been able to forget about his troubles for a while. But now he was back down to earth he had to face up to reality again. And that meant worries and fears and all the dangers of a new, unfamiliar country.

There was a crowd of photographers, television cameramen and reporters waiting for them outside the arrivals terminal. Max and Consuela posed patiently for some pictures and answered a few questions, then went to the limousine that Herb Feinstein had sent to pick them up. A driver in a black uniform and peaked cap took their luggage and loaded it into the boot. Max had never ridden in a limo before. The interior was luxurious – deep leather seats, air conditioning, a television and a bar with a bottle of champagne on ice for Consuela and a selection of soft drinks for Max. Neither of them touched the drinks. They were both too tense.

This wasn't the way they'd planned their trip to San Francisco. Rusty and Zip should have been with them on the flight, but they'd been detained by security men at Heathrow and taken away for questioning. Max hadn't seen them since. The plane had left without the two bodyguards, making Max feel very vulnerable. Nor was Chris there to protect him. Chris was wanted by the British police, so he'd taken the Eurostar to Paris on a false passport and flown from there to San Francisco the day before Max and Consuela. If everything had gone according to plan, he would be at the hotel waiting for them to arrive. *If*... Max thought anxiously, praying that nothing had gone wrong.

They took the freeway north, the eight-lane highway cutting through ugly industrial suburbs, occasionally hugging the shore of the bay, then Max saw skyscrapers on the horizon – tall pillars of glass and concrete rising up the slopes of a hill, their bases hidden by clusters of lower buildings. The traffic began to thicken. The limousine slowed and crawled through a series of lights into the downtown area. Office blocks towered up alongside them, sunshine glinting on their windows. A cable car chugged sluggishly away from a stop up ahead and began to climb a steep hill. The limo followed it, overtaking so that Max could see the passengers hanging precariously from the cable car's sides.

A few minutes later, they were at the top of the hill, turning off onto the forecourt of the Fairmont Hotel, an elegant seven-storey stone building with a long row of international flags dangling above the entrance. A uniformed doorman hurried forward to open the door of the limousine, then two bellboys in brown and gold livery and spotless white gloves removed their luggage from the boot and carried it into the hotel. Max felt awkward. He wasn't used to this kind of treatment; he would have preferred to open the door himself, carry his own suitcase, but that wasn't how things were done at the Fairmont.

There was a canopy over the forecourt to protect guests from the weather, then a high, pillared, classical entrance with a red carpet on the steps beneath it. Max and Consuela went through a revolving door into a lobby so opulent that Max stopped dead, staring around with his mouth open in amazement. He'd never seen a hotel foyer like it. There was gold and marble every-where: polished marble floors, marble pillars supporting the gold-embossed ceiling, rococo gilt-framed mirrors on the walls, gilt armchairs and sofas and chaises longues in the seating areas, everything lit with table and standard lamps that bathed the whole lobby in a soft, golden glow.

Stretched out in an armchair by the staircase was Chris Moncrieffe. He appeared to be reading a news-paper, but looked up as Max and Consuela came in. His eyes met Max's for an instant and he gave a discreet nod. Max nodded back, then turned away, pretending he hadn't seen him. An immense feeling of relief coursed through his body. Chris had made it here safely. Max could stop worrying now.

He followed Consuela to the reception desk and

checked in, then they took the lift up to the seventh floor, the two bellboys accompanying them with their luggage. They had a two-bedroom suite, each bedroom with its own separate bathroom and a spacious sitting room in between. The sitting room was less showy and formal than the lobby downstairs. It had a thick cream carpet, a long sofa and armchairs upholstered in pale blue, and French windows opening onto a small balcony which afforded a spectacular view of the city and bay.

Max barely had time to explore the room before there was a knock on the door. Consuela checked through the peephole, then snapped back the lock to let Chris in. He smiled at them both, dropped his holdall on the floor and gave Max a high five.

'How're you doing?'

'We're OK,' Max replied.

Chris hugged Consuela. Max turned away, giving them a moment to themselves. When he looked back, they'd broken apart and Chris was glancing around the suite, pursing his lips appreciatively.

'Not bad,' he said dryly. 'You're becoming quite a celebrity, aren't you, Max?' He wandered across the room, checking the balcony, then testing the cushions of the sofa. 'I'll bed down here, it feels pretty comfortable.'

He picked up the room service menu from the coffee table and flicked through it, pulling a face. 'My God, you seen the prices? It's a good job someone else is paying for all this.' He tossed the menu down and looked at Consuela, suddenly serious. 'Where are Rusty and Zip?'

'They were detained by security at Heathrow,' Consuela replied. 'We don't know what happened to them after that.'

'Convenient,' Chris said. His tone was light, but there was a flicker of worry in his eyes. 'You have any trouble on the flight? Or when you arrived?'

Consuela shook her head. 'No. How about you?'

'No problems.'

'Are we going to be OK?' Max asked. 'Without them, I mean.'

Chris gave him a reassuring smile. 'We'll be just fine. It would have been kind of crowded with five of us in here, anyway.' He went across to the phone on the desk next to the window. 'But all the same, I'd like to know they're all right.'

He dialled the number of Rusty's flat in London and let it ring for a long time. No one answered. Then he tried Rusty's mobile and got his voicemail. He left a message – 'You know who this is. Give me a call' – and hung up. 'It's been a long twenty-four hours,' he said, picking up his bag. 'I think I'll take a shower.'

Chris disappeared into one of the bathrooms. Max sat down in an armchair, feeling suddenly tired. He looked at the clock on the sitting-room wall, then checked his watch. They'd left London at two o'clock in the afternoon and endured an eleven-hour flight, then the journey in from the airport. His body clock told him it was nearly two o'clock in the morning, but in San Francisco it was only approaching six p.m.

'Feeling jet lagged?' Consuela said.

Max nodded. 'It's weird. It feels like the middle of the night to me, but it's broad daylight outside. Should I go to bed?'

'Better to stay up. Try to adjust to the new time and go to bed when it's dark. Why don't you take a shower too? It'll freshen you up, help you get through the next few hours.'

'OK.'

Max went into his bathroom and had a long shower. Consuela was right – it did wake him up, make him feel better. When he came back out into the sitting room, he picked up the phone and dialled the number of San Francisco General Hospital which he'd brought with him. He asked the main switchboard for the human resources department and a young woman's voice came on the line. Max had phoned the hospital several times from London, but he didn't recognize this voice. It was warmer, more pleasant than the others had been. He explained that he was trying to get in touch with a Dr Halstead, whom he believed worked at the hospital.

'Just a moment,' the young woman said. She put him on hold for a few seconds. 'I'm sorry, but Dr Halstead doesn't start his contract with us until next week.'

'I really need to speak to him now,' Max said. 'Could you possibly give me a contact number for him?'

'I'm afraid I can't give out the phone numbers of staff members. It's hospital policy.'

Max already knew that – it was what he'd been told every time he'd called – but he wasn't going to give up.

'Please, this is important,' he said pleadingly. 'I've come all the way from England to find him.'

'I'm sorry, I can't give you his number,' the young woman repeated, but she sounded more hesitant this time.

'Then could you pass on a message to him? Ask him to call me?'

'Well, I'm not sure—'

'*Please.* I have to speak to him. My name's Max Cassidy. I'm staying at the Fairmont Hotel.'

There was a silence on the line. Then the young woman said, 'OK, I suppose I could do that. Which room are you in?'

Max gave her the number and thanked her, then

hung up. Tracking down Dr Halstead was proving a frustrating task, but it was one that he had to accomplish. The doctor knew where his dad was, Max was sure of that.

He went to the window and stepped out onto the balcony, looking out over the city. There must have been thousands of buildings in San Francisco, hundreds of thousands of people. If you wanted to lie low for a time, it was a good place to choose. Was his father out there? he wondered. If he was, would he see the press coverage of Max's stunt off the Golden Gate Bridge and maybe try to make contact? Or was that just wishful thinking on Max's part? He had flown five thousand miles, yet now he was here, he was beginning to realize he was still a very long way from finding his father.

At ten o'clock the next morning, the local show-business promoter, Herb Feinstein, met them in the hotel lobby. He was a small, bird-like man in his mid-forties, with a sharp beak of a nose and big black-framed glasses that seemed to cover half his face. His hair was thick and curly, worn long so that it brushed the shoulders of his tan leather jacket; his stick-thin legs were encased in tight blue jeans, and on his feet he sported a pair of white sneakers with purple trim around the lace holes.

'Hi, Max, hi, Consuela. Good to meet you,' he said warmly, holding out a thin, bony hand. 'You have a good night? You like your room?'

'Yes, very much, thank you,' Consuela replied. She introduced Chris, calling him Alan Montgomery and describing him as Max's security adviser.

Feinstein looked momentarily nonplussed. 'Hi, Alan. I wasn't expecting you. Sheldon didn't say anything about a security adviser. That's why I only booked rooms for Max and Consuela.'

'Don't worry, I made my own arrangements,' Chris said.

'You did? Well, make sure you bill me for them. I'm taking care of all expenses. Hotels, meals, whatever you like. You're my guests. OK?'

Feinstein turned and headed for the exit. 'My car's just outside. This is a great hotel,' he added. 'You been up the tower block at the back yet? You should, it gives you a terrific view of the city. This is the highest point in San Francisco, you know – Nob Hill. So called because this is where all the nineteenth-century millionaires built their mansions. People like Collis Huntington, Leland Stanford and Mark Hopkins. You heard of any of them? The Robber Barons, they were called. The Fairmont is named after another nob, James Fair – his daughters built the hotel after his death. It was finished in 1906, and two days later it was gutted in the fire that followed the great earthquake. But it was rebuilt using the original white terracotta façade.'

They came out of the hotel, the promoter still talking about the earthquake and the damage it had done. He pointed across the road to a square imposing building made of dark, reddish stone.

'That was James Flood's mansion. He was known as the Bonanza King – made a packet from silver mining. The house is now the Pacific Union Club. And beyond it you can see Huntington Park and Grace Cathedral, which is modelled on Notre Dame, in Paris. You should go in there, if you have time. It's well worth a visit.'

They climbed into Feinstein's car, a grey Lexus convertible with the top down. Max tried to get in the back, but the promoter insisted he take the front passenger seat next to him. Max sighed inwardly. He was already beginning to realize that Feinstein – like Sheldon Mackenzie – enjoyed the sound of his own voice.

'Why don't I show you some of the sights of the city on our way to the bridge?' he said. 'You been here before? No? It's the most attractive city in the whole US. And don't just take my word for that, look around you. Where else do you get views like this? The Pacific Ocean that way, the bay over there, hills up to the north.

An hour's drive and you're in the wine country of Napa and Sonoma. An hour after that and you can be skiing in the Sierra Nevada mountains. That's why people love to live here.'

Feinstein started up the car and pulled off, maintaining his almost continuous monologue as they toured the city, going up a hill to Haight-Ashbury, which the promoter said was where all the hippies had gathered for the 'Summer of Love' back in the 1960s. Max listened politely, though he'd never heard of the Summer of Love, and the 1960s seemed to him as long ago as the Stone Age.

After that, they drove through a huge stretch of open parkland that Feinstein called Golden Gate Park, the road sweeping in long curves between lawns and gardens and imposing stands of redwood trees.

'This park goes all the way to the ocean,' the promoter said. The wind was gusting in through the car's open top, blowing his long hair into his face. 'There's everything here. Lakes, a golf course, botanical gardens, a Japanese tea garden, even a paddock full of buffalo. Imagine that, *buffalo* in the centre of a densely populated city like San Francisco.'

The road began to descend a gentle hill and Max saw the Pacific Ocean directly in front of them. There were surfers in wet suits out in the breakers, people sun-bathing and flying kites on the long beach, but there was almost no one swimming in the sea – it looked too dangerous for bathing.

Feinstein turned right onto the coast road and headed north. The Golden Gate Bridge came gradually into view, the tops of the towers first, then the rest of the superstructure. Feinstein drove through a short tunnel and they emerged into a car park beside the toll plaza for the bridge.

'We have to leave the car here and do the next bit on foot,' he explained.

They got out of the Lexus and walked across the car park. Feinstein pointed to an orange metal container, about the size of a garden shed, that occupied one of the parking bays. 'That contains all your equipment from London,' he said. 'I'll have it moved up onto the bridge tomorrow.'

They walked up past the toll plaza and along the footpath next to the freeway, the cars racing past only a couple of feet away. Max could smell exhaust fumes, feel the ground shaking beneath him. The vibrations got worse as they walked further out onto the bridge. So did the roar of the traffic. The footpath was three metres wide and there was a chest-high fence between it and the carriageway, but the vehicles speeding by produced a draught strong enough to buffet Max's body and ruffle his hair.

It took them nearly ten minutes to reach the middle of the bridge. Max leaned on the guard rail, looking down at the green, opaque water. It was a long drop.

'It's quite an engineering feat, isn't it?' Feinstein said proudly. 'It was the biggest in the world when it was built, back in 1937. It's one point seven miles long, the towers are seven hundred and forty-six feet high and the roadway we're standing on is two hundred and twenty feet above the water – that's about seventy metres.'

Max nodded, though he already knew all those facts. He also knew the water was just over a hundred metres deep, that there was a difference of nearly four metres between high and low water and that the tide rushed in under the bridge at sixty miles an hour. He'd done his research thoroughly before he left London, needing to know exactly what this stunt was going to entail.

He turned his head, looking along the footpath to a phone on the side of a lamppost. A sign above the phone read: *Emergency phone and crisis counselling. There is hope. Make the call. The consequences of jumping from this bridge are fatal and tragic.*

'It's a favourite spot for suicides,' Feinstein said,

seeing where Max was looking. 'Jump off the side into the water. From this height, it's like hitting concrete.'

Max knew that too, though he didn't want to be reminded of it. He was going to be lowered off here in a wooden crate suspended from a rope. If the rope snapped, he knew he would never survive the fall.

'Let's go through the timetable again,' he said. 'I do the stunt at ten p.m. tomorrow night.'

'That's right. But two of the northbound lanes will be closed from eight p.m. All shipping traffic under the bridge will also cease at that time. There'll only be two safety boats down there – one on the east side of the bridge, one on the west, both with teams of divers on board in case anything goes wrong. Not that anything will, of course,' Feinstein added hurriedly. He gave a reassuring smile. 'I have complete confidence in you, Max.'

'Thanks,' Max replied, trying to look and sound equally confident, though inside he was beginning to feel nervous. Now he was here on the spot, he was realizing just what a daunting task he'd taken on. It was a very long way down to the water, and then there were winds and a strong tide to contend with too. It all made Tower Bridge look like a stroll in the park. 'What's the weather forecast?' he asked.

'Reasonably good. Clear skies, not too much wind,

no rain. But I should say that the conditions here are unpredictable, always liable to change.'

'The crane will be where?' Consuela asked.

'About where we're standing,' Feinstein replied. 'The local carpenters will build the wooden crate on the freeway. Then the crane will winch the crate up and lower it over the side, with you at the controls, of course.'

'And the spectators?'

'This middle section will be closed off with barriers, but the rest of the east side of the bridge will be open to spectators. There'll be more over there on the shore of the bay, watching on a giant TV screen. There are going to be thousands of people here.'

Max and Consuela wandered off together, inspecting the area – the guard rail along the edge of the bridge, the drop to the water – and discussing in detail how they were going to do the stunt. Then they had a talk with Feinstein about tides and currents and wind speeds, making sure they were fully informed about the conditions in the area. The Golden Gate was a notoriously treacherous stretch of sea, a narrow opening through which huge volumes of water flowed. It was vital that they were properly prepared to deal with any problems that might arise.

Chris stayed in the background during this, not saying anything. This was Max and Consuela's show, not his. It wasn't his role to join in discussions about the technical aspects of the stunt. But he was alert and vigilant, watching every vehicle that went past on the freeway. He was all too aware of how exposed they were on the bridge, how vulnerable to attack. And when the others had finished talking, he asked Feinstein what measures had been taken to ensure Max's safety, before and after the stunt.

'Will there be police present?'

'Lots,' Feinstein replied. 'Max will get a police escort to and from the bridge. There will be cops manning the barriers and controlling the crowds, a helicopter over-head and a police launch down on the water. Don't worry, we're taking good care of him.'

'Thanks, I'm glad to hear it,' Chris said.

Max took a last look around. This was certainly a magnificent spot from which to admire the city. He let his gaze rove across the shoreline, taking in the old brick fort underneath the southern end of the bridge, then the beach and fields and nature reserve that fringed the bay before the real built-up area began – the houses and apartment blocks, the piers and wharves along the waterfront, the skyscrapers climbing the slopes behind. From this distance, white and dazzling in the sunshine, San Francisco looked stunningly beautiful.

Out in the bay, the water was dotted with yachts and the foaming wakes of motorboats and, rising up in the middle, a couple of miles away, was a small, rocky island topped by a long white building and a lighthouse.

'Is that Alcatraz?' Max said. He'd read about the famous prison in a San Francisco guidebook, knew that it had been America's most secure penitentiary before it was closed and turned into a tourist attraction.

'That's it,' Feinstein confirmed. 'Intimidating-looking place, isn't it? Al Capone was a prisoner there, and Machine Gun Kelly.'

'Is it true that no one ever escaped from it?' Chris asked.

'No,' Feinstein replied. 'A few guys did manage to get away. The most famous were three convicts who chipped through the back walls of their cells, left dummy heads in their beds and used home-made life-vests to get off the island. That's the tricky bit – getting across the bay, with its dangerous currents and tides. The guys were never seen again. No one knows for sure whether they got away or were drowned.' He grinned at Max. 'I reckon even *you* would have had trouble escaping from Alcatraz.'

Feinstein took them for lunch at a restaurant in Chinatown, then the afternoon was taken up with a press conference and interviews with the major television networks to promote the following night's stunt. By the end, Max was flagging and bored with having to smile and answer the same questions over and over again. His body clock had still not fully adjusted to the new time zone and he longed to go back to the hotel and sleep.

But when the promoter finally dropped them off at the Fairmont, there was a message waiting for Max at the reception desk that put all thoughts of resting out of his mind.

It was a single sheet of paper in a sealed envelope. The message on it read: *Call me on this number. Don't use your room phone, or a cellphone, use the payphone in the hotel lobby.* It was signed *Tony Halstead*.

Max gazed at the words, feeling his pulse increase. At last, he was in contact with Dr Halstead, the man who had helped his father fake his own death in Borneo and then – Max was sure – had helped him go into hiding again.

He showed the note to Consuela and Chris and they went across to the payphone together where Max dialled the number. It was answered on only the second ring.

'Max?' a man's voice said urgently.

'Yes, is that Dr Halstead?'

'We can't talk now. Be outside the hotel at ten o'clock tonight. Alone.'

'I have friends with me.'

'Leave them behind.'

'But they're here to protect me.'

'You won't need protection.'

'Where's my dad? Is he with you?'

'Not on the phone. I'll tell you tonight.'

'You know where he is?'

'Yes, I know where he is. Ten o'clock, OK? Just you, Max, you got that?'

'Yes.'

'I'll pick you up.'

The line went dead. Max hung up and checked his watch. It was twenty to six.

'What did he say?' Consuela asked.

'Not here,' Max replied, glancing warily around the lobby. 'Let's go upstairs.'

They took the lift up to their room. Max slumped down into an armchair.

'Well?' Consuela said.

'He's picking me up at ten tonight. Just me.'

'Now hang on a minute—' Chris began.

'*Alone*, he said,' Max broke in quickly.

'I don't like that. We don't know who this guy is, whether he can be trusted.'

'He's on our side,' Max said firmly. 'He helped my dad. I know we can trust him.'

'I still think we should come with you,' Consuela said.

Max shook his head. 'I've got to follow his instructions. He's being cautious – he sounded on edge. If he sees you two with me, he might drive straight past.'

'But we're all in this together,' Consuela protested. 'We're looking after you.'

'I told him that, but it didn't make any difference. I'll be OK. Halstead is important. I've spent weeks trying to track him down. Now I've found him, I don't want to blow it.'

Consuela and Chris exchanged concerned looks.

'Max, people are trying to kill you,' Consuela said anxiously. 'You're in a strange city. You're going to be getting in a car with a man you've never met before. That doesn't sound very sensible.'

'I don't care what it sounds like,' Max said defiantly. 'He said he knows where Dad is. I have to go with him. And no one's going to stop me.'

He got up and went into his bedroom, putting an end to the discussion. But Consuela wasn't prepared to let the matter drop. She followed him into the room and sat down on the end of his bed.

'Listen, Max,' she said gently. 'No one wants to stop

you finding your dad. I want it as much as you do. But you have to be careful.'

'I *am* being careful.'

'Are you? Are you sure?'

'*Yes*,' he insisted. 'I can look after myself, you know.'

'But you don't have to. Chris and I are here to protect you. You know that.'

Max softened his tone. Consuela was like a stand-in mother to him; he didn't want to upset her. 'Yes, I know. And I appreciate it. But Halstead was quite clear. He said I had to be alone. I know what I'm doing, Consuela. Stop worrying about me.'

She gazed at him for a long moment. Then she sighed and shook her head. 'It doesn't look as though I have a choice, does it? But you take care, Max. Don't do anything reckless. Make sure you have your mobile with you, and phone us if you get into trouble. You promise?'

Max nodded. 'OK, I promise.'

# ELEVEN

There were two men inside the dark green Ford saloon that pulled into the forecourt outside the Fairmont. The one in the front passenger seat had his window rolled down. He looked up at Max standing on the steps by the hotel entrance and held out his hand.

'Max? I'm Tony Halstead. Good to meet you. Get in.'

Max hesitated for a fraction of a second. He didn't know what Halstead looked like, but the voice was the one he'd heard on the phone.

'Get *in*,' Halstead repeated impatiently. He was glancing nervously around the street, turning his head from side to side. The driver kept the car engine running, his foot revving the throttle. Max pulled open the rear door and slid in. The car started moving immediately, while he was still fumbling for his seat belt.

They took the first left, the car accelerating rapidly. Max saw Huntington Park and Grace Cathedral flash past, then they turned right, then left, then right again in quick succession, going round the same block a couple of times to shake off tails, before turning into a broader road. Max saw a sign on a lamppost – Van Ness Avenue.

They drove downhill for several blocks, then turned right and began to climb a hill. The houses at the side of the road started to give way to shops and restaurants that looked familiar to Max. He realized he'd been there that morning with Herb Feinstein.

'Where are we?' he asked.

'Haight-Ashbury,' Halstead replied.

The Ford turned right into a side street and down a narrow lane into a cramped little yard behind the shops. Max got out and followed Halstead and his companion back round onto the main road. They went up a flight of stairs in between a bookshop and a vegetarian café. Halstead unlocked a door and led them into an office above the café. He went to the window and pulled a blind down, before clicking on a lamp on the desk.

Max got a proper look at him for the first time. He wasn't particularly tall – maybe only five eight or nine – but his build was solid and muscular, a broad chest and shoulders and thick biceps beneath his checked shirt. His face was tanned and he had a close-trimmed black beard and moustache. He looked like a hiker or a mountaineer, someone who spent his spare time outdoors.

'Sit down,' Halstead said. 'You want something to drink?'

Max shook his head, pulling out a chair by the desk. It was obviously the office of some kind of environmental organization, maybe a wilderness protection group if the posters on the wall were any indication. They were a mixture of photographs of beautiful pristine mountain lakes and forests and ugly open-cast mines and stripped hillsides where trees had been felled – a sort of 'before' and 'after' of what man was doing to the world.

'This is Jimmy,' Halstead said, nodding at his companion.

'Hi,' Jimmy said.

He was a small, skinny man in his mid-twenties, everything about him a marked contrast to Halstead. His chest was hollow, his arms like twigs and his clean-shaven face had a pale, pasty complexion, as if he spent too much time indoors.

'Hi,' Max replied. He looked at the doctor, who had sat down in the chair behind the desk. 'I've been trying to find you for weeks.'

Halstead raised an eyebrow in surprise. 'Yeah? I didn't know. Not until the hospital passed on your message yesterday. How did you trace me?'

'I was in Borneo, at the hospital in Pangkalan Bun just after you left. They said you'd gone to a new job in San Francisco.'

Halstead was staring at him in astonishment now. 'You were in Pangkalan Bun?'

'Looking for my dad. I went to his grave. I dug it up and found the empty coffin. Where is he? Is he here in San Francisco?'

'Yes, he's here,' Halstead replied.

Max's heart gave a jolt. He stared at the doctor. He couldn't believe he'd heard him correctly. His dad was in the city. The excitement pulsed through him like a drug.

'Where? In this building? I have to see him. Where is he?' The words tumbled out in an almost incoherent flood. 'How is he? Please, let me see him, now.'

Halstead held up his hand in a calming gesture. 'You will see him, Max. But I need to talk to you about him first.'

'Talk to me about what?'

The doctor studied him for a moment. His eyes were gentle and compassionate. 'I have to tell you that your dad isn't the person he used to be. How much do you know about what's happened to him over the last couple of years?'

'I know he was kidnapped by Julius Clark and held prisoner on Shadow Island, off Santo Domingo,' Max said. 'I know he was given a brainwashing drug called Episuderon and then somehow managed to escape from the island. After that, it's all a blank until I picked up his trail again in Borneo.'

Halstead pursed his lips, letting out a soft whistle.

'Wow, you have been busy, haven't you? I'm afraid your dad hasn't been well, physically or mentally. After he escaped from Shadow Island, he had a complete breakdown – caused by the Episuderon. He lost his memory, didn't know who he was. He was given help by a local man, a political activist named Luis Lopez-Vega, who took your dad to his sister, Maria, in a remote village in the north of Santo Domingo.'

'Lopez-Vega? I met him,' Max said quickly. 'He came to London to tell me Dad was still alive. Then he was murdered.'

Halstead nodded. 'A very sad event. Shortly after Lopez-Vega met your father, he was arrested on a trumped-up drugs charge and imprisoned for two years. When he was released, he went to see his sister. She had been hiding your dad, nursing him back to health all that time. By then, he had gotten much better. His memory had returned. He asked Lopez-Vega to go to London and find you.'

Suddenly things started to slip into place for Max. Those gaps in his knowledge were no longer so big.

'Dad left me a letter in northern Santo Domingo, hidden under some rocks on the coast. That must have been near the village where he was in hiding. He said he hadn't been well.'

'He still hasn't fully recovered. He's better than he was, but he's physically weak and he has momentary lapses of memory. His condition isn't helped by his reluctance to rest. He's overdoing it, determined to defeat Julius Clark.'

'Why hasn't he come home?' Max asked in bewilderment. 'Why hasn't he got my mum out of prison? She's been locked up for two years now and is really suffering.'

'I know this is hard for you, Max,' Halstead said sympathetically. 'But your father daren't come out of hiding or he'll be killed. Your mother would be in danger too. She's safer remaining in prison for the time being.'

'And how long is that going to be?'

'Not long, we hope. What do you know about Julius Clark?'

Max shrugged. 'I know he's a billionaire tycoon who makes money out of oil and minerals. I know he's kidnapping his opponents – environmentalists, scientists, lawyers, journalists, anyone who is a threat to his business interests – and brainwashing them, then releasing them so they can secretly work for him. Fifth columnists, he calls them – his supporters in the enemy camp.'

'You've met him?'

'He tried to kill me in Borneo. And on Shadow Island.'

Halstead's jaw dropped. He gaped at Max in surprise. '*Kill* you?'

'I'm a threat to him. I know too much about him, about what he's doing. And I'm going to find out more and see him put behind bars.'

The doctor looked worried. 'Max, you're only young. Your father wouldn't want you to take risks, to put your life in danger.'

'It's too late now,' Max replied. 'Where is my dad? What's he doing here in San Francisco?'

Halstead glanced at Jimmy, who was sitting to one side of the desk, sipping Coke from a can he'd got from a refrigerator in the corner of the office. 'Julius Clark isn't the only one with fifth columnists,' the doctor said. 'Jimmy Abbott here is ours – our mole inside Rescomin headquarters. Jimmy is an environmentalist, but he's managed to get himself a job working for Clark, in the Rescomin accounts department.'

Jimmy nodded. He was leaning forward in his chair, the can of Coke cupped in his hands. He was fidgeting nervously, his head moving from side to side, his sneakers tapping softly on the floor. Max noticed that he had a slight twitch in his left eye.

'I'm doing what I can,' Jimmy said. 'You know, for the Cedar Alliance.'

'You know about the Alliance?' Halstead asked Max.

'Yes, I know it's a secret organization that's trying to stop the Earth being destroyed by greedy businessmen like Clark. I know my dad is one of its leaders.'

'Jimmy is looking for evidence we can use against Clark,' Halstead said. 'We know he's been bribing politicians in developing countries, and here in the United States. We know he's broken laws, committed crimes. We just have to prove it.'

'Prove it how?' Max asked.

'By finding documentary evidence, following the paper trail, uncovering records of illegal payments to people, bank transfers, memos to Clark's employees in the countries where he does business.'

'I'm getting close,' Jimmy said. 'But I have to be care-ful, not draw attention to myself.' He took a long swig of Coke and stared down at the floor. His toes were still jiggling up and down, his left eye twitching occasionally. Max thought he looked under stress; the pressure of working undercover was obviously affecting his health.

'It takes a hell of a lot of guts to do what Jimmy's doing,' Halstead said admiringly. 'If Clark finds out he's working for us, he'll kill him.'

Max was suddenly concerned for his father's safety. 'What about my dad?' he said. 'Is it wise for him to be here, in the same city as Clark's headquarters? What if Clark's men find him?'

'They won't find him,' Halstead said reassuringly. 'He's in a safe house, just a couple of blocks from here. Only I know the location.'

'Can I see him now?'

The doctor nodded. 'Jimmy, you want to bring the car round to the front?'

'Sure.' Jimmy stood up and tossed his can into a recycling bin by the window. 'Which direction are we going?'

'Shrader Street. Number five two four.'

Jimmy went out of the office. Max and Halstead followed, Max barely able to control his mounting excitement. At last he was going to see his dad again. The doctor paused to set the alarm and lock the door behind them.

'You'd better prepare yourself, Max,' he said as they walked down the stairs. 'Your father's aged a lot over the past two years. He's lost a lot of weight, his hair has turned grey – you might not recognize him.'

'But he'll recover, won't he? Get back the way he was?'

'I don't know,' Halstead said, shaking his head

grimly. 'Episuderon is a very nasty drug. Who knows what its long-term effects might be.'

They emerged onto the street. It was dark now, but there were still a lot of people around. Loud music was blaring from a bar across the street; adjacent to the bar, a tattooist's parlour was still open for business, its front window lit up, showing examples of the elaborate designs customers could have inked into their skins. A scruffy man shuffled past, pushing a supermarket trolley piled high not with groceries but with what looked like his entire worldly goods.

'How did you meet my dad?' Max asked Halstead.

'Through the Cedar Alliance. I first met him, oh, ten or twelve years ago, not long after I'd finished medical school. I was working as a doctor in Seattle, but in my spare time I was very active in the environmental move-ment, campaigning to stop all sorts of things – the over-fishing of the seas, the killing of whales, the destruction of the wilderness by multinational oil and mineral corporations. Your dad recruited me for the Alliance, as an area coordinator for the northwest USA.' He glanced up the street. 'Jimmy's taking a long time . . . Anyway, then I got a job in Borneo, working at a hospital in Pangkalan Bun, and really got interested in how the rainforest was being destroyed, how it was affecting not just the local people, but the whole world.

I became the Cedar Alliance's coordinator for Indonesia, organizing protests, publicizing what was happening, helping local groups to be more effective in opposing the big logging and palm-oil companies like Rescomin – all behind the scenes, of course. The Alliance, as you know, always stays in the background, guiding things from a distance . . . Let's go find him. He should be here by now.'

They walked round into the side street and paused at the mouth of the access lane to the yard. There was no sign of the car coming out.

'He must be having trouble,' Halstead said, turning into the lane. 'Your dad trusted me – that's why he came to Borneo. He knew about Clark's fifth columnists. He was trying to find out how many there were around the world, trying to identify who they were and—' The doctor came to a stop. They'd reached the yard and he was peering around in the darkness, a puzzled frown on his forehead. 'What the . . .'

The dark green Ford was nowhere to be seen. Max looked around, too, wondering whether they'd somehow missed the car going past, or whether Jimmy had already been parked out at the front and they hadn't noticed him.

'Where the hell has he gone?' Halstead snapped. He sounded confused and irritated.

Max was also confused. But his confusion was rapidly giving way to more sinister thoughts. *What if something had happened to Jimmy?* Like what? Had he been kidnapped? Had someone taken both him and the car? Max felt suddenly alarmed. He sensed danger. 'I think we should get out of here,' he said urgently.

'What?' Halstead didn't seem to have heard him.

'Something's wrong. We shouldn't hang around.' Max turned and walked quickly back along the access lane and round to the front of the building, feeling safer under the street lights. He looked around for the Ford, but it wasn't on the street, either. Halstead came up next to him. He seemed more alert now, as if he were sensing danger too.

'Jimmy's a reliable guy,' he said tensely. 'He wouldn't just disappear.'

Max glanced up and down the street, watching out for people or vehicles approaching. He felt very exposed. 'What if Clark's men snatched him?' he said.

'That doesn't make sense. Jimmy would've put up a fight. We'd have heard or seen something.'

'Then where *is* he?'

Max's brain was in overdrive, working feverishly through all the possibilities, searching for an explanation. Why would Jimmy have vanished like that? If he hadn't been abducted – and Halstead was right, there were no signs of a struggle – then he must simply have driven off of his own free will. But why? Why drive off when Max and Halstead needed the car to go and see Max's father?

*My father*, Max thought abruptly. He's in a safe house, a place known only to Dr Halstead. No, not just Halstead. Jimmy knew where it was now. The doctor had given him the address. Five-twenty-four Shrader Street.

*Jimmy Abbott?*

*Oh my God, no!* Max's stomach turned to ice. Why hadn't he thought of it earlier? He spun round to face Halstead, feeling sick.

'Jimmy is short for James, isn't it?'

'What? Why are you—?'

'*Isn't it?*'

'Yes,' Halstead said.

'James Abbott. He was on Shadow Island.'

'Shadow Island? Jimmy? Max, you must be—'

'I saw his name in the files,' Max broke in. 'His and four others. James Abbott was taken to the island and brainwashed. He's not *your* fifth columnist, he's Julius Clark's.'

'Clark's? Max—'

'Don't you see? He's not working for you, he's

working for *Clark*. And you've just given him my dad's location. *That's* where he's gone.'

Halstead stared at him, horror-struck. 'You think—'

'Where's Shrader Street?' Max demanded.

'That way.' Halstead pointed west. 'Two blocks.'

Max took off along the street, running flat out. He heard the thud of Halstead's feet behind him, but didn't look round. He had to get to Shrader Street, get to his father. How could he have been so stupid? He should have worked it out the moment he heard Jimmy's name. It was one of the five. Three he'd already traced: only James Abbott and Sergei Alekseev had remained unidentified. Until now, that is.

Never before had he run so fast, with such ferocious determination. Jimmy had a head start on him – and he had a car – but Max had his strength and fitness, his speed honed over hundreds of training runs around the local park in London. Halstead couldn't keep up with him; Max glanced over his shoulder as he reached a junction and saw the doctor thirty metres back.

'Straight on!' Halstead yelled.

Max sprinted across the side street, narrowly avoiding a turning car. There were people on the pavement, coming out of restaurants and bars or just loitering around in groups. He dodged around them without slowing, accidentally bumping into a man's shoulder and earning a mouthful of abuse for the collision. He could feel the pain in his chest. He was gasping for air, his pulse off the scale. He was desperate. He *had* to get to his father. He was so near him. So near. To have him snatched away now would be a devastating blow.

He passed more shops, had to leap over the feet of a tramp who was stretched out in a doorway, wrapped in a blanket. Then he looked up and saw a sign on a lamp-post – SHRADER.

'Go right,' Halstead called.

Max turned into the street and paused, looking at the buildings, trying to see their numbers. Which side was 524 on? He saw 542 to his right, so even numbers were on this side. 524 couldn't be far away. Then he saw them. Five men coming out of the front door of a four-storey Victorian house fifty metres ahead of him. He recognized Jimmy Abbott, but not the other four. Then he realized that the man in the centre of the group was being held by his arms, forced down the steps against his will. He was struggling to escape, but the others were too strong for him. Max stopped dead, realizing who it was.

'Dad!'

The cry escaped from his lips without him being aware he'd spoken. The men turned their heads and Max caught a glimpse of his father's face. He was almost unrecognizable as the dad he remembered – his face was haggard, with hollow eyes and prominent cheekbones, his hair thin and grey as smoke.

'Max?' he called out weakly. 'Max, is that you? Get away from here.'

Max heard Halstead running up behind him, heard the rasp of his laboured breathing. He didn't look round. His eyes were fixed on his father, on the men who were taking him away. One of them broke apart from the group, his right hand reaching under his jacket and bringing something out. Max saw the glint of metal in the lamplight and instinctively threw himself sideways behind a parked car. The pistol fired once, then again.

Max rolled over on the tarmac and glanced round in time to see Halstead tumbling to the ground, a dark patch of blood on the front of his shirt. There was another gunshot. A bullet pinged off the bodywork of the car only inches from Max's head. He pulled himself up into a crouch and scuttled away across the road, keeping low and zigzagging to offer less of a target to the gunman. He heard another report, felt a bullet whine past his ear. He dived into the cover of a van parked on the far side of the street and twisted round. He could hear his father protesting, his voice faint and croaky. Then car doors slammed, an engine started up and the dark green Ford came speeding past. Max saw Jimmy at the wheel, a man in the back he didn't recognize, with Alexander Cassidy next to him. Alexander turned his head and for a split second his eyes met Max's, father and son communicating with each other, almost identical emotions fleeting across their faces – fear, anxiety, love.

Then the car was gone and Max was staring across the street at Halstead's lifeless body, aware that there were still two men unaccounted for – men who were intent on killing him too. He knelt up and cocked an eye round the side of the van. The men were coming warily out across the street. They were tall and powerfully built, but light on their feet. Both had automatic pistols outstretched in front of them, holding them in two hands like soldiers or policemen – professionals who were used to handling firearms.

Max knew he had to move fast. Scrambling to his feet, he raced out from behind the van and sprinted away along the pavement, veering into a parking lot on the corner of the street and running diagonally across it, using the parked cars to shield himself. When he came out of the lot, he turned right along the main road and kept running for a block until the buildings petered out. A street cut horizontally across his path, and on the other side of it was what looked like a park, a large open space with dense shrubberies and pockets of trees that would provide good places to hide.

He looked back. The two men were running towards him, moving easily like athletes. One of them had a phone pressed to his ear. Max felt a sharp stab of fear in his guts. He turned and dashed across the road into the park.

# TWELVE

There was grass underfoot, a copse of tall redwood trees towering over him. Max ran in a straight line, not caring where the path was, just trying to put as much distance as he could between himself and the men behind.

He trod on something soft, heard a yelp and stumbled to the ground, realizing he'd tripped over a tramp sleeping rough. The tramp sat up, flailing his arms and yelling incoherently, so close that Max could smell the strong odour of alcohol on his breath. He rolled away and pulled himself to his feet.

'Sorry,' he murmured, and sprinted off, pushing past a large bush and breaking out onto a patch of open grass. There was a road on the far side of the grass, intermittent headlights moving along it. Max recognized where he was: Golden Gate Park. Herb Feinstein had driven him through it that morning.

Max raced across the open space. If he could get to the road, maybe he could stop a car, get help. He looked back. He couldn't see the men, but that didn't mean they weren't there. It was so black that they could have been just a few metres away and he wouldn't have noticed them. The thought made him accelerate. He knew he was running for his life. These men had gunned down Dr Halstead in a well-lit suburban street. They wouldn't hesitate to kill Max in this dark, secluded park.

He reached the road and paused, looking both ways for headlights. But the cars he'd seen earlier had all passed by and the road was deserted. Glancing over his shoulder, he could now make out two shadowy figures jogging across the grass towards him. They didn't seem to be in any hurry. Max found that lack of haste almost more terrifying than the guns he knew they were carrying. It showed how confident they were, how completely sure of their superior force. They didn't need to rush. They had Max where they wanted him – alone and defenceless in a park at night. It was only a matter of time before they caught up with him and finished the job.

Max felt his anger start to simmer. These men thought they could do anything. They'd kidnapped his father, they'd shot Tony Halstead and now they were going to kill him. Well, they weren't going to find it easy. He was young and fit and determined, and was fighting for his very survival. There was no way he was going to let them catch him.

He sped across the road and crossed another open

patch of grass, the ground underneath it uneven and pitted with hollows. It was too dark to really see where he was going. He had to run blind, feel his way across the field using his other senses.

He came out onto a second road and paused to draw breath. There was a high chain-link fence on the far side of the road, blocking his path, so he turned right and ran along the carriageway. There were no cars around, no pedestrians. He looked over his shoulder. The two men had reached the road and one of them was now talking into his mobile.

The sight reminded Max that he had a phone too. In the panic and agitation of getting away from the gunmen, he'd forgotten all about it. He felt in his jacket pocket, increasing his speed around a bend in the road. He could hear the sound of his own breathing, the pad of his trainers on the tarmac. He was getting tired. Then he heard the faint noise of an engine, saw the flicker of headlights on the trees and a car came cruising into view a hundred metres in front of him. Max let out a sigh of relief. Help was at hand.

He ran out into the middle of the road, waving his arms frantically. The car headlights hit him in the face and something about the vehicle suddenly struck him as wrong. It was going very slowly, prowling like a police patrol car. But it wasn't a police car, and this wasn't a built-up area. Why was it going so slowly? Then he remembered the man talking into his phone and realized with a sickening jolt what he'd been doing. This car wasn't help – it was back-up for the killers on his tail.

For an instant, Max froze. The road was blocked in both directions. He pulled his phone out of his pocket and switched it on. The car accelerated, heading straight for him. Max dived out of the way, the phone slipping from his fingers and skittering away into some bushes. The car had stopped just up the road. Max heard doors slamming, the pounding of feet. There was no time to look for his phone. He leaped up at the chain-link fence, scrambled over the top and dropped to the ground on the other side. As he landed, he saw two men in dark suits running towards the fence, guns in their hands. He scuttled away into the undergrowth and burst out onto a path. The fence would slow the men up, give him a chance of getting away.

The path went up a slight incline past flowerbeds and formal gardens. Max wondered about hiding some-where, but rejected the idea – it was far too passive for his liking. Better to keep on the move and try to outrun his pursuers. He entered a wood, huge sequoia trees blocking out what little light was filtering in from the streetlamps on the nearby road. He was starting to feel the pain now; the hill was sapping his energy. His legs and chest aching, he paused briefly, looking back the way he'd come, listening hard. He could detect no signs of the men. Had they come over the fence after him? Or were they circling around the perimeter – maybe using their car – waiting for him to come out? The thought made his heart beat faster. He had to keep running, get out the far side of the gardens before the men got there.

The terrain levelled out as he left the wood, easing the pressure on his body. He could see an orange glow in the sky – the lights of the city that was all around the park. There were thousands of sleeping citizens only a short distance away, but they were out of reach for Max, out of earshot. If he shouted for help, no one was going to hear him except the gunmen who wanted him dead.

As the ground began to slope gently downhill, Max got a second wind and increased his speed. The path was soft and yielding, bark chippings rather than the concrete of the earlier paths. It cushioned his legs, made running easier. His eyes had fully adjusted to the darkness now. He could see the edges of the path, the shapes of the plants in the borders and, up ahead, a harder, more defined line that he realized was the perimeter fence.

He sprinted up to it and stopped, panting for breath. There were bushes on the other side of the wire mesh, blocking his view. Were the gunmen out there some-where, waiting for him to emerge? It was impossible to tell. Grasping the mesh with his fingers, he climbed up the fence and down the other side. Then he pushed his way cautiously through the bushes, pausing where they came to an end to survey the ground beyond. There was a strip of grass next to another road and across it a steep, wooded hill. Max looked around intently, his gaze probing the shadows, the trees on the far side of the road. He saw nothing suspicious, nothing to alarm him.

Keeping low, he edged forward, then burst out and dashed across the strip of grass. He was crossing the road when a car suddenly appeared around the bend to his right, its headlights momentarily illuminating him before he broke out of the beams and plunged into the wood.

It was tough-going up the hill. The gradient was steep, almost vertical in places, and the ground was soft, the soil slipping away beneath his feet. Max scrambled up on all fours, using his hands to assist him, clinging onto bushes and tree roots. Down below, the car had stopped and two men had leaped out and followed him into the wood.

Max tried not to panic. The men were only thirty or forty metres behind him. He could hear them snapping twigs, breaking through the undergrowth. He was hurting badly. His lungs and muscles were burning, crying out for relief, but he didn't slow down. He made himself keep going at the same punishing pace. To give up now meant certain death.

He clambered up to the top of the hill and stopped. There was open ground in front of him. At least, that was what he thought at first. Then he saw that it wasn't ground at all, it was water. He was standing on the edge of a lake.

He had no choice. Every second he waited the gunmen were getting nearer. He waded out into the shallows, the cold water creeping up his legs. He let it reach his thighs, then dived forward and started swimming – on the surface for a few strokes, then he took a deep breath and ducked under to conceal himself from the gunmen.

He struck out under the water, but he could feel his muscles struggling. In ideal conditions, he could swim a hundred metres underwater, but not tonight. He was too tired, there wasn't enough air in his lungs. Fortunately, it wasn't a big lake. After only a short distance he felt it getting shallower. His fingers touched vegetation, the stems of reeds that were growing along the shoreline. He swam through the stems and let himself float to the surface, making as little noise as possible. He sucked in air and lay there motionless, the reeds forming a screen around him.

He could see the two men on the far shore. They were scanning the water. They would guess that Max had swum out into the lake, but they couldn't know exactly where he was now. It was too dark, he was too well hidden in the reeds.

What would they do? Max wondered. Would they swim out after him? A cold lake in the middle of the night, the water ruining their smart black suits, probably wasn't an appealing prospect for them, unless there was no alternative. They were obviously discussing what to do, murmuring quietly to each other. Max watched them, wishing they'd make up their minds. It was freezing lying there in the water and he could feel his body temperature plummeting, his teeth starting to chatter.

Finally, the men seemed to come to a decision. They split up, one going left along the lakeshore, the other going right. Max shivered, and it wasn't the cold water that caused it: it was fear. The men were going to circle around the lake from both directions and try to pick up his trail on the other side.

As quietly as he could, he floated through the reeds and dragged himself out onto the bank, lying flat on the ground while he took in his surroundings. There was a dirt path running along the edge of the lake – a flat strip about three or four metres wide. Beyond it, the ground rose steeply up another tree-covered hill. Max couldn't face a second climb – he didn't have the strength. He'd have to skirt around the base of the hill where the going was easier.

Pulling himself to his feet, he paused to glance around. He could no longer see either of the gunmen, which was worrying. He didn't know how far the lake extended. Were the two men even now reaching his side, trapping him in a pincer movement? He had to keep running, weary though he was. Every second he waited gave them more time to catch him.

But which way to go? Left or right? It didn't seem to make any difference. He chose left, jogging away along the path. His clothes were heavy with water, his feet squelching in his trainers. He knew the extra weight would slow him down, but he couldn't afford to stop to wring them out.

The path curved around to the right, the hill rising up on one side, the water on the other, the lake following the same curve as the path, never getting any wider or narrower. Its shape was more like a bend in a river than a lake, only it couldn't be a river, there was no current. Max had the sudden, frightening realization that he wasn't on the other side of a lake – he was on an *island* in the middle of one.

He pulled up abruptly. He could see the faint silhouette of a bridge up ahead, spanning the water from the shore to the island. A man was moving across the bridge. Max was trapped.

There was no point in retreating, or trying to climb the hill. He would still be on the island if he did that. To have any chance of escape, he had to go back into the water. Dropping to the ground, he slithered down the bank into the lake, gliding out through the reeds, then ducking down beneath the surface once he'd reached open water. He swam slowly and smoothly, trying to conserve his remaining energy, but also to avoid leaving any telltale ripples that the gunman might spot. The lake wasn't very wide at this point, probably no more than thirty metres. Max's hands touched the bottom, then found the stems of reeds and he knew he'd reached the other side.

He lifted his head, gulping in air, and the world erupted suddenly around him – there was a deafening honking noise, a ferocious flapping of wings as a flock of geese he'd disturbed lifted off. Max took a moment to recover from the shock, then he splashed rapidly to the shore and heaved himself out onto the bank. The gunman couldn't have failed to notice the geese taking wing and would know it meant only one thing.

Max heard a gunshot and a bullet hissed past his

head. He scuttled across the bank, keeping low. There was another gunshot. This time, something zipped through the flap of his jacket. Max ducked lower and hurled himself into a clump of bushes, tumbling down the hill on the other side. But he was going too fast to control his descent, and he rolled over and over, smashing through the undergrowth, narrowly missing several tree trunks before coming to a stop in a heap at the bottom of the slope. Battered and bruised, he staggered to his feet and stumbled away.

Every part of his body was hurting now – his legs, his arms, his chest, his lungs. A fast jog was the most he could manage. Sprinting was out of the question. If the gunmen caught him in the open, even saw him from a distance, Max knew they would quickly catch up with him. So he had to make sure that didn't happen. He had to stay undercover, yet keep moving at the same time.

Sheltered by a line of trees, he headed west across the park, emerging only when he had no alternative. Each time he encountered a patch of grass or other open terrain, he tried to find a way round it without coming out from cover. He crept through woods, dashed from bush to bush, did anything he could to stay out of sight.

Then he came to another of the empty roads that crossed the park. All his cover was gone. There was a fence along one side of the road, a broad area of grass on the other. He hesitated. If he kept going, he would be dangerously exposed, but if he stayed put, he risked being caught. He hadn't seen or heard the gunmen since he'd left the lake, but he knew they would still be searching for him. They might not be far behind.

He checked the road. Like all the others, it was quiet at this time of night. If he was quick, he wouldn't be out in the open for long. Glancing carefully around once more, he started jogging along the verge between the road and the fence. His clothes were still sodden, his trousers and shirt sticking uncomfortably to his skin.

He'd gone less than fifty metres when the car came out of nowhere. He didn't hear it, didn't see it until he looked over his shoulder and the headlights blinded him. It was moving fast along the road, too fast to outrun. He knew they were going to try and knock him down again, make it look like a hit-and-run accident. He did the only thing he could in the circumstances: he veered across the verge and clambered over the fence. Looking back, he saw the car come to a stop, two men in suits jumping out. Max accelerated, surprising even himself with his turn of speed. But he knew it was his last gasp. He couldn't keep it up for long, he was too drained. He gritted his teeth, forcing himself through the pain barrier.

He was in a field covered with thick tufts of grass. No shrubs or trees. No cover of any kind, except the darkness all around. It was that, he guessed, that was stopping the men from opening fire again. They couldn't see him well enough to take aim.

They were over the fence now, about sixty metres back. Max tried to speed up, but his legs wouldn't respond. Nor would his lungs. He was struggling to breathe and his pulse was hammering away furiously, making his head throb. The men were gaining on him. For a fleeting moment, Max wondered why he was still running. What was the point now? Then he pulled himself together. *Don't be so gutless*, he thought. *There's still hope.*

The field started to slope uphill. That hurt even more. Max was in agony, gasping painfully for air, his legs leaden and on fire. Something loomed up out of the darkness in front of him – another fence, this one higher than the first. He didn't have the strength to climb it, or to keep running. He slumped to the ground and leaned back on the wire mesh. Waiting for the gunmen to come and finish him off.

He closed his eyes, feeling his heart pounding, hearing the wheeze of his own breathing. Then he heard something else, something shuffling around on the other side of the fence, and he became aware of a pungent smell – an animal smell of dung and musk. He opened his eyes and twisted his head round. There was an animal pressing against the wire mesh with its muzzle. No, not one animal, but several, maybe more. Big animals with long, shaggy coats. He was beside the buffalo enclosure that Herb Feinstein had told him about that morning.

Max saw a metal rod directly in front of his eyes and took a second to work out what it was. A bolt. This wasn't a fence. It was a gate. And beyond the gate was a herd of buffalo. He looked round. The gunmen were coming up the slope, walking slowly now – they didn't need to run any more. There was just enough light for Max to see the pistols in their hands.

He reached behind him, grasped hold of the bolt and rammed it back hard, pulling open the gate and rolling sideways out of the way as the buffalo charged through into the field. For such huge animals they were surprisingly fast. They surged by with a thunder of hooves, crammed tightly together in a moving wall of solid muscle. The two gunmen didn't stand a chance. The buffalo hit them like a tidal wave, knocking them to the ground, then trampling over the bodies. Max heard a muffled cry, then nothing.

He waited for the stampede to end, the buffalo to disperse across the field, then got up and walked over to the bodies lying sprawled in the grass. Neither man was moving. Max couldn't tell whether they were alive or dead, and didn't want to touch them to find out. He wanted only to get away from the area as quickly as possible. But he couldn't just leave the men there, either. What if they were only injured and needed urgent medical help? Would their mobile phones have survived the stampede?

Bracing himself, Max crouched down by the nearest body. He patted the man's jacket and felt a lump in one of the side pockets. The man stirred and Max pulled back abruptly. So he wasn't dead. Max didn't know whether to be relieved or alarmed, but he waited a moment, then leaned over again and gently removed the phone from the man's pocket. It seemed to be intact. He dialled 911.

'There's been an accident,' he said when the emergency operator answered. 'Outside the buffalo enclosure in Golden Gate Park. The animals are loose too.'

Max rang off and tossed the phone down. Then he ran across the field, scrambled over the fence and disappeared into the trees.

# THIRTEEN

Max was a quarter of a mile from the buffalo paddock when he heard the distant sounds of sirens and guessed that the emergency services were on their way. He was shaken by what had happened. He hadn't wanted to injure the gunmen, but they'd left him with no choice. He'd acted purely in self-defence; opening the gate had been an impulse decision, the only action left to him. He'd thought it might create a diversion, give him the chance to slip away. It hadn't occurred to him that the buffalo would charge out and trample the men. In retrospect, he would do the same thing again, he realized. They'd tried to kill him. Why should he feel sympathy for them? If they'd had their way, it would be Max lying there dead in the enclosure.

He jogged across the fairway of a golf course, then paused in a copse to strip off his wet clothes, wring the water out of them and then put them back on. They were cold and clammy. He shivered and kept running, knowing he wasn't out of danger yet. There had been four men in total pursuing him across the park. Two of them were no longer a threat, but what of the other two? Were they still searching the area for him?

Max stayed vigilant until he reached the edge of the park and came out onto a well-lit street. Even there, he didn't feel completely safe as he headed east towards the downtown area, walking as fast as his exhausted body would allow and keeping his eyes skinned for any signs of the other two men.

As he walked, he thought about what had happened in Haight-Ashbury just an hour or so earlier – the shock he'd felt as he watched Tony Halstead being gunned down, his father taken away. He could still see his dad's face, his expression as the car went past. The memory cut into his heart like a knife. He'd been stunned by his dad's appearance, how frail and ill he looked. Where had the men taken him? Why had they taken him away at all? Why hadn't they simply killed him in the house in Shrader Street? There had to be a reason.

Had they gone to Rescomin headquarters? It was possible, maybe more than possible. Max had intended going there, in any case, to see if he could find out what had happened to the consignments of Episuderon that had been sent there from Woodford Down Laboratories, but looking for his dad now gave him another good reason to check it out. And he couldn't afford to delay. If his dad *was* there, Max had to find him quickly.

Should he try to do it alone? Maybe not. Maybe he should go back to the hotel and consult Chris and Consuela, let the police look for his father. But would the police be interested? Would they believe Max's story, which had all the hallmarks of fantasy, the product of a teenage boy's over-active imagination? A man who'd disappeared two years earlier in Central America suddenly resurfaces in San Francisco and is kidnapped by gunmen working for Julius Clark, one of the world's richest, most respected businessmen. Did that sound likely?

And could the San Francisco police even be trusted? Clark had friends in very high places, his tentacles of power stretched everywhere. Rescomin was an important company in the city. Who was to say whether the local police weren't in Clark's sphere of influence. Max had learned over the past few months to rely on no one except his closest allies. The betrayal by Jimmy Abbott, whom Dr Halstead had trusted implicitly, had only reinforced those lessons. Trust no one. If you want something done, do it yourself.

He increased his pace, looking back to see if there were any buses on the horizon. He'd passed a couple of stops, but seen no one waiting at them. Maybe the buses in San Francisco didn't run this late. Then over the road, he saw a yellow cab dropping off a man and woman outside a house. He sprinted across and caught the driver before he pulled away.

'I need to go downtown,' he said. 'Can you take me?' He pulled out a wad of damp dollar bills. 'I can pay.'

The driver looked at the money. He barely glanced at Max, didn't seem to notice – or care about – his rather bedraggled state. 'Get in,' he said. 'Where d'you wanna go?'

Max gave him the address and collapsed back into the seat, finally able to relax, finally feeling safe. But it was only a brief respite. His mind was focused on what he was about to do – on the dangers of venturing into his enemies' lair. It was a terrifying prospect, but he knew he had to take the risk.

The Rescomin headquarters was in the Financial District, on the east side of the city, a densely built-up area of office blocks and skyscrapers. None of it was on a New York scale – the buildings were mostly less than forty storeys high – but there were enough of them to create an oppressive feeling of size, of soaring glass and concrete towers broken up by deep, shadowy canyons.

Max got out of the taxi on California Street, paid the driver and gave him a generous tip, which he hoped would make up for the mess his wet clothes had left on the rear seat. The area was quiet, empty of people and traffic. There were metal tracks running along the centre of the street, but it was too late for the cable cars to be running and most of the buildings were in darkness, although their corporate signs and logos were still illuminated. There seemed to be a lot of banks in the office blocks, with the ground floors occupied by the kinds of smaller businesses that were always found in financial districts – courier services, restaurants, copy shops, florists.

Rescomin Tower had a small plaza in front of it, containing a fountain and flowerbeds and four massive stone urns, taller than a man, that overflowed with ferns and trailing vegetation. The building itself was a smooth, shiny glass box stretching high up into the sky. Max counted the storeys: there were thirty-five, the bottom two of which were taken up by an opulent, brightly-lit lobby. What interested him most was the reception desk near the rear wall. A uniformed guard was sitting behind it, a barrier to one side giving access to the lifts that could not be reached without the guard's authorization.

Max wasn't surprised by the security – it was no less than he'd expected in a corporate headquarters. He'd have to find another way of getting inside.

Walking across the plaza, he went down the street at

the side of the building – straight into a strong head-wind that knifed through his wet clothes, chilling his body and making him shiver. At the rear of the tower, there was a ramp leading down into a subterranean section, probably a car park, and a row of big industrial waste bins. Next to the bins was a high metal roller door that looked like a loading bay entrance for delivery vehicles, with a smaller door in the wall beside it. Max looked around. He could see no sign of any CCTV cameras. He tried the door. It was locked, so he went to the waste bins, lifted the lid of one and rummaged inside it until he found a thin strip of metal that had been thrown away. He returned to the door and used the strip to pick the lock.

He paused. Would the door have an alarm on it? Probably, but he'd just have to deal with it. He grasped the handle and pushed the door open. Inside was a vast, cavernous space, with a concrete floor and a ceiling so high that, in the darkness, Max couldn't see exactly where it began. What he could see, however, was the alarm keypad on the wall beside the door. He knew he had only a few seconds before the alarm went off. He didn't waste time punching random buttons, trying to guess the code for disabling the system. Instead, he glanced quickly around the area, light trickling in through the door. He took in the raised concrete platform for loading and unloading lorries, the stacks of cardboard boxes and crates on the floor and, in the wall to one side, a door and wide glass window that looked like an office.

He closed the external door behind him. The loading bay was immediately plunged into blackness. Max crouched down and relocked the door. As he finished, he saw that the indicator light on the keypad had changed from green to flashing red. No bells started ringing, which surprised him, but he guessed that somewhere in the building – maybe on the desk in the lobby – another light was also flashing red and a security guard would soon be coming to investigate.

He walked across the bay as quickly as he dared in the pitch-darkness, his hands outstretched in front of him. His fingers touched a large wooden crate and he felt his way round it, going deeper into the bay until he found a collection of small cardboard boxes grouped together in stacks a couple of metres high. He slid one of the stacks aside and squeezed through the gap, re-arranging the boxes to create a space in the middle big enough to conceal him.

He was only just in time. The loading-bay lights clicked on. Max blinked, shielding his face from the glare for a few seconds to let his eyes adjust. He heard footsteps – a lone man walking across the bay towards the external door. The footsteps stopped. The door handle rattled. The man was trying it, finding it still locked. What would he do now? Just reset the alarm, assuming there'd been some malfunction in the system, and go away – that was what Max hoped. He held his breath, listening hard and detecting the faint tap of a finger on the keypad. Then the man came back across the bay and into the stacks of containers. He passed only a metre away from where Max was hiding, but didn't stop. A walkie-talkie crackled and the man spoke into it, talking to a colleague somewhere.

'Looks OK,' he said. 'The door's secure. Must have been a glitch in the power supply. Put it in the log and we'll get the engineer to look at it in the morning.'

The footsteps grew fainter. The lights went out. Max stayed where he was for a few minutes, then crept out and felt his way across to the office door he'd noticed earlier. It wasn't locked. Going inside, he fumbled around and located a switch on the wall. A bare bulb in the ceiling came on, flooding the room with harsh light.

It wasn't a big office, maybe four metres wide and three deep, containing a desk and chair, a computer terminal and two filing cabinets. The outer wall was taken up almost entirely by the window overlooking the loading bay and on the inner wall was a huge calendar showing every day of the year, the date squares marked with coloured stickers and neat felt-tip pen writing. A sign on the door read, DISPATCH OFFICE.

Max sat down at the desk and turned on the computer. Access to the files required a password. He knew he'd never be able to guess it in a million years, so he hunted around the desk for a few minutes, just in case someone had been careless enough to write it down somewhere. They hadn't.

*Never mind*, he said to himself. *It was always going to be a long shot.* He switched off the computer and turned his attention to the in-tray on the desk, which was over-flowing with paper. He sifted through the documents. Most of them related to cargo shipments – machine parts, engineering accessories, foodstuffs and other goods that were being sent to a place called Zaliv Myertvetsa.

Max had heard that name before. It took him a moment to realize where: in the *London News Chronicle* offices when Dan Kingston had shown him the locations of Rescomin's operations around the world. Zaliv Myertvetsa had been in Kamchatka, on the east coast of Russia. Rescomin had a platinum mine there, if he remembered correctly.

The cargo was being shipped to Kamchatka on a vessel named the *Reunion Star* which, according to the paperwork, was berthed at Pier 80, Cesar Chavez Street, in San Francisco Bay. Max twisted round to look at the wall calendar. On the date square for Monday 27 July, only two days away, were written the words, *Reunion Star sails, 9 a.m.*

Max went carefully through the pile of documents, but found nothing that really interested him, in particular no mention of Episuderon, so he moved on to the filing cabinets. They were both locked. He could have picked the locks, but he didn't need to bother since the keys were in a tray on the desk.

He opened the first cabinet and looked in the files beginning with the letter 'E'. There was no mention of Episuderon there either. Disappointed, he sat back down and stared out through the window at the towers of boxes in the loading bay. He knew from the files at Woodford Down that three hundred ampoules of the drug had been sent to this building only two weeks ago. Had the ampoules already been dispatched to some other location? Or were they still here, awaiting dispatch. *Are they out there in one of those boxes in the loading bay?* he wondered. He thought about checking them all, then realized what an unrealistic idea it was. There must have been a thousand or more boxes and many of them were out of reach – high up in the stacks or buried beneath other containers. Examining them all was out of the question.

So what now? Were there more files somewhere else, maybe upstairs in the main offices? That was possible, but finding them was not going to be easy. Where did he begin? Rescomin Tower was thirty-five storeys high, with dozens of offices on each floor. There was no way he could search such a huge building, especially in the dark.

Then he thought suddenly of that night he had gone through the files at Woodford Down. The Episuderon sales hadn't been filed under the name of the drug itself, they'd been filed under the name of the company buying it – Rescomin. So the reverse should apply here: the purchases would be filed under the name of the company selling the Episuderon – Phobos Pharmaceuticals.

Max went back to the cabinet and rummaged through the 'P' file. There it was: Phobos Pharmaceuticals. He took out the wad of documents and spread them out on the desk. Some were 'Goods In' papers – the invoices and notes that had accompanied the Episuderon to San Francisco. They told him nothing he didn't already know. But others were 'Goods Out' papers. Now that was what he wanted. He put them all in a pile and sorted through them. The earlier invoices showed that Episuderon had been flown from San Francisco to Santo Domingo, presumably for use on

Shadow Island. But for the past few weeks every cargo of Episuderon that had arrived from the UK had been sent on by air freight to a Rescomin office in Petropavlovsk-Kamchatskiy, and from there to Zaliv Myertvetsa.

Max put the documents back in the cabinet and locked it. He'd answered one of the questions that had been nagging away at him. Now for the other question: had his father been brought here to Rescomin head-quarters? There was only one way to find out – go upstairs and look.

Leaving the light on in the dispatch office so he could see what he was doing, he went out into the load-ing bay and explored its furthest reaches, discovering two service lifts and a door to the emergency stairs at the rear. He decided against taking the lift – the security guards might possibly use them – and took the stairs instead. They were in a well on the north side of the tower, enclosed by glass windows that gave a clear view of the surrounding area.

Max ran up to the first floor, pushed open the door from the stairwell and found himself in a large, open-plan office space that was divided up into cubicles by shoulder-high partitions. There were no lights on any-where. It was the small hours of the morning now, so he didn't think that anyone would be working at this time

– even the cleaners would have come and gone. Therefore any light burning in an office would be easy to spot, and almost certainly suspicious.

He went back to the stairs and headed up to the second floor. That was similar to the first – another huge open-plan office in complete darkness. The third and fourth floors were the same, but the fifth had corridors with smaller individual offices opening off them. Max checked every corridor, looking for light seeping out under the doors, but saw no sign that there was anyone there.

Slowly, he worked his way up the building. Too slowly. After an hour, he'd only reached the fifteenth floor. That left another twenty storeys to go. It would be daylight before he'd finished. He decided to speed things up by using one of the service lifts. He'd just have to take the risk of encountering a guard. *Was* his father in the building? Max was beginning to wonder. But by the thirtieth floor, he'd seen no sign of anybody, let alone his dad. The place appeared to be deserted.

On the thirty-first floor, he discovered how wrong he was.

The lift doors opened and Max was startled to see Jimmy Abbott waiting just outside. Jimmy was taken by surprise too. He gaped at Max and yelled out, then stepped forward, but Max was too quick for him. He jabbed the button on the control panel and the doors started to slide shut. Jimmy thrust his arm and a leg into the closing gap, trying to hold the doors open. Max shoved him back and kicked him hard on the leg. Jimmy cried out in pain and Max kicked him again, pushing Jimmy's shoulder back with all his strength, then withdrawing his hands just before the doors snapped shut.

Max hammered on the nearest button – for the thirty-fifth floor – and felt the lift surge upwards. Moments later, the doors slid open and he darted out. Glancing up and to the side, he saw that the floor indicator panel above the second lift was illuminated, reading thirty-three, then thirty four. They were coming up after him.

Max stared around desperately, trying not to panic. He ran across to the stairwell door and hurled himself through. He was about to race down the stairs when he heard rapid footsteps echoing up from below. He peered over the handrail. Two men were running up from the thirty-fourth floor – his escape route was cut off. He had no choice; he had to go up. Spinning round, he sprinted up the stairs and burst out onto the roof of the tower.

The first thing he saw were other skyscrapers surrounding the building and the tall, slim Transamerica Pyramid lit up in the distance like the spire of a cathedral, a red light winking on its top to warn away low-flying aircraft. Then he turned his gaze to the roof itself. It was flat and broad, with a waist-high concrete parapet around the edges. In the centre was a two-storey high block housing the lift shafts and the services for the building – water tanks and air conditioning units. Max ran around to the other side of the block and paused, panting for breath.

He was trapped. There was only one way off the roof – the stairs he'd just come up – and his pursuers were on them. They might even be emerging from the stairwell right now. Max knew he couldn't evade them. There was nowhere to hide up here, and nowhere to run. He would just have to give himself up.

But everything in his nature rebelled at the thought. Giving up wasn't something that he did, especially as he knew that giving up wasn't just defeat – it was death. They would kill him for certain. They'd tried and failed on Shrader Street and then again in Golden Gate Park, but they'd finish him off this time. Max had no doubt about that. But what alternative did he have? Could he fight them? They were grown men, and they had guns. What chance did he stand against them? They wouldn't even give him the opportunity to fight. They would shoot him down the moment they saw him.

But Max wasn't going to go quietly. And he wasn't

going to wait meekly for them to come for him. If he was going to die, he was going to do it on the move, resisting to the very last.

The stairs were blocked, but maybe there *was* another way off the roof. Maybe he could attempt to climb down the outside of the building. Tower blocks like this had window frames and ledges that could provide hand- and footholds. It was crazy, but it was the only option he had.

He sprinted across the roof and looked over the parapet. It was a long way to the ground. He felt his stomach lurch at the prospect of trying to climb down a thirty-five-storey skyscraper. One slip and . . . he didn't let himself finish the thought.

He looked to his right and something caught his eye. What was that? Suspended on wires just below roof level was a small platform with a metal fence around its edges. His heart leaped, stirred by a sudden burst of hope. It was a window-cleaning gondola that could go up and down the sides of the building, with enough space inside it for a couple of people to wash the glass panes. Maybe he didn't have to climb down, after all.

He raced along by the parapet, noticing the thick steel girder embedded into its surface. He should have spotted it earlier. It was the track that the hoist supporting the gondola used for moving sideways across the tower.

*Bang!* A gunshot reverberated around the roof and a bullet ricocheted off the top of the parapet only inches in front of Max. He twisted his head and saw a man training a pistol on him, lining up for a second shot. Max threw himself to the ground and heard another bullet thudding into the concrete wall. He scrambled to his feet and kept running, calculating the position of the gondola by the framework of the hoist that protruded out from the edge of the roof.

He glanced sideways and saw the man heading towards him, wanting to get in closer for another shot. The man raised his pistol. He was only twenty metres away. From that range he couldn't miss. His finger tightened on the trigger. And at that moment, Max hurled himself over the parapet.

He did it blind, just hoping and praying that he'd calculated correctly. He felt himself falling through space and braced himself. His shoulder, then his hip hit something hard. There was a clang of metal, a vibration as the platform swung out a little from the building. He'd done it! He was on the gondola.

He had to move fast. The gunman would be closing in, readying himself for a shot over the parapet. Max was a sitting duck. He scanned the inside of the gondola, taking only a fraction of a second to register and identify its features: a solid metal base, metre-high mesh sides with a metal guard rail around the top, reels of thin steel cable at each end connected to the over-hanging hoist, a control panel and a long lever beneath it that looked like a brake.

Max grabbed hold of the lever and released it. The reels of cable immediately began to spin, unwinding so rapidly that Max was thrown to the floor. He flung out his arms and hooked them around one of the metal stanchions, clinging on for dear life as the gondola plummeted down the side of the tower. He looked up, saw the gunman leaning over the parapet, aiming his pistol, but the gondola was already out of range, the gunman blurring, receding into the blackness around the roof.

The windows flashed past, too fast for Max to register the floors. He was pinned to the base of the gondola by the force of the descent, the wind howling past his ears, the drums of cable rattling, making the gondola shudder and sway – it wasn't built for this kind of punishment. The cables were screaming and the gondola was out of control. If it hit the ground at this speed, it would shatter into pieces and Max would be pulped like a ripe tomato.

How far had it dropped? It must be halfway down by

now. Max twisted his head round and squinted through the wire mesh, saw the ground racing up to meet them. He tried to get to his feet, but the force was too great. It was like a rock pressing down on his head. He made it to his knees and stretched out his arm. The brake lever was just out of reach.

The gondola was juddering violently, the vibrations throbbing through Max's body, making him grimace in pain. The ground was getting nearer and nearer. He crawled forwards, every centimetre a struggle, and reached out with his arm again. His fingers closed around the lever. He hauled back on it. He felt, and heard, the brake engage and the steel cable screech in response. The lever started to jump and jerk. Max hung on tight, gritting his teeth, his muscles knotting under the strain. The gondola was slowing, the cables emitting a high-pitched shriek. Max prayed they wouldn't snap. His arms felt as if they were breaking, while the noise pierced his eardrums like a skewer – but he refused to let go.

The ground was looming up beneath him, only fifteen metres away. From somewhere, he found a morsel of extra strength and threw it all onto the lever. The gondola shuddered to a stop, swinging to and fro a mere two or three metres above the pavement. Max let go of the brake, gasping for air, his whole body trembling. Then he clambered over the side of the gondola and dropped to the ground.

He looked around. The descent from roof to street had taken only a few seconds. His pursuers, even using the lift, would take much longer. That gave him time. He stumbled away across the street and into the labyrinth of skyscrapers.

An hour before dawn, when most of the city was still sleeping, a sleek black saloon pulled into the car park by the toll plaza on the southern approach to the Golden Gate Bridge. A man in a dark sweat top and running shoes got out. He looked like a keen, early-morning jogger about to set off on a training run down to the shore of the bay. He glanced around cautiously. The car park was deserted, no other people, no other vehicles. On the freeway and bridge, the traffic was light. A damp, grey mist was blowing in from the ocean, creeping over the water and reaching out onto the land in cold, hazy tendrils. The man shivered and zipped his sweat top up to the neck. Then he jogged easily away across the car park.

On the far side, in the shadow of some trees, stood an orange metal storage container. The man took a thin steel implement out of his pocket and used it to pick the lock on the container door. He glanced around once more, to check he was unobserved, then pulled open the door and stepped inside the container.

The beam of his pencil torch lanced around the interior, picking out the stacks of timber planks on the floor and a neatly-coiled rope in one corner. The man went to the rope and knelt down. From his pocket he took a tiny explosive device no bigger than a sunflower seed. Opening up the strands of the rope with the blade of a knife, he inserted the device deep into the fibres, then inspected his handiwork carefully. The device was completely hidden – it was impossible to tell that the rope had been tampered with in any way.

The man stood up and eased open the container door a couple of centimetres, putting his eye to the gap. The car park was still deserted so he stepped out and re-locked the door behind him. Then he jogged back to his car, climbed in and drove away.

# FOURTEEN

'You said you'd phone us, Max. You *promised*.'

'Yes, I know, but—'

'You almost got killed. Several times. Why didn't you contact us?'

Max had never seen Consuela so angry. She was pacing across the sitting room of their hotel suite, her mouth tight, her face flushed.

'I couldn't,' Max protested. 'I told you. I lost my phone.'

'That was when you were being chased through Golden Gate Park. You could have found a payphone after that and rung us. Or you could have come back to the hotel. But no, you had to go to Rescomin Tower, didn't you. *On your own*. You didn't need to do that.'

'I was looking for Dad. I couldn't afford to wait, I had to go straight there.'

'You didn't have to go alone. Have you any idea how worried Chris and I have been? You've been out all night. We didn't know where you were, we didn't know what had happened to you.'

'Look, I'm sorry,' Max said meekly. 'Really, I am.'

He meant it. He could see how upset Consuela was. He knew he'd behaved recklessly, thoughtlessly, and wanted to make amends. 'I didn't want to delay, that's all,' he said. 'In case they moved Dad to another place.'

'If you'd come back here, we could have contacted the police and let them deal with it. All you've done is give Clark and his men the time to spirit your dad away and hide him somewhere we don't know about. Hasn't he, Chris?'

Consuela glanced across at the armchair in which Chris was slouching. He'd said very little since Max had returned. He'd left all the talking – and all the anger – to Consuela. He nodded phlegmatically.

'I'm afraid so. Consuela is right, Max. Your dad won't be there any longer. They'll have moved him to a safe house elsewhere in the city. They might have moved him out of San Francisco altogether.'

'You put your life in danger,' Consuela said. 'And for what? Why don't you let us help? Why did you have to rush in like that?' She slumped down onto the edge of the settee and covered her face with her hands. Her shoulders began to shake with silent sobs.

Max looked anxiously at Chris, unsure what to do, his eyes asking for guidance. Chris glared at him, then jerked his head at Consuela. The message was unmistakable: *You caused this mess, mate. Now you sort it out.*

Max got up and sat down beside Consuela. He hesitated for a moment, then put a tentative arm around her shoulders. 'I'm sorry,' he said softly. 'I didn't mean to upset you.'

Consuela took her hands away from her face. Her cheeks were wet with tears, her make-up smudged. 'I know you didn't, Max.'

'Sometimes I don't think. Sometimes I do stupid things. I'm sorry. I shouldn't have done what I did.'

Consuela twisted round on the settee and gave him a long hug. 'You've got to understand,' she whispered in his ear. 'You're only fourteen. I'm your guardian. I'm responsible for you. I *care* about you, Max.' She wiped her cheeks with the back of her hand. 'But you're alive. That's the important thing.'

She stood up and went across the sitting room into her bathroom, closing the door behind her. Max watched her, feeling bad about making her cry.

Chris gave him a reproachful look. 'What were you thinking, Max? I'm here to look after you. Your safety is paramount to me. That's why I roped Rusty and Zip in to help. We've heard from them, by the way. Rusty called an hour or so ago. The police held them for forty-eight hours, then released them without charge.'

'Are they coming over to join us?'

'There's no point now. It's too late. But *I'm* here, Max. You know you can always call on me. Don't go running off on your own again like that, OK? Enough said.'

Chris went across to the television set and switched it on, flicking through the channels until he found the local station.

The shooting in Haight-Ashbury was the lead item on the breakfast news. There was a reporter at the scene, a tall, elegant woman in her thirties, with a lot of blonde hair and very white teeth. She was standing on Shrader Street, just outside an area that had been cordoned off. In the background, the camera picked up police vans and cars, officers moving around under bright portable arc lights. The reporter described what had happened, how a white male, identified from his driving licence and other papers as 38-year-old Anthony Halstead, a doctor about to take up an appointment at San Francisco General Hospital, had been gunned down on the sidewalk. Neighbours had heard two or three shots, seen cars and several un-identified men running away from the scene.

Max listened to the report, going suddenly cold as he relived the experience – seeing Halstead going down again, seeing the blood on his chest, then seeing the gunmen coming after him, chasing him through the park.

'You OK with this?' Chris asked. 'I can turn it off, if you find it disturbing.'

'I'm OK,' Max replied.

'I think we should know what the authorities are saying, what the official story is.'

Max nodded in agreement. He wanted to keep watching. It had taken place only a few hours ago, yet it seemed so much longer. He remembered every part of it in vivid detail, but he felt detached from it now, as if it had all happened to someone else.

Consuela came out of the bathroom, her face washed, her make-up repaired. She sat down next to Max and watched the news with them. From the shooting of Dr Halstead, the programme moved on to another incident in the west of the city that the police believed might be connected to it. Two men, so far unidentified, had been seriously injured in what appeared to have been a buffalo stampede in Golden Gate Park. The men were in a stable condition in hospital, with police guards outside their rooms. A police spokesman, interviewed on camera, said that the two men had both been carrying automatic pistols and tests were currently underway to establish whether the guns had been used in the Shrader Street shooting.

At the end of the report, Chris turned the television set off.

'You're a one-man news-creation machine, Max,' he said dryly. 'That entire bulletin was generated by your antics.'

Max didn't dispute the facts. It was undoubtedly true, but he'd had enough of the previous night and all the explanations and apologies that had followed. He wanted to move on now.

'So what do we do about my dad?' he asked. 'Why did those men take him away? Why not kill him there and then?'

Chris shook his head. 'I don't know.'

'Do you think they've killed him now? Taken him somewhere and shot him?'

Consuela winced. 'Max, don't think about such things.'

'But I have to think about them. It's important.'

'I know it's important,' Consuela said. 'To all of us. But you have other things to deal with today.'

'My bridge stunt, you mean?' In all the excitement, Max had almost forgotten that he was performing on the Golden Gate Bridge that evening.

Consuela nodded. 'And you've been up all night, had no sleep. You look absolutely terrible. I think you should go to bed for a few hours.'

'I don't want to go to bed.'

'Max, this is the biggest show of your life. Do you want to cancel it?'

'I don't know. Maybe we should pull out. I don't really feel like performing.'

'You don't *feel like it*?' Consuela said incredulously. 'Max, have you thought about how big this event is? Why you are getting such a huge fee, and all our expenses met like this? They've closed part of the Golden Gate Bridge to enable you to do this stunt, the mayor of San Francisco has given it his personal support, the police department is providing hundreds of officers to help and there are going to be thousands of spectators watching here in the city and millions around the world. There's no way you can pull out now – unless, of course, you are too ill to do the stunt . . . ?'

'What about those men who just tried to kill me?' Max said, ignoring her concern about his health. 'They could try again.'

'Not on the Golden Gate,' Chris said confidently. 'Not with all those police officers around, plus Feinstein's own security men, not to mention the TV cameras. They'd have to be stupid, or crazy, and I don't think they're either. The bridge is going to be the safest place for you. Now go to bed. You need to be sharp and alert tonight.'

'And my dad?' Max said.

'Consuela and I will discuss what we should do about your dad.'

Max considered for a moment, then gave a reluctant nod. The previous night was catching up with him. He needed some sleep, if he was going to be ready for his show.

He went into his bathroom and stripped off his clothes. They'd dried almost completely since his immersion in the lake, but they were still tainted with dirty water and made him feel unclean. He took a shower, then got into bed.

Sleep didn't come easily. He'd got through the night on a mixture of adrenaline and determination. Now he was back in the security of his hotel suite, he was realizing how drained he was, how shaken by those terrifying events. Three times they'd tried to kill him and three times – through luck and skill – he'd escaped. Rupert Penhall's parting comment came back to him. 'You lead a charmed life at the moment, Max. I wonder how much longer you can keep it up.'

Max was wondering too, now. How many lives did he have left? Not many, if he kept taking such foolhardy risks. He was bitterly disappointed not to have made contact with his father. He'd been so close. Their eyes had met for a brief moment, and then his dad had gone. Max found that immensely distressing. Alexander Cassidy had looked so feeble and infirm. Max desperately wanted him back home with him and his mother where he could be properly looked after. But now he'd disappeared again.

Max's thoughts strayed back to the questions he'd asked earlier. Why had the gunmen abducted his dad? If he was such a threat to Julius Clark, why hadn't they just killed him in the house on Shrader Street? He could think of only one reason why Clark wanted his father alive: to interrogate him. But about what? Again, there seemed to be only one answer: about the Cedar Alliance, the secret organization that was fighting Clark's global ambitions and whose clandestine leadership included Alexander Cassidy. Did Clark want to find out who the other leaders were so he could destroy the Alliance? Did he intend to drug Alexander with Episuderon again, to finish off the job he'd started on Shadow Island two years ago?

Max had a feeling he did. But where would he do it? Max's reckless escapades at Rescomin Tower had failed to find, or rescue, his father, but it had succeeded in its other aim: he'd discovered where the Episuderon was being sent – to Zaliv Myertvetsa. Max was certain that Clark was continuing the brainwashing programme that he had originally conducted on Shadow Island before Max destroyed his laboratory. Kamchatka, like Shadow Island, was remote and unpopulated. Clark could do whatever he liked there.

If the brainwashing drug was being used at Zaliv Myertvetsa, then maybe Max's father was also being taken there. The more Max thought about it, the more the idea became a conviction. And in San Francisco harbour was a ship named the *Reunion Star* that at nine a.m. the following morning was setting sail for Kamchatka.

# FIFTEEN

Max had never experienced such a phenomenally high level of public and media interest in one of his shows. He was used to a certain amount of press coverage for his theatre performances as the Half-Pint Houdini, and his Tower Bridge stunt *had* been televised in the UK. But San Francisco was something different altogether. Here, he was being treated as a real global celebrity.

He'd already done a press conference and a few television interviews and he'd caught a glimpse of a trailer for his show that one of the networks was running regularly in between programmes, but nothing had prepared him for the sheer scale of the media circus that surrounded him that Sunday evening.

The lobby of the Fairmont was crowded with photographers and reporters and television crews. Stepping out of the lift with Consuela, Herb Feinstein and Chris – who, after the events of the night before, was sticking to him like a magnet – Max was so taken aback by the barrage of flashguns and cameras that he stopped dead, his face frozen into a mask of stunned surprise. It took a reassuring squeeze of his arm from Consuela and a murmured, 'Smile,' to prevent him diving back into the lift and retreating upstairs to their room.

'How're you feeling, Max?' a reporter yelled.

'You all set for the show?' called another.

'Hey, Consuela, look this way,' shouted a third.

Max recovered himself. He forced his features to relax and beamed at the cameras. 'I'm fine. I'm looking forward to it,' he said brightly.

'You scared?' one of the reporters asked.

'You bet,' Max replied, with a grin, though it wasn't his forthcoming stunt that frightened him, but this seething mass of journalists and cameramen, all jostling and fighting for position so aggressively that he feared he might be crushed in the scrum.

Two big security men in dark suits stepped forward, pushing the crowd back to allow Max and his companions a clear path to the exit. The media people followed, pouring out through the doors and clustering around Max and Consuela as they ducked inside the limousine that was waiting for them on the forecourt.

Max sagged back into the soft leather seat and let out a deep breath, relieved to have the metal doors and tinted windows between him and the mob. Consuela and Feinstein settled down next to him. Chris took one of the fold-down seats opposite, his back to the glass panel that separated them from the driver.

'You OK?' he asked Max.

Max nodded. 'Just a bit shocked. I never expected that. So many people, all those cameras.'

'You're like a rock star,' Feinstein said. 'The media are wild for you. They've been hyping your show round the clock. Didn't you notice?'

Max glanced out of the window. The photographers were pressing close to the glass, still snapping away. The attention made him feel exhilarated, but uncomfortable. He wasn't a rock star, and didn't want to be treated like one. A blue flashing light and a siren started up and he noticed a police patrol car in front of the limousine. There was another one behind, too. A police escort – that was a new experience for him as well.

The convoy pulled off, going west past Grace Cathedral, then turning north a few blocks later to head over to the Golden Gate Bridge. They drove fast, the police sirens giving them an uninterrupted run through the traffic.

On the flyover near the bridge, Max looked out of the window and saw dense crowds of people down on the shore of the bay. 'They've not all come to watch me, have they?' he asked, astonished by the numbers.

'Why else do you think they're there?' Feinstein

replied. He seemed amused by Max's question. 'You'd better get used to it. This is a first for San Francisco – a stunt like this off the Golden Gate Bridge, and done by a fourteen-year-old kid from England. *Everyone* wants to see it.'

Max felt the stirrings of a few butterflies in his stomach. He wanted people to take notice of what he did, but this was really rather overwhelming.

Consuela sensed his nerves and reached out to touch his hand. 'You'll be fine,' she said with a smile. 'You've done this before. You can do it tonight too.'

'But in front of so many people!' Max said.

'One person, or a thousand, what difference does it make?'

In theory, none, Max thought. The stunt was still the same regardless of how many people were watching. But, of course, it *did* make a difference. It increased the pressure on him. He had to be good. He had to be better than good, he had to be superlative, if all these spectators were to go away satisfied. And he had to be good to survive too – he was putting his life on the line with a stunt this dangerous, no matter how well prepared he was.

The limo slowed as it passed through the toll plaza, then stopped at a metal barrier that had been erected at the southern end of the bridge. A police officer swung open the gate and waved them through. The limo accelerated behind the leading police car. The two near-side lanes of the northbound freeway had been closed to traffic. One was rapidly filling up with spectators, but one had been fenced off to allow police, fire and ambulance access in the event of an emergency, and to let Max through to the middle of the bridge. The central section of the two lanes was also cordoned off with barriers manned by police officers. No one was allowed past except Max and his team, Feinstein's people and the television network staff who were covering the event.

Max had never seen so many uniformed police officers in one place. It made him feel secure. Chris was right; Clark's men wouldn't be able to touch him here. He got out of the limo and looked around. It was getting dusky. The bridge was bathed in bright light from portable spot lamps. The city, too, was lit up. Max could see the skyscrapers in the Financial District, the street-lights on the hills behind. Out in the bay, Alcatraz was also visible. The old cell block that dominated the summit of the rock was illuminated and next to it the light at the top of the lighthouse was rotating, flash-ing its warning beam every few seconds.

A television crew came across towards him – a cameraman with a hand-held camera on his shoulder, a sound technician with a microphone on the end of a boom – and Max prepared himself for another interview. A reporter asked him questions and Max did his best to answer. Then Feinstein led him away to a big caravan that was parked at the side of the freeway.

'This is your trailer,' he said, opening the door of the caravan and showing Max the interior.

It was huge: it had a sitting room, a bathroom with a shower and a kitchen in which fruit and sandwiches and other food had been laid out. Max gazed around, impressed by the way Feinstein was looking after them.

'I hope you like it. It's the kind of trailer they give movie stars on location,' the promoter explained. 'You can chill out here before the show, take a shower and relax afterwards. You need anything, just let me know.'

'Thanks,' Max said.

'I'll be back later.'

Feinstein went out of the trailer. Max wandered across the sitting room and stared out of the window. He could see the spectators flooding onto the bridge, rushing to get a position by the railing where they would have the best view of the show. There seemed to be thousands of them. The knot in his stomach tightened. He'd never undertaken anything with such a high profile before. Tower Bridge had been daunting, but it seemed pathetically small scale compared to this.

The Golden Gate was a massive bridge, the audience was going to be huge – not just on the spot but around the globe too. Feinstein had already told him that the syndication rights had been sold to more than sixty countries. Millions of people would be watching. If Max failed, he would do so in front of the whole world.

'You want something to eat?' Chris asked.

Max turned and moved away from the window. 'No, thanks.'

'Maybe you should,' Consuela said. 'You need to keep your energy up.'

'I don't feel like eating.'

Consuela regarded him with a mixture of affection and sympathy. 'Don't worry about nerves,' she said. 'It's only to be expected in the circumstances.'

'There's a lot riding on this,' Max said.

'And you can cope with it,' Consuela said firmly. 'Now have something to eat. Settle your stomach.'

Max shook his head. 'I'll feel better if we check over the equipment now. I need something to do.'

'OK.'

They went back out of the trailer. The bridge was swarming with police officers and security guards employed by Feinstein, but Chris was nevertheless staying close to Max.

They went to the orange metal container that had

been brought up from the toll plaza car park and went inside it, leaving the door open to let in light. All the equipment for the show had been flown over from England: the planks for the crate, the nails, the rope, the handcuffs. Everything had to be just the right specification. The planks had to be strong, but springy, the nails rigid but soft enough to be severed with a pair of cutters.

Consuela counted out the planks, checking that they were all there and in good condition. Then she went through the bag of nails, making sure there were no duds. Max was going to be sealed inside a crate built from these materials. It was vital that they were strong enough to hold together and take his weight.

Max examined the rope, twisting it between his fingers and inspecting every centimetre of it for weaknesses, but found none.

'You happier now?' Consuela asked as they left the container.

Max nodded automatically, but he still had a tightness in his stomach that was more than just the nerves one would expect before a show as big as this. He was uneasy, though he couldn't put his finger on exactly why. Everything was as it should have been. The equipment was in order, he was fit and well and feeling confident about his ability to perform the stunt. So why did he have this unsettling sense of foreboding, this sense that something was going to go wrong?

It was the moment Max had been waiting for. He was in the trailer with Chris and Consuela. He'd changed into the black suit he wore for his performances. The key to the handcuffs that would shortly be locked around his wrists was securely hidden in the thick hair behind his right ear, and behind his left ear were taped the three nails he would need to close up the crate once he'd escaped from it. Consuela, too, had changed into her show clothes – a sparkly red and gold top and tight black trousers. She smiled at Max and checked her watch.

'It's time. You ready?'

Max took a deep breath and nodded. 'Yes.'

'Then let's do it.'

Chris gave Consuela a light kiss, then slapped Max on the back. 'Good luck. You're going to be terrific.'

'I hope so.'

Chris pulled open the trailer door and stood back to let them pass. A camera crew was waiting outside. They backed away as Max and Consuela came down the steps, then stayed with them, filming as they walked away towards the side of the bridge. A loud cheer went up from the spectators on the carriageway, then Max heard a fainter, more distant, cheer from the people lining the shore of the bay, who were seeing him on a giant television screen. He waved his arms and smiled, feeling the crowd lift his mood.

The weather had changed in the couple of hours Max had been on the bridge. It had got cooler, and a damp mist was drifting in from the sea, curling around the steel cables and girders, then floating away across the bay in translucent clouds. Visibility was deteriorating. Max could still see the crowds on the shore, the glow of torches and barbecue fires on the field behind the beach making it look like some kind of military encampment. But the mist was getting thicker, the wind picking up. Max didn't like it. He still had that queasy feeling of unease in his stomach and he was anxious to get on with the stunt before the conditions got any worse.

The team of local carpenters had finished constructing the wooden crate. Standing beside the crate was the mayor of San Francisco. He gave a short speech, welcoming Max to the city and wishing him well. Then he checked Max's pockets and gave him a pat-down search before putting the handcuffs on him. Max held up his hands for the television camera, then stepped onto the low wooden block next to the crate. Consuela grasped his hand to help him climb inside the crate and slipped him the tiny nail-cutters at the same time. Max palmed the cutters like a magician and sat down against one of the wooden sides, holding up his manacled hands again and smiling confidently for the camera.

The wooden lid was manoeuvred into place and the carpenters nailed it down, saving the final nail for the mayor to hammer in.

'I'm no expert at this – you should see the shelves I've put up at home,' the mayor joked, 'but here goes.'

He raised the hammer and banged it down hard onto the nail three times until the head was buried in the wood. The rope was then fastened around the crate like a sling and attached to the hook of the mobile crane that was parked at the side of the carriageway. Consuela was already standing beside the crane's control panel, close to the edge of the bridge so she could see the crate as it was lowered down into the bay. She pressed one of the buttons and the steel cable on the winch began to reel in, lifting the crate up off the ground. When the crate was three metres up, Consuela stopped the motor and pressed another button. The boom of the crane swung round ninety degrees until the crate was over the side of the bridge, suspended seventy metres above the water. She touched the motor button and the cable started to unwind. Slowly, the crate descended towards the sea, a spotlight illuminating it, making the surrounding darkness even blacker.

Inside the crate, Max had already unlocked the manacles and freed his hands. He knelt up, holding the nail-cutters tight, counting the seconds and readying himself for the next stage of his escape.

A mile away, standing on the south shore of the bay with several thousand other spectators, a man in a black windcheater and jeans was watching the crate's progress carefully. He put his hand into his pocket and pulled out what looked like a mobile phone. No one around him paid any attention; their gazes were all fixed intently on the bridge. The man held the device to his ear, as if he were making a call, and pressed the transmit button. Deep inside the fibres of the rope tied around the crate, the tiny explosive charge detonated, severing the rope cleanly, with a flash and a bang so small that no one, either on the shore or on the bridge, noticed.

Max felt it, though. He felt the rope snap and the crate suddenly lurch violently to one side. But it didn't fall immediately. Only one section of the rope had broken – the other strands of the sling were still intact. But it wouldn't be long before the crate *did* fall. It was sliding slowly out of the sling, tilting over at a dangerous angle.

Crouching blind in the darkness, Max didn't know what had happened. He'd been thrown into a corner of the crate and could tell it was about to plummet down into the sea. He scrambled desperately to balance the box by moving his body weight to the other side, but he couldn't do it. The floor was sloping up at too great an angle. All he did was make the crate rock, loosening it further from the sling.

On the bridge, and along the bay, the spectators had seen it now. The TV cameras zoomed in close, showing the snapped rope, the crate dangling over and about to fall. Terrified screams and gasps of horror reverberated through the crowd. If the crate fell from that height, Max Cassidy was dead.

Consuela reacted instantly. Someone slower-witted might have tried to raise the crate, get it back up onto the bridge before it could fall, but Consuela did the opposite. In that split second as she saw the rope snap, she had already judged that there was no time to bring the crate back up. What she had to do was get it as near to the water as possible before it slipped out of the sling.

She thrust the control lever of the crane around from 'slow' to 'fast'. The steel cable unwound with lightning speed, sending the crate hurtling down towards the sea.

Max was thrown back into the corner, his legs above him, his body doubled up. He struggled to right himself.

He knew he had to get ready, but he was winded, gasping for breath. He wriggled around frantically, getting his legs beneath him again, kneeling up and sucking in air.

Consuela eased the lever back, slowing the cable. She was leaning out over the railing at the side of the bridge, watching the crate with her heart in her mouth, knowing that her actions would decide Max's fate. Her head was throbbing, the nausea rising in her throat, but she didn't panic. She'd been Max's assistant for two years, his father's assistant for twelve years before that. She knew all about staying calm in life-threatening situations.

The crate was more than halfway down now, maybe twenty metres above the sea. It was still dangling precariously from the sling, tilting over at an ever-increasing angle. Consuela slowed the cable further, doing it gradually, trying to avoid any sudden jerks. But it was no use. The crate was going, slipping out from the sling, and nothing was going to stop it. Consuela let out a cry of distress – she couldn't help it – and watched in agony as the crate plunged down towards the water.

Max felt the box tilt over and start to fall. He straightened up, getting to his feet, his knees bent, his arms stretched out to steady himself. He could feel the wind rushing up through the gaps in the planks, feel his stomach churning. How far above the water was he? He didn't know, and there was no point in guessing – he just had to brace himself for the impact. He took a long gulp of air, then held his breath, closed his eyes and tensed every muscle of his body.

The crate hit the water with such velocity that it disintegrated, the planks splitting apart and shattering into pieces. Max was thrown clear and sank like a stone, blacking out for an instant, then coming round and realizing he was underwater. He kicked out instinctively, not knowing which way was up and which down, and felt himself being swept along by some massive force that could only have been the tidal current beneath the bridge. He didn't try to fight it – he didn't have the strength. His whole body felt as if it had been hit with a piledriver. He was bruised, aching all over, but he was alive.

His eyes were open now, but he could see nothing but blackness all around. He could tell from the pressure on his ears that he was deep down, being pushed irresistibly forward by the tide. He needed air badly, could feel himself getting faint through lack of oxygen. Sweeping back his arms and kicking hard, he surged upwards and broke the surface. He trod water, filling his lungs, then looked around, wondering what had happened to the rope, and how he'd managed to survive the fall.

He was stunned to see how far the tide had taken him. He was out in the middle of the bay, a quarter of a mile from the shore and two hundred metres from the bridge. Through the thickening layer of mist, he could see spotlights shining on the place where the crate had smashed into the sea, the two safety boats circling the area. A couple of divers were dropping over the side, going down to search for him. This far outside the circle of light Max was as good as invisible.

It was at that moment that he made his decision. He could have waved his arms and shouted for help, but he didn't. He suddenly saw this as his chance to disappear, as his father had done in Borneo – to do what he had to do without his enemies on his tail. Fate had dealt him this hand and he was going to play it to his advantage. Ducking back down beneath the surface, he started swimming east, letting the current sweep him further and further away from the Golden Gate Bridge.

# SIXTEEN

The tide was still coming in. That was one of the main reasons why Herb Feinstein had chosen ten o'clock at night for Max to do his stunt. If anything went wrong, he wanted him to be swept into the shelter of San Francisco Bay, not dragged out into the Pacific Ocean. High water was eleven p.m. Max wasn't wearing a watch, but he guessed it must be about ten-thirty by now. That gave him half an hour to get to the shore, half an hour before the tide started to turn and the currents began to pull him back towards the bridge and the open sea beyond it.

He couldn't swim to the nearest bit of the shore – that was the area occupied by the thousands of spectators. He had to head further into the bay, towards the city itself. He was on the surface now, swimming in an easy freestyle. Occasionally he stopped to rest, treading water, and looked back. The mist had thickened, lying low over the bay in a dense blanket, so he couldn't see clearly what was happening, but once or twice the wind tore a hole in the mist and he could make out lights, vague movements under the bridge which he guessed were the safety boats still trying to locate him.

He felt a pang of guilt at his deception, at the distress it would cause to a lot of people – to the crowds on the spot, to the audience watching at home, but most particularly to Consuela and Chris, and to his mum too. They would believe him to be dead, would grieve for him. Max didn't want to inflict that kind of pain on them, but he was sure he was doing the right thing. He had to think about the bigger picture, about rescuing his father from Julius Clark's clutches – and he couldn't do that with Clark's gunmen breathing down his neck.

It was cold in the water and Max was getting tired. But it was the mist that worried him most, as it was becoming worse by the minute. He could no longer see the Golden Gate Bridge, but more disturbing, he couldn't see the lights of the city either. Everything had disappeared into the fog.

He was swimming blind, trusting to his sense of direction. He was confident he was going the right way, but aware also that there were hidden currents tugging at his body, pulling him off course. He tried to compensate, to adjust his stroke to take account of them, but couldn't tell whether he was succeeding. The wind, too, was a problem. It was breaking up the surface of the water, creating waves that splashed in his face and slowed him down. And it seemed to be blowing from the southwest, pushing him further out into the bay.

His right hand grazed a rock and he lifted his head and stopped swimming. Lowering his legs to tread water, he was astounded to find solid ground only a metre below him. He stood up, feeling elated. He'd reached the shore. He waded out through the shallows onto a small, rocky beach, a few metres deep and bounded on the far side by a sheer cliff. He looked around. The mist was so thick he could see only a couple of metres in any direction. The top of the cliff was completely obscured – it could have been five metres high, or fifty, for all he could tell. The shore was coated in slippery seaweed, large boulders interspersed with rough shingle. He was puzzled. It wasn't what he expected. San Francisco was a well-developed port city; its waterfront consisted of concrete piers and wharves for loading ships, not beaches like this.

Max got a sinking feeling in his stomach, realizing suddenly that this wasn't the edge of the city he'd reached. He was somewhere else, on some other piece of land that had a rocky shore and a cliff. Round here that could only be one place. He was on Alcatraz.

The shock took his breath away. How could he have swum so far off course? The currents and wind must have been much stronger than he'd thought. Alcatraz!

The Rock! He was on the notorious island in the middle of the bay, the island that had once been a prison from which very few people had escaped and of those who had, most had drowned attempting to reach the mainland.

He slumped down onto a boulder, dispirited and exhausted, all his remaining energy draining away with the water that was running off his body. He couldn't face another gruelling swim. He was too tired, too cold. He needed to warm up, to refuel with food, but that wasn't possible on Alcatraz. The island was un-inhabited. Trippers and tourists came out to visit it during the day, but there was no one there at night.

Max didn't know what to do. He couldn't go back into the water. If he attempted to swim to the mainland in his present condition, he would surely drown. But if he stayed put, the tide would turn, making it even more hazardous for him to get off the island. And he *had* to get off. He had to reach the *Reunion Star* before it sailed.

Whatever he did, Max knew he had to get his bearings. If he *was* on Alcatraz – and there was still a tiny element of doubt in his mind – then he needed to know where on Alcatraz, which side of the island. To start swimming again without that basic information would be suicidal. He could end up heading out to sea, or across to the wrong side of the bay. Down here by the water, he could see almost nothing. He had to get above the mist and try to work out where he was.

Pulling himself wearily to his feet, he picked his way along the shore, clambering over the slimy green boulders until he came to a low stone wall with a metal guard rail along the top of it. He pulled himself up onto the wall and climbed over the rail. He was on a dirt path that seemed to run along the base of the island, close to the sea. At the point he'd joined it, there was a flight of stone steps leading up the cliff. Max walked up them, shivering in his dripping clothes, the mist swirling around his head.

At the top of the steps, the visibility was better, the mist thinner with the wind blowing it around, tearing it into vaporous strands that straggled over the ground like shredded gauze. Max saw that he was on the edge of a large, flat, open area, its surface bare earth and gravel, mounds of rubble that looked like demolished buildings heaped around the perimeter.

There was no doubt now. He *was* on Alcatraz. Beyond the open space was another sheer cliff, on the top of which were the lighthouse and a ruined house that had no roof and gaping holes in its walls. Behind the lighthouse, lit up by floodlights, was the massive concrete cellblock, looking sinister and ghostly in the drifting mist. Max shuddered involuntarily, thinking suddenly of the prisoners who'd been locked up for years on this bleak little outcrop of rock, many of them dying here in captivity. Did their tormented spirits still wander the island, looking for peace?

Suddenly Max wanted to be somewhere else. Anywhere but here in this creepy, fogbound place that was haunted by memories of dead convicts and murderers, men who'd taken other people's lives and paid for it with their own. He walked away quickly, glancing around nervously, half expecting to feel a spectral hand reach out and grab him by the throat. His tiredness had gone – fear had seen to that – and he was desperate to get back in the water again.

He knew which way to go now. He could see the lights of San Francisco in the distance, maybe only a mile away. That wasn't too far to swim, assuming he could deal with the currents, of course. He went downhill along a paved road, wide enough to fit a couple of cars, and around a sharp curve that took him through a short tunnel between two buildings. It was pitch-black here and he had to slow down and almost feel his way along the tunnel.

As he stepped back out into the open, he stopped dead, his heart giving a sudden jolt of terror. A figure was walking up the road towards him, the mist half shrouding his outline. He was wearing a uniform with a peaked cap, a torch in his hand.

Max ducked back into the shadows of the tunnel and pressed himself against the wall, his pulse racing, his legs shaky. It was a ghost: the ghost of one of the guards who'd worked in the prison years ago.

Max heard footsteps, saw the beam of the torch penetrate the tunnel and pulled himself together, getting a grip on his nerves. Ghosts didn't carry torches, their feet didn't make a noise on the ground. This wasn't some phantom guard from the past, it was a modern-day security guard going out on patrol. That made sense. Alcatraz was a protected site. Of course they'd have some kind of security there at night.

Max shrank back as the guard walked past, praying that he wouldn't examine the sides of the tunnel too closely. And he didn't. He just kept going, shining his torch straight ahead. Max waited until he could no longer see the beam, then slipped out of the tunnel and padded softly down the hill, alert and watchful now. Would there be just one security guard on the island, or more? Max had to make sure he didn't accidentally bump into another one.

At the base of the hill was a quayside, with a long, imposing four-storey building along the back of it that looked like a military barracks and a high metal-framed watchtower at one end which Max reckoned would have been manned by armed guards when the island was a prison. There was no one on the tower now, but there was a light burning at the other end of the quay, on the ground floor of the barracks-like building.

Max walked warily across towards it, skirting a much smaller, more modern structure that, from the signs, was obviously a toilet facility for the tourists visiting Alcatraz. The light he'd seen was in a tiny block attached to the base of the barracks. A door plaque identified it as the Golden Gate National Park Rangers' Office. Max peeped cautiously in through the window and saw a desk and chairs and a kitchen unit with a sink and a coffee maker, an open packet of chocolate cookies placed neatly next to a stack of paper cups. There was no sign of another guard.

Max opened the door and slipped quietly into the office. He didn't like coffee, but he needed something to warm himself up. He poured a cup from the pot on the hotplate and added four sachets of sugar to take away the bitterness. Then he helped himself to three cookies and went back out onto the quayside, hiding out of sight behind the toilet block. He sipped the coffee. Even with the sugar, he still didn't like the taste, but it went down easily, the liquid warming his throat and stomach, the glow spreading out through his chilled body. He wolfed down the biscuits and started to feel better. He was still cold and tired, but the prospect of another swim didn't seem so daunting now.

The edge of the quay was only a few metres away. In the light from the rangers' office, Max could see a floating dock where the tour boats tied up to unload their passengers. Something on the dock caught his eye: a red and white life belt attached to a wooden post.

Finishing his coffee, he dumped the paper cup in a litter bin and went across to the dock. He lifted the life belt down from the post and slipped it over his head and shoulders, holding it in place around his waist. He stepped to the edge of the dock and paused. The mist lifted just enough for him to see the lights of San Francisco. He stared at them, locking the bearing into his brain, then jumped into the water and struck out for the shore.

Without the life belt he would probably not have made it across the strait. The turning tide and the ferocious currents would have swept him west across the bay, maybe sucked him under to his death even before they carried him out into the ocean. But the belt kept him afloat. It allowed him to save his energy and channel it into his swimming. Even so, it was the hardest physical challenge he'd ever faced. A mile and a quarter of open water – cold, choppy water – with the wind and the tide against him. Max was a good swimmer, but nearly all his training had been done in a warm municipal pool. He wasn't properly prepared for these conditions – a night swim across one of the world's most dangerous bays, fully clothed and already dog-tired from his previous exertions.

Several times, he almost gave up it was so hard. He stopped swimming, too worn out to continue, and just floated for a few minutes, the life belt holding him up, preventing him sinking straight down to the bottom of the bay. When he'd recovered enough, he swam on for another few hundred metres before pausing again to rest. Only his sheer stubborn determination kept him going. He had to get to the *Reunion Star*, he had to find his father. Nothing else mattered. Not the pain in his arms and legs, not the biting cold, not the relentless tide. He was going to do it, no matter how difficult.

As he neared the shore, he found encouragement in the lights that were drawing slowly closer. *Not far to go now*, he told himself. *Just a few more strokes. Dip the arms in, pull back, turn to breathe, pull again. Forget the pain, it doesn't really hurt. You can do it, Max. You can.*

He noticed the wind dropping, the surface of the water getting smoother. The undercurrent seemed to slacken. Swimming was easier. He was in the shelter of the wharves that ran along the edge of the city. Almost there. Just the thought gave him the strength to cross that final hundred metres. Then his fingers were touching a rough wooden mooring post on one of the piers jutting out into the bay. His hands gripped a metal ladder and he clung onto it for a long time, panting with exhaustion, until he summoned the energy to discard the life belt and climb up onto the pier.

He was on one of the small commercial wharves to the south of the main tourist centre, a pier still used by fishing and other working boats, though not at this time of night. The area was in darkness, the warehouses all closed up. Max lay on the ground for a while with his eyes closed, letting his body recover, letting the water trickle out of his clothes. He'd never felt so drained before.

After a few minutes, he sat up and looked around. He could see the lighthouse on Alcatraz poking up through the mist. Had he really swum from there? It didn't seem possible. There were other lights up the bay, on the tourist piers where there were restaurants and shops, and he could hear the sound of jazz music playing somewhere. He felt too tired to move, but he knew he had to get going. His body was cooling rapidly, and he had to find Pier 80 and the *Reunion Star*.

He got unsteadily to his feet and stumbled away along the wharf. His legs were heavy, his muscles barely strong enough to hold him upright. On the road at the end of the wharf, he paused. Which way was Pier 80? It had to be south, away from the tourist attractions and deeper into the bay. He turned left and kept walking. He saw cars passing by, but very few pedestrians. It didn't feel like an area where people went at night.

He went past a large stadium that had a sign saying it was the home of the San Francisco Giants. He'd never heard of them, but guessed they had to be a baseball team because there was a statue of a baseball player on the forecourt outside. Soon the landscape gave way to a more industrial zone, a desolate area of parking lots and warehouses. There were even fewer people out here, Max was relieved to discover. He didn't want anyone to see him, anyone to remember a teenage boy in wet clothes.

It took him almost an hour to reach a crossroads where Cesar Chavez Street turned off to Pier 80. Max went left, walking past a streetcar depot and a truck hire firm. Pier 80 was at the end of the street, a huge floodlit dock area enclosed by a high chain-link fence, with only one entrance – a checkpoint manned by security guards in a cabin. On the other side of the checkpoint was a wide, open concrete apron and a long, windowless building like an aircraft hangar which, presumably, was used for storing freight. Beyond the hangar was a quayside at which a ship was moored, tall gantry cranes loading it with cargo. That had to be the *Reunion Star*.

Max stayed well away from the entrance to the pier, turning left down a street which took him round to a derelict industrial site at the side of the docks. He walked over to the perimeter fence and felt in his trouser pocket. He still had the tiny nail-cutters he'd been going to use for his stunt off the Golden Gate Bridge. Crouching down, he used the cutters to make a hole in the wire mesh, then crawled through to the other side, pausing only to snip off a ten-centimetre length of wire, which he slipped into his pocket.

The hangar-like warehouse was only thirty metres away. Max flitted across to it and headed down to the quayside, sticking close to the back wall of the building. When he reached the end of the warehouse, he stopped and peered round the corner. It was the early hours of the morning, but the port was bustling with activity, the dock workers hurrying to get the *Reunion Star* loaded in time for her nine a.m. departure.

The quayside was flooded with light. Forklift trucks were moving in and out of the warehouse carrying crates and boxes, which were stacked on the apron, then lifted up by a crane and lowered into the hold of the ship. A second, larger crane was picking up metal containers the size of caravans and loading them on board too.

Max calculated his chances of getting across the quayside and up the gangplank of the *Reunion Star* without being spotted. He reckoned they were zero. There were too many people around, the area was too brightly lit. He would have to find another way of getting onto the ship.

Retreating sixty or seventy metres, he paused by a door in the wall of the warehouse. He tried the handle. The door swung open. Max peered cautiously through the gap, then slid inside. The warehouse was enormous, like a football pitch with a roof, and every inch of it was crammed with freight – great stacks of it reaching right up to the ceiling. Max moved off along one of the aisles. This part of the warehouse was quiet. All the activity was down at the far end, nearer the quayside. He moved stealthily, using the towers of boxes and packing cases as cover, keeping a sharp eye out for people.

He noticed that all the crates and cases were labelled with the names of the ships on which they were to be transported. He looked out for ones that said *Reunion Star*, but didn't see any until he was approaching the end of the warehouse. There he found a section that contained nothing but cargo for the ship. He sneaked round behind the stacks and inspected the crates. He could hear the forklift trucks moving around, the shouted orders from someone out on the quayside.

Then he heard the ringtone of a mobile phone nearby and froze. There were footsteps on the concrete floor. Max threw himself behind a packing case and lay still as a young man in jeans came past, not five metres away. The young man rummaged in a denim jacket that had been thrown casually over a wooden pallet and pulled out a phone. He had a short conversation, obviously talking to his wife or girlfriend, then replaced the phone and walked away.

Max stayed where he was for half a minute, the phone reminding him suddenly of Consuela and Chris, of the phone call he'd failed to make the night before and how angry Consuela had been with him as a result. She would be distraught now, believing him to be dead. His mum, when she heard the news, would be equally upset and grief-stricken. Could he really leave them in that state? He realized how selfish he was being, how cruel. He couldn't subject them to that kind of anguish.

He stood up and checked that the young man had gone, then he darted over to the jacket and took out the phone, crouching down with it behind a container. He didn't dare make an actual call, in case anyone heard him talking, but he sent a short text message to Consuela's number. Then he deleted it from the sent box, switched off the phone and put it back in the jacket.

His conscience was clearer now: he felt he'd done the right thing. He went back to the stacks and resumed his inspection of the freight, looking for a container big enough to hide in. The cardboard boxes were out of the question. They were too small. Most of the wooden crates were also unsuitable. Their lids were nailed shut and Max had no way of fixing them back in place once he was inside.

Or had he?

He suddenly remembered the three nails taped behind his left ear. He reached up and was astonished to find that they were still there. Somehow they had remained lodged in his hair throughout his two long swims. Going to the nearest crate, he used his cutters to sever the nails in the lid and lift it off. There were polythene bags inside, containing some kind of clothing. Max pushed the bags apart, compressing them to open up a space in the middle of the crate. Then he climbed in, put the lid back on top and used the nails behind his ear to fix it in place, tapping them through into the flange of the lid with the back of the cutters. It was warm and comfortable curled up next to the soft bags of clothing. Max lay back and relaxed, waiting for the crate to be loaded on board the *Reunion Star*.

It was getting cold on the Golden Gate Bridge. The mist had turned into a thick grey-white fog that clung to the girders and cables and swirled across the freeway, forcing the traffic to slow to almost a crawl.

Chris and Consuela were standing by the guard rail on the eastern side, looking down at the water, at the safety boats that were continuing their search of the area. Splintered pieces of timber, the remains of the wooden crate, had been salvaged from the sea, but there was still no trace of Max – alive or dead.

Consuela was shivering, droplets of water on her bare arms from the moisture in the mist. Chris had tried several times to persuade her to go inside their trailer, or at least to put on his jacket to protect herself from the elements, but she had refused. She was tense, distressed, using all her willpower to hold back her tears.

Chris put his arm around her shoulders and tried again to get her to seek shelter. 'They're doing all they can,' he said gently. 'Let's go inside the trailer.'

Consuela shook her head. 'No, I want to stay here,' she said stubbornly.

'You're freezing. It's not doing you any good. Come on, I'll make you a cup of coffee.'

He pulled her away from the guard rail. She put up a token show of resistance, but then gave in and let him lead her to the trailer. It was warm inside. Chris got a towel from the bathroom and made her sit down and dry her damp hair while he poured them both cups of hot coffee.

'I need to be out there,' Consuela said.

'Why? If they find anything, you'll be the first to be told. Let the police do their job. Now drink your coffee.'

Consuela took a sip, then gave a little hiccup and started to cry, the tears pouring down her cheeks. Chris took the cup from her hand and put his arms around her, holding her silently while she wept. 'He's dead, isn't he?' she said eventually, pulling away and wiping her eyes with her hands.

'You don't know that,' Chris replied firmly.

'It's been nearly two hours. Where is he? He can't have survived.'

'There are strong currents down there. They could have swept him a long way. That's why the police, the coastguards are still out there looking. They're doing everything they can.'

'You think there's still hope?'

'Max is a very tough kid, a survivor. Of course there's

still hope,' Chris said, trying to sound optimistic, though he knew that the longer they waited, the less hope there was. Consuela knew it, too. She found a handkerchief and blew her nose, then drank some coffee.

'I must let Helen know,' she said abruptly. 'Max's mum. This will be on the news all round the world. I don't want her to hear it from anyone but me. What time is it in England?'

Chris checked his watch. 'Just gone eight in the morning.'

'I'll call the prison, see if I can speak to her.'

Consuela stood up and went to her handbag, taking out her mobile. She switched it on and stared at it for a moment, frowning. Then she touched the screen with a finger and gave a cry of surprise.

'What's the matter?' Chris asked.

She was gaping at her phone, speechless, her hands trembling.

'Consuela?'

She held out the phone to him. Chris saw the text message on the screen.

Its max. Don worry im alive need 2 dispear 4 time 2 find dad. Btr if Clark thinks im ded. Plz tel mum. Soz 4 all the trubl

'He's alive!' Consuela exclaimed, starting to cry again. 'Max is alive.' Then her face clouded over. 'What the hell is he playing at? Half the San Francisco police force are out there looking for him. Boats, divers, helicopters.'

Chris read the message again. 'Whose number is that? Where's it been sent from?'

Consuela punched in the number and listened. 'Voicemail. The phone's switched off. Is this genuine? It's not a hoax, someone playing games?'

'It looks genuine. How many people have your mobile number?'

'Not many. No one who would pretend to be Max.'

'Then it's him all right.'

'What do we do?' Consuela asked, bewildered. 'Do we show this to the police, tell them to call off their search?'

Chris gave the question some thought. 'Maybe not,' he said. 'Max is playing for very high stakes. His father's life is at risk. He wouldn't do this unless he felt he had no alternative.'

'So we do nothing?'

'For the time being, yes.'

'How could he do this? Put us through all this suffering?'

'I don't know,' Chris replied. 'But I know one thing. If he comes out of all this alive, *I'm* going to kill him.'

# SEVENTEEN

Max waited until the *Reunion Star* had been underway for several hours before he dared emerge from the crate. Forcing off the lid, he climbed out. His wet clothes were completely dry now, but it was cold in the ship's hold. If he was going to survive the voyage to Kamchatka, he needed to find a way of keeping warm.

He ripped open the plastic bags he'd lain on in the crate and discovered they contained overalls and fleece jackets with the blue and white Rescomin company logo on them. The overalls were all way too big for him and the fleece jackets were also on the large side, but if he rolled up the sleeves of the smallest size, they just about fitted him. And they were very warm, obviously designed for the Russian climate.

Then he set about exploring the hold. He knew he was going to be on the ship for some time. How long did it take to sail from San Francisco to Kamchatka? He had no accurate idea, but it was certainly going to be several days. He'd need somewhere to sleep, and he'd need to find food and drink.

Luckily, there was enough light trickling in through ventilation slats in the deck hatches for him to see what he was doing. The hold contained a lot of cargo, but it wasn't completely full. There were spaces through which Max could squeeze, boxes and packing cases which he could access. He opened a few and found more clothing with the Rescomin logo on it – clearly intended for the workers at the company's platinum mine at Zaliv Myertvetsa. He found medical supplies and blankets and a whole crate packed with cigarettes and vodka. Vodka? Didn't the Russians make that themselves? He opened two of the big metal containers and discovered machine parts and pneumatic drills and hard hats. Then, in a corner of the hold, he found some boxes of food and bottled water. There were sacks of flour and rice, bags of pasta and cartons of pizza bases, cans of beans and other vegetables. He inspected them longingly, realizing just how hungry he was, but also with a sense of frustration. It was food, but he couldn't eat raw rice or pasta, and he couldn't get into the cans without some kind of tin opener. He broke into another box and saw packets of biscuits and chocolate bars. That was more like it. He ripped open a chocolate bar and ate it greedily. Then he went through a whole packet of cookies and washed them down with some of the bottled water. It wasn't a very healthy diet, but he could live on it, if he had to.

Feeling better, he sat down on a wooden crate and thought about what he was going to do next. He had food and water and blankets. He could sleep in one of the crates or on the floor. Would anyone check the hold during the voyage? He couldn't see why they would, but he would have to be careful, just in case – make sure he had somewhere to hide if someone came, and ensure he left no signs of his presence: no wrappers or empty bottles out in the open.

He could survive, that was what counted. What he had to think about now was his father. Max was sure he was being taken to Kamchatka for more brainwashing, but was he on the *Reunion Star*? Max would have to search the entire ship to find out. But how should he do it without being caught?

Max pictured the ship lying alongside the quay in San Francisco. It hadn't looked a particularly large vessel, certainly nothing like as big as an oil tanker or even one of the car ferries that Max had been on across the English Channel. Most of the space was taken up by the cargo holds, but Alexander Cassidy wouldn't be being held in a hold – he'd be locked up in a cabin somewhere, possibly with a guard on the door. Max would have to find the crew's quarters and check every cabin. Doing it at night would be safer. The ship never stopped, of course; it kept going round the clock and there would always be someone on duty, particularly on the bridge, but Max reckoned there would be fewer people around after dark.

He removed another packet of biscuits, some chocolate and a bottle of water from the box he'd opened, then closed it up, grabbed a blanket from the other box and went back to his crate. He climbed inside, pulling the lid back into place above him, wrapped himself in the blanket and closed his eyes.

He dropped off almost immediately. He'd been up for more than twenty-four hours and had endured two long, gruelling swims. He was shattered, utterly exhausted. He didn't know how long he slept for, but when he woke up he sensed it was night. His body clock told him so. He clambered out of the crate and saw at once from the darkness that he was right. There was no light coming in anywhere, though high above him in the hatches he could see the pale strips of the ventilation slats.

He felt his way across to the hold door and opened it. The gangway outside was brightly lit. Down here in the bowels of the ship, Max guessed that the lights would be on all the time. It made sense if there was an emergency and the crew had to get out in a hurry.

The cargo holds occupied the middle and rear of

the ship and the bridge, from where the vessel was controlled, was at the front – the bow. The crew's quarters had to be below the bridge – there was nowhere else to fit them in – so Max made his way forward. He could hear the throb of the engines, feel the vibrations through his feet. There was a strong smell of diesel, which gradually started to blend with another odour – the pungent reek of fried onions and garlic. He heard the clank of pans and realized he must be nearing the galley, the ship's kitchen.

There were doors along the left side of the gangway, one every three or four metres, that he guessed were cabins. Then he reached a wider opening on the right. He paused just before it and peered cautiously round the corner, seeing stoves and stainless-steel worktops, two men in greasy white aprons dishing out food through a serving hatch to a group of men, a couple in oil-stained overalls who must have come from the engine room and three in smarter, pressed white shirts – part of the above-deck crew who actually sailed the ship.

Beyond the serving hatch, on the wall of the dining room, was a television screen showing a CNN satellite news programme. Max did a double take, astonished to see pictures of himself, footage that had been taken on the Golden Gate Bridge just before his stunt, then a clip of the wooden crate crashing down into the sea and shattering. The report cut to Consuela returning to the Fairmont Hotel looking pale and strained, declining to give any comment to the waiting reporters, then a police spokesman came on camera to say that the search for Max Cassidy would go on throughout the night. It had been nearly twenty-four hours since the teenager had disappeared, but they still hadn't given up hope of finding him alive.

Max felt a sharp stab of guilt – he was going to have a lot of explaining to do when he finally reappeared. When? Maybe that should be *if* he ever reappeared, since he still had a lot to do, all of it potentially hazardous. He put the negative thoughts out of his mind. One thing at a time. First he had to find out whether his father was on the ship.

He ducked back out of sight. How many crew did the *Reunion Star* have? he wondered. He suspected it wasn't all that many. Some would be up on the bridge, steering and keeping watch. If these others down here were having their evening meal, it probably meant that most of the cabins would be unoccupied. He retreated along the gangway and tried the first door he came to. It wasn't locked. Max glanced inside. It was, indeed, a cabin – a cramped little space containing a pair of bunk beds and a chest of drawers. But no people. He tried the other two cabins. There was no one in any of them either.

There had to be more cabins, he thought. Probably on the other side of the ship. He crept softly back along the gangway and turned left into another corridor that took him over to the starboard side. There were three more cabins there, all empty.

Max decided he'd done enough for the time being. No doubt there were other cabins further forward, but he couldn't reach those without going past the galley and dining room, and that was far too risky to attempt now. *Don't push your luck*, he said to himself. *You can continue your search later.*

He returned to the hold and, settling back down in his crate with another bar of chocolate and some biscuits, he tried to map the layout of the ship in his head. How many decks were there? Two, maybe three down below, then the bridge up above. His father wouldn't be on the bridge – that wasn't somewhere you could hold a man prisoner. He had to be below deck. Max had searched part of the bottom deck; if he waited a while for the crew to finish their meal, then he could go and search the rest of it.

A few hours later, he ventured back out into the gangway. The galley and dining room were deserted, though the lights were still on. Max went across into the bow section of the ship and found more doors that looked like cabins. It was half past twelve – he'd noted the time from the clock in the dining room – so the night watch would be up on the bridge, but some of the crew would certainly be in their bunks by now. That made checking the cabins a potentially tricky operation. Max would have to watch his step.

He tried the first door, pushing it open a fraction. The room beyond was in darkness. Max opened the door wider, then stopped dead. Someone was inside. He could hear the faint sound of snoring. He closed the door quickly and moved away around a corner, his heart rate increasing. Maybe this wasn't a good idea. But how else was he going to find his dad?

Then something occurred to him. He didn't need to actually enter any of the cabins, or even open their doors. His father was being held against his will. He wouldn't be in an unlocked cabin. Therefore, if a door was unlocked, his father couldn't be behind it.

Reassured by the thought, Max tried the next door and felt it give a little. It was unlocked. He released the handle softly and moved on along the gangway. Two more doors were also unlocked. Max crossed them off the list and kept going until, at the very front of the ship, he came across a door that *was* locked. He looked through the keyhole. He could see no light. He put his ear to the panel. No sound. His hopes rose. Maybe this was the one. Maybe his dad was here, probably drugged to keep him quiet. Max took out the piece of wire he'd cut from the fence around Pier 80 and used it to pick the lock, surprised to see his hand shaking a little. He grasped the handle and paused, trying to hold in his excitement, then pushed open the door. The disappointment hit him like a wave, throwing him back a step. His father wasn't there: the cabin was just a storeroom, full of cans of paint and tarpaulins and old ropes.

It took a few moments for him to recover, to get his mind back on track. One setback wasn't going to deter him. He'd tried every door on this deck, so he went back to the dining room and up the stairs to the deck above. There was no one about here either. He checked more doors, ignoring the ones that were unlocked and picking the locks on those that weren't. But he still didn't find his father.

Finally, he decided he'd done enough for one night, taken enough risks. It was time to retreat to his bolthole. He went back down the stairs and made a detour to the galley to see if there was any food he could scavenge. There was a large bowl in one of the fridges containing a chicken stew that must have been left over from the evening meal because it was still lukewarm. Max ate a good helping of it, but not so much that anyone would notice it had gone, then cut a chunk off a block of cheese and ate that too. There were plastic-wrapped loaves of sliced bread and small packs of butter and jam on the serving counter, obviously put out in advance for breakfast. Max took a couple of slices of bread from three of the loaves and resealed the plastic bags, then he helped himself to butter and jam and borrowed a knife from one of the drawers. He noticed a tin opener in amongst the other utensils and fingered it thoughtfully. Would anyone miss it if he removed it? He glanced around the galley. There was another, more sophisticated can opener on the wall that had to be the main one the cooks used. This opener in the drawer was surely just a back-up. No one was going to notice if it disappeared, and even if they did, they'd simply assume it had been misplaced, not taken by a stowaway on the ship. Max put the opener into his pocket and headed back to the hold.

The following night, he made another foray out into the ship, focusing this time on the higher decks. He went up two flights of stairs and began to try doors again, creeping quietly along the gangways, listening hard for sounds inside the cabins before he tested the handles. Just two of the doors he checked were locked, but when he picked them and peered inside he found only empty offices. Puzzled and frustrated, he paused underneath a staircase to consider his next move. Was there somewhere he'd missed? Was his father being held in one of the holds – there were at least two others apart from the one in which Max was hiding – or even in the engine rooms down below the bottom deck?

He heard men's voices, footsteps on the stairs above him. Someone was coming down. He caught a glimpse of shoes through the open treads. They were very close, only seconds away. There was no time to run – he'd be spotted for certain. Hiding was his only option. But where? There was a long locker, like a bench, against the wall beside him. He whipped open the lid and saw life jackets inside. The men were almost at the bottom of the stairs, still talking loudly. Max scrambled into the locker and wriggled down among the lifejackets, then pulled the lid shut and lay still, holding his breath. Had they heard him? Maybe not. They hadn't stopped talking, at any rate. He heard them go past, then waited a few minutes before he dared open the lid. The gangway was deserted. He climbed out, his pulse throbbing, and went quickly back down to the hold. The experience had shaken him, reminded him that there were crew around at all times of the day and night. He had to be patient, not get over-confident. If his dad was on the ship, he had plenty of time to find him.

He ventured out again the next night, and the night after that, searching all the holds, going down into the engine rooms, even once sneaking up to the bridge and taking a peep through the window at the control room. By the end, he was pretty sure he'd explored every corner of the *Reunion Star* and had come to the depressing conclusion that his father was not on board.

That was a blow. Max wondered if he'd made a huge mistake stowing away on the vessel. He'd been so sure that his dad was going to be taken to Kamchatka. Maybe he was. Just not by ship. Maybe he'd been flown there instead and was already being injected with Episuderon by Julius Clark's sinister scientists. The thought made Max feel even more despondent. His father was in great danger, probably being drugged and interrogated, and Max was stuck on a ship in the middle of the Pacific Ocean, no use to anyone.

Not that there was anything he could do about it. He just had to sit tight, make sure he wasn't discovered and hope he got to Kamchatka in time to save his dad.

The days went by with tedious slowness. Max didn't leave the hold; he lived off tinned meat and tuna, canned vegetables and biscuits and chocolate; he didn't wash, and a bucket he'd taken from a storeroom served as his toilet.

On the morning of the sixth day, he felt a change in

the ship's engines. It was slowing down. The dipping and rolling motion of the open sea that he'd got used to eased off and he knew that they were in more sheltered waters. The vessel slowed further. Max heard movement on the main deck above him, orders being shouted, then the engines went into reverse, the power coming on and off as the *Reunion Star* manoeuvred its way into port. The side of the ship scraped against the dock, there was a rattle of the anchor being dropped, then the engines stopped completely. For the first time in nearly a week, there was silence. No vibrations, no throbbing, no noise at all. They had arrived in Kamchatka.

Max felt an immense sense of relief mixed with apprehension. He was in Russia now, and he didn't know what to expect. He'd tried to plan a course of action for when he arrived, but how did you plan for the complete unknown? He would just have to take his chances and hope for the best. He hid his slop bucket and all the empty cans and food wrappers in a container, then climbed inside his crate and listened as the deck hatches were opened, flooding the hold with daylight. Stevedores came on board the ship and began to unload the cargo. Max could hear them moving around, talking to one another in Russian.

The big metal containers were winched out first,

then the smaller boxes and crates, including Max's. He felt himself being lifted into the air, the crate swaying in a sling, and for a moment he was back on the Golden Gate Bridge – the heart-stopping terror of those few minutes, when he'd been dangling precariously from the crane, then plummeting down into the sea, returned with chilling intensity. He felt sick, his pulse began to race and he had to slow his breathing, force himself to calm down. It wasn't the same, he assured himself. The Golden Gate trauma was over and done with. This was just a routine unloading of a freighter. Nothing was going to go wrong.

He stayed tense, however, until he felt the crate touch down on the quayside, felt a forklift picking it up again and moving it away to a storage area. He was safely off the ship. But now the really difficult bit began. He had to get out of the crate without being seen, then find out exactly where he was and, hardest of all, find his father and rescue him.

Waiting until after dark would have been the safest course of action, but Max didn't want to wait that long. He couldn't afford to. He'd been at sea for a week. Now he was in Kamchatka, he needed to get moving as quickly as possible.

He listened for signs of activity nearby – forklift trucks moving to and fro, stevedores shouting – and when there'd been a prolonged period of silence carefully eased off the lid of his crate and slid it aside a few centimetres, creating a gap wide enough for him to see out. He was in an open-air cargo holding area at the back of the quayside, surrounded by boxes and packing crates. There was a long, aluminium-sided warehouse to his left, with an opening in the wall through which trucks were moving, transporting containers out onto the waterfront where they were loaded onto the *Reunion Star*. The ship brought in supplies for the Rescomin platinum mine, Max guessed, then returned to San Francisco with a cargo of the metal. But where *was* the mine? It certainly wasn't here by the sea. Max could see no buildings other than the warehouse, no houses, no accommodation blocks for the workforce or any other signs of industrial activity. This was just a port facility – a place where goods were loaded and unloaded – and nothing more.

He surveyed the area. There was no one nearby, the stevedores all busy on the other side of the quay. He climbed out of his crate. He was still wearing the navy blue Rescomin fleece jacket, and was glad of it since the air was cool, a damp breeze gusting in from the ocean. He crouched down for a second, checking that he hadn't been spotted, then crept away through the stacks of freight until he reached a chain-link fence at the back of the site. There was a road on the other side of the fence, an unmade dirt road with a rough, potholed surface. It headed inland away from the port, cutting through a dense forest of coniferous trees.

Max snipped a small hole in the fence with his nail-cutters and wriggled through it, closing the mesh up behind him to hide what he'd done. Then he ran across the road and into the forest, going just deep enough into the trees to be out of sight but still close enough to the road to use it as a guide. He took a deep breath, then stretched his limbs. It felt good to be out in the open again, to feel fresh air on his face. Staying roughly parallel to the road, he made his way through the forest. There was very little undergrowth so he was able to move quickly and easily.

He'd gone more than a mile when he heard the noise of an engine getting louder. He ducked behind a tree trunk and looked out cautiously, seeing a truck with a container on the back clattering up the road from the port, leaving a white cloud of dust in its wake. Four more trucks followed close behind.

Max gave them a couple of minutes to disappear over the horizon, then kept walking. The ground was beginning to slope uphill now, the forest clinging to a low range of coastal hills. The road doubled back on itself, twisting up the hill in a series of hairpin bends.

Max decided to save time and energy by cutting across the road in a straight line instead of following the bends. The gradient was steep and by the time he reached the top of the hill he was panting for breath and so warm he had to remove his fleece jacket and tie it around his waist.

Climbing out of the forest onto a rocky ridge to spy out the land ahead, he was stunned by the scenery. It was probably the most spectacularly beautiful view he'd ever seen: the land dropped away into a broad valley in which a crystal lake nestled, its waters reflecting the pine and birch trees that framed the shore. From one end of the lake a river emerged, a wide, shallow stream that meandered across the flood plain through pools and channels, whose edges were marked by boulders and tiny crescents of shingle beach. Behind the lake, the mountains rose up in a long, jagged line, in the centre of which was a high, conical peak topped with brilliant white snow. From the summit of the cone, puffs of steam were belching, lingering for a while in the blue sky before fading away to nothing. Max realized he was not looking at a mountain, but an active volcano. He gazed at it with slight trepidation, wondering how dangerous it was.

The only thing spoiling the view was the road, which cut across the valley at the lower end, crossing the river on a man-made causeway before disappearing through a notch in the hills. But even that was just a minor blemish on the landscape, a barely noticeable imperfection in the midst of such pristine, natural beauty.

Max climbed down off the ridge, crossing another bend in the road and plunging back into the forest. Half an hour later, he stopped to get his bearings. He'd strayed away from the road, but he'd nearly reached the valley floor. The river could only be half a mile away, the lake maybe double that.

In front of him, winding away through the trees, was what looked like a well-used animal track, a distinct ribbon of worn ground that stood out from the surrounding land. Max followed it for twenty or thirty metres, then paused. He could see a clearing in the forest up ahead and lying on the track just before the clearing was a hare. The creature didn't move as Max walked closer. It just turned its head and looked at him with big, frightened eyes. One of its hind legs was caught in a wire snare. It had struggled to free itself, but only pulled the snare tighter. The wire was cutting deep into the flesh and there was blood on the fur around the wound; it looked very painful.

Max crouched down and loosened the snare, pulling apart the wire and gently extricating the hare's foot. The animal lay still for a moment, as if it couldn't believe it was free, then it limped slowly away into the clearing, dragging its injured leg behind it. Max watched, wondering if he'd done the right thing. Could the hare survive in the wild in that condition?

He was so absorbed with the creature that he didn't hear the faint sound of feet behind him, didn't sense there was anyone there until he felt a heavy blow on his back that sent him sprawling forward on to the ground. An angry male voice yelled at him in a language he didn't understand – Russian, he thought – and a foot slammed into his ribs. Max grunted and rolled sideways out of the way. Looking up, he saw a tall, thin man stride over to the injured hare, which had only managed to shuffle a few metres away across the clearing, pick it up and, with one violent twist, snap its neck.

The man came back to Max, the dead hare dangling from his hand. He was wearing boots, faded jeans and a jacket made out of animal skins. His cap was fur, with flaps to protect his ears from the cold. Slung across his back was a hunting rifle and a leather knapsack. He bawled something else in Russian and took another swing at Max with his foot, obviously still furious with him. Max avoided the blow and scrambled to his feet, his fists clenched, ready for a fight. Was this one of Julius Clark's men?

'What the hell are you playing at?' he shouted. 'Why are you attacking me?'

The man stepped back in surprise. He stared at Max. 'You speak English?' he said, a strong Russian flavour to his accent.

'I *am* English,' Max replied. 'What're you doing? I mean you no harm.'

'What are *you* doing?' the man fired back. 'Messing with my snares. Letting my catch go.'

'It was hurt,' Max said. 'It was in pain.'

'This is my food,' the man snapped, holding up the hare. 'It's what I live off. Who are you to interfere, eh? What're you doing out here anyway, a kid like you?'

Max didn't answer. He'd seen something move on the far side of the clearing. The man turned to follow his gaze and froze. Coming out through the trees was a huge, shaggy brown bear.

# EIGHTEEN

Max stayed completely still, hoping that the bear hadn't seen them, that it would simply wander back into the forest. But it *had* seen them. Its head came up and it stared directly at them, its eyes cold and black and expressionless. Max shivered. His chest was tight. He was finding it difficult to breathe. The bear watched them intently. It looked a big, powerful creature, but Max realized that a lot of that was its dense fur coat, underneath the fur, its body was actually quite lean and underfed. Its face, too, was markedly thin. *A hungry bear*, Max thought. *Very bad news.*

'Don't move an inch,' the Russian man said softly. 'Just stay calm.'

Max did as he was told, trying to remember what he'd read in books or seen on the television about dealing with wild bears. Never try to run away from one, they said. A bear could easily outrun a human. Never climb a tree either. Bears were equally good at climbing trees. Lying down and pretending to be dead was sometimes advised. The bear might leave you alone then. But

Max didn't fancy that option. Lying down, it seemed to him, would just be an invitation to the creature to come and eat his fill.

Maybe if they did nothing, the animal would go away. But it wasn't going away. It took a couple of tentative steps towards them, a trickle of saliva glistening at the corner of its mouth. Max could see it was preparing to strike. The Russian must have realized that too for he suddenly stepped forward, throwing up his arms and puffing out his chest to make himself look as big and frightening as possible, and screamed loudly at the animal.

'YAAAAH! YAAAAH!'

The bear hesitated. The Russian yelled at it some more, taking another step forward.

'YAAAAH!'

The bear backed away a little, then stopped. Its eyes were still fixed on them. There was no fear in them, just wariness. The Russian took another pace forward, waving his arms and shouting. The bear stayed where it was. Its head dipped down, its shoulders came forward. Max realized it was about to attack. There was nothing they could do. There was nowhere to run. This was it.

The Russian said something terse in his own language that sounded to Max like a swear word, then swung back his arm and threw the dead hare across the clearing. It landed on the ground with a thud right in front of the bear, which fell on the carcases greedily, tearing it apart with its huge, yellowish teeth.

'Back away slowly,' the Russian said.

Max shuffled backwards, still watching the bear. It was gorging itself on the hare as though it hadn't eaten in a long time. He felt a tree trunk behind him and stepped round it into the fringes of the forest. The Russian was already heading off along the path. Max followed him. The man moved fast, but silently, his feet making almost no sound on the ground. He seemed to belong in the forest, seemed in some way to be part of it. They went across the slope of the hill for a quarter of a mile, then the man stopped in another clearing and turned to look at Max. The sunlight was full on his face now and Max was stunned to see that he wasn't a man at all, but a boy. A boy not much older than him. He had long, unkempt black hair, watchful brown eyes and a tanned, weather-beaten face ingrained with dirt. Above his lip and along his jaw were smears of dark, teenage stubble.

'You'd better get back to Zaliv Myertvetsa,' he said curtly. 'You shouldn't be out here, you don't know what you're doing.'

'Zaliv Myertvetsa?' Max said.

'The platinum mine. That's its Russian name. Didn't you know? Dead Man's Bay, it means in English.'

'You think I've come from the mine?'

'Where else could you have come from? There are quite a few foreigners there – English, Americans, Germans.' He pointed at Max's fleece jacket, the company logo clearly visible. 'Your parents work for Rescomin?'

'I haven't come from the mine,' Max said. 'I was on the ship, the *Reunion Star*.'

'The *ship*?' The boy eyed him narrowly. He seemed perplexed. 'You're too young to be crew, so is your dad the captain or something? Did he bring you along for the trip?'

'I stowed away.'

The boy stared at him. 'You stowed away? To come to Kamchatka? Are you crazy? Why?'

'It's a long story,' Max said. He wasn't sure about this Russian boy – he could still feel the ache in his ribs where he'd been kicked – but he was beginning to realize that he might need some help in this strange, hostile country, so he tried to be friendly. 'Look, I'm sorry about what happened just now,' he said. 'The snare. I didn't think about what I was doing. I come from a city, so I'm not used to seeing animals caught for food. And thanks for dealing with the bear. You saved my life.'

The boy shrugged, not interested in thanks.

'I'm sorry you had to give him the hare,' Max went on. 'Are you going to go hungry now?'

'I've another hare in my bag,' the boy said. 'I have snares all over the forest.'

Max held out his hand. 'I'm Max.'

The boy hesitated, then took the hand. 'Dmitri.'

They shook. Dmitri's hands were rough and calloused, covered in muck and a reddish stain that Max suspected was blood from the hares. *This is really weird*, he thought. *I'm in the middle of a Kamchatka forest, shaking hands with some wild Russian boy who speaks fluent English. What on earth is going on here?*

Dmitri's expression softened. He looked guilty for a second. 'I'm sorry too,' he said. 'For hitting you.' He paused. 'Are you hungry?'

'A bit,' Max admitted.

'Come with me.'

Dmitri headed off through the forest. Max went after him, struggling to keep up. The Russian boy seemed to know every inch of the terrain: the paths, the fallen logs, the gullies that dissected the area. They crossed a stretch of scree below a sheer rock escarpment, then forded a stream and climbed a tree-covered bluff to a clearing in front of a cave. On the ground just outside the cave a wood fire smouldered, the smoke trickling lazily up into the air. Dmitri unslung his rifle and took the other dead hare out of his knapsack. He picked up a blackened cooking pot and gave it to Max.

'You get the water.'

Max went down the hill to the stream and filled the pot. He bathed his face and drank some of the water. It was cool and refreshing. When he got back to the cave, Dmitri was skinning and gutting the hare, using a flat stone as a butcher's block. He chopped the carcass into pieces and tossed them into the cooking pot. Then he knelt down by the fire and nursed it back to life, stoking it with logs until it was burning fiercely. He disappeared briefly into the cave and returned with a couple of onions, a tin of tomatoes and a can opener. He threw the tin opener to Max, then peeled the onions, cut them in half and added them to the cooking pot. Max opened the tin and Dmitri poured the tomatoes in on top of the hare and onions. Then he put the lid on the pot and placed it on the fire.

'A couple of hours, it should be ready,' he said, wiping his hands on his jeans.

Max was in a dilemma. He didn't want to hang around for two hours. He wanted to get on and find the platinum mine. But he was tempted by the prospect of his first decent meal in a week, and also aware that he was out of his depth here. He didn't want to blunder over to the mine and get caught by Clark's men. Maybe talking to Dmitri, getting some local knowledge from him, would be a sensible idea.

He glanced around the clearing. 'You live here? In this cave?'

'Yes.'

'Alone?'

Dmitri nodded. 'That's a long story too.'

'Where did you learn such good English?'

'Geneva.'

Max was momentarily taken aback. It wasn't the kind of answer he'd expected. What did that mean? Geneva was in Switzerland, thousands of miles away from Kamchatka.

'Geneva?' he said. 'I don't understand.'

But Dmitri was going into the cave again. He reappeared with a bottle in his hand, picked up his rifle and moved off towards the trees. 'Come on,' he called. 'There's somewhere better we can talk.'

They went down the slope through the forest and walked for about fifteen minutes until they came to a hollow in the hillside that was filled with water. Max could see steam rising off the surface of the pool, smell the faint odour of sulphur.

'Hot springs,' Dmitri explained. 'You ever been in one?'

'No,' Max replied. He looked uncertainly at the pool.

It was a couple of metres deep, with rocky sides and a fissure at the bottom through which the water was bubbling up from underground. 'How hot is it?'

'Just nice. You'll see.'

Dmitri put down his rifle and the bottle on a rock at the edge of the pool, stripped off his clothes and jumped in. Max waited a few seconds, then did the same. The water was warm and soothing, about the temperature of a hot bath back home in London. *London?* Max thought. That was about as far away from here as it was possible to imagine. Far away in a geographical sense, but also far away in every other sense. *How much bigger a contrast could you get?* he wondered. The cramped, dirty, urban streets of London and this untouched wilderness of lakes and forests and hot springs.

'Good, eh?' Dmitri said.

'Very good.'

'I come here all the time. It's particularly nice in winter. Snow all around, temperatures below freezing, but this pool is always hot.'

'The mountain at the top of the valley,' Max said. 'Is that a volcano?'

'Yes.'

'Active?'

'Did you see the steam coming out of it? Sometimes

286

it rumbles, throws red-hot cinders up into the sky. It's really spectacular at night.'

'Is it in danger of erupting?'

'I hope not,' Dmitri said, and laughed. It made him look younger, more boyish.

'But you don't know?'

'This area is full of active volcanoes and hot springs and geysers. I wouldn't worry about them. Just enjoy them.'

Max rubbed his arms and legs under the water, washing off the grime and sweat that had built up during his six days on the *Reunion Star*. It felt wonderfully relaxing, floating around in this hot pool, the clear sky up above, the air fresh and clean, the snow-capped volcano visible on the horizon above the birch and pine trees. Dmitri seemed more at ease too, as if he were enjoying having company.

'What did you mean when you said you'd learned English in Geneva?' Max asked.

'Just that,' Dmitri replied. 'I went to school there.'

'In Switzerland?'

'My father was a diplomat, attached to the United Nations in Geneva. I went to an international school with kids from all over the world. The only common language we had was English.'

'How old are you?'

'Seventeen.'

'So how come you're here in Kamchatka now, living all alone in a cave? Where are your parents? Still in Switzerland?'

'My mother died when I was four. My father's dead too. At least I think he is.'

'You think?'

'He just disappeared one day. I don't know what's happened to him.'

'He *disappeared*?' Max said, feeling a sudden empathy for Dmitri. How strange was that, both their fathers vanishing without explanation?

Dmitri pushed off across the pool, floating on his back, gazing up at the sky. He was silent for a long time, then he said: 'My dad was very interested in environmental issues – around the world through his work for the UN, but especially in Russia. He was concerned about how much we're destroying our environment. He made noises about it which the government didn't like, so they sacked him. He came here to Kamchatka to run a small environmental action group and I came with him. We lived inland, about eighty kilometres from here, in a small town near the main road north. Do you know much about Kamchatka?'

'Not a thing,' Max said.

'It's still pretty much a wilderness. Mountains and

forests and volcanoes and lots of wildlife – bears, wolves, sea otters, sable, beavers. My dad was fighting to keep it that way, but there were others – businessmen, corporations, politicians – who didn't agree with him, who wanted to develop the area commercially, make money out of it.'

'Like Rescomin, you mean?'

'Yes. Rescomin is the worst of them. The river near their mine has become polluted with chemicals from their processing plant. So has the sea. That bear we met earlier – it would usually keep well away from people, but it's hungry, desperate to find food. You know why? At this time of year, it would normally be fat and contented, building up its reserves for winter by feeding on the thousands of salmon that swim up the river from the sea to breed. But this year there aren't many salmon. They've been declining for the past two or three years, almost certainly killed by the pollution from Zaliv Myertvetsa. So the bears are starving. Two miners have already been killed by them this summer.'

Dmitri rolled over onto his front and swam to the edge of the pool, sitting on a submerged rock shelf so only his head was above the surface. Max paddled gently to and fro. He could feel the hot water bubbling up below him, swirling around his legs. Dmitri picked up the bottle he'd brought, removed the cap and took a drink. Then he held it out to Max.

'You want some?'

'What is it?'

'Vodka.'

'No, thanks.'

Dmitri took another sip, keeping the bottle in his hand. 'My dad was campaigning to get Zaliv Myertvetsa closed down,' he continued. 'Gathering evidence of pollution, of severe damage to the environment, of bribes paid to politicians by Rescomin. He left our house one morning about eighteen months ago, but never showed up at his office. He just disappeared. I haven't seen him since.'

Max stopped paddling, a sudden suspicion taking shape inside his head. He stared intently at Dmitri. 'What's your second name? Your family name.'

'Alekseev. Why?'

'And your father's name. Was it Sergei?'

Dmitri started, gaping at him in astonishment. 'How did you know?'

'I think I know what happened to him.'

'You? How could you possibly know that?' Dmitri said sceptically.

Max swam to the rock shelf and sat down next to

him. 'What do *you* think happened to your father?' he asked.

Dmitri shrugged. He drank some more vodka and wiped his mouth with the back of his hand. 'I think he was murdered.'

'Who by?'

'I don't know. He had a lot of enemies, people who didn't like what he was doing, who wanted to protect Zaliv Myertvetsa.'

'You think Rescomin had a part in it?'

'I'm certain of it. But I have no proof. That's why I came out here. My dad used to bring me with him when he came to do his research – to monitor the mine, to take water samples from the river and the sea, to collect dead fish and other animals for the laboratory to analyse for poison. We'd camp out, cook over a wood fire. I loved it. When he disappeared, there was no one to look after me. I was on my own, but as I believed in what he'd been doing, I came out here to try to continue his work, to watch what they were doing at Zaliv Myertvetsa. I even got a job there under a false name, worked all last summer and autumn in the mine. I thought I might somehow find out what had happened to my dad.'

'But you haven't?'

'No.'

'How long have you been here?'

'About fifteen months.'

'And you've discovered nothing?'

Dmitri glanced away, a look of guilt and self disgust in his eyes. 'I haven't been trying as hard as I could, I suppose. After Dad disappeared I was all right – or I thought I was. Then last winter I cracked up. Had some kind of breakdown. I started drinking. Couldn't find the energy to do much. Maybe I've given up, I don't know. I survive. I live off the land, catching my own food, stealing what I can't catch. But I've done nothing about Rescomin or the mine.'

He took another long swig of vodka and stared into the distance, his face twisted as if he were in pain.

'I think you're right about your dad,' Max said gently. 'He *was* murdered. But not here. He was taken to a place in Central America called Shadow Island. The island is owned by Julius Clark, the boss of Rescomin.'

'Shadow Island?'

Max nodded and told him about it. How he'd been held prisoner there, how Clark had been kidnapping his opponents and brainwashing them, turning them into his fifth columnists – people who would then work *for* him, rather than against.

'I only saw a few of the files on the island,' Max said. 'But Sergei Alekseev was one of the names in them. That has to be your dad.'

Dmitri said nothing for a while, gazing down through the limpid water. Then he turned his head to look at Max. 'So the brainwashing killed him? This drug you mentioned, Episuderon.'

'I don't know for sure,' Max replied. 'Some people – maybe a lot – survived the brainwashing. But if you haven't heard from your dad in eighteen months, it doesn't look good, does it? I'm sorry.'

He kept quiet then, sensing that Dmitri needed some time to himself, some time to come to terms with what had happened to his father. Dmitri gulped down more vodka, as if it were water.

'You drink a lot, don't you?' Max said.

Dmitri flared up immediately. 'So? Why shouldn't I?' he snarled angrily. 'If I want to drink, I will.'

He put the bottle to his lips again defiantly and took another long gulp. When he lowered the bottle, there were tears in his eyes. He blinked a few times, then heaved himself out of the water and turned away so Max couldn't see his face. He dried himself on his shirt and got dressed. Max climbed out too and put his clothes back on.

'I'm sorry I got angry,' Dmitri said eventually. 'I was pretty certain he was dead, but, well, I suppose I hoped he might not be. That there might be some other explanation.'

'I know,' Max said sympathetically. 'That's how I felt when *my* dad disappeared without trace.'

Dmitri's eyes opened wide in surprise. '*Your* father too?'

Max told him. The whole story – from his dad going missing in Santo Domingo to his own arrival in Kamchatka.

'I think Clark has moved his brainwashing programme here,' he said. 'I think my dad's being held prisoner at Dead Man's Bay. Probably other people too. He didn't come on the ship from San Francisco so they must have brought him here some other way.'

'There are other, smaller boats that come up the coast from Petropavlovsk-Kamchatskiy,' Dmitri said. 'But I'd guess he came by air. There's a helipad at the mine. The helicopters come and go all the time.'

'I want to go over there and look for him,' Max said. 'How well do you know the area?'

'What is it you say in English – "like the back of my hand"? That's how well I know it. I've worked there, been there dozens of times.'

'Can you describe it to me – the layout of the site, the buildings?'

'I can do better than that,' Dmitri replied. 'I'll take you there and show you.'

\* \* \*

They went back to the camp first and ate some of the hare stew that had been slowly cooking on the fire, followed by a bowl of cloudberries Dmitri had picked the previous day. The stew was delicious and after a week of living on canned food and biscuits, Max relished the luxury of a proper meal. Then they went into the cave. Max was impressed by the way Dmitri had turned it into a home: he had his sleeping bag on a raised platform constructed out of pine branches, and a table and stool he'd made from a couple of thick silver birch stumps. Stacked against the rock wall were tins of vegetables and corned beef and bags of rice and flour and other provisions.

'All "liberated" from the store at the mine,' Dmitri said dryly.

'How did you carry it here?' Max asked.

'Bit by bit, in a rucksack. I'm careful. I go in at night, just take a few items at a time. They have so much that they'd never notice any of it was gone.'

'And they've never caught you? Aren't there guards?'

'Not many. They aren't needed. The site's very isolated – the nearest town is eighty kilometres away along a road that's only passable for three months in summer. Who's going to break in? The only secure part of the area is the store where they keep the refined platinum before it's shipped out.'

Dmitri went to an airtight plastic container that was sitting on a rock ledge, opened it and removed a folded sheet of paper. 'My dad had a plan of the site. We'll look at it when we get there. It'll make more sense then.'

He put the paper and a torch in a small rucksack, picked up his rifle and they headed off down the hill. On the valley floor, they avoided the road and kept to the safety of the forest. Dmitri said that the trucks went regularly from the port to the mine and vice versa. You could usually hear them coming, but it was better to be cautious and not get caught in the open.

They forded the river where it started to turn north and followed its bank for twenty minutes before branching off and climbing a steep incline to the top of a ridge from which they had a good view of the land ahead. The contrast with the valley they were leaving was immediately – and depressingly – noticeable. The plain below the ridge must once have been green and verdant, carpeted with grass and trees and meadow flowers. Now it was just a massive hole in the ground, a black, ugly scar on the landscape. The surface had been stripped away to form a huge open-cast mine the size of a small town. It stretched far into the distance, across the plain and into the side of the mountains whose slopes were being gradually blasted away, as if some colossal rock-eating monster were biting chunks out of them.

Max had never seen anything like it before, never seen such an awesome example of environmental destruction, of what man could do to nature when it stood in his way. It brought home to him the importance of what his father, and the Cedar Alliance, were fighting for. This mine could have been the surface of the Moon, or of Mars, it seemed so alien to the Earth. The only signs of life were the diggers scooping up the rocks and the trucks transporting them away from the mine, but they, too, were somehow alien and unnatural. The diggers were like mechanical giants, dwarfing their surroundings, and the trucks, their headlights blazing in the twilight, were like huge bug-eyed insects crawling over the carcass of a slaughtered animal.

'That's the platinum mine,' Dmitri said.

Max stared across the terrain, too stunned to respond for a moment. Then he said, 'I never imagined it would be so big. They're taking away the whole mountain.'

'That's how they do it. You only get a few grams of platinum from a tonne of ore. That ring or brooch in a jeweller's shop in London or New York, it's taken truckloads of rock to produce. You see over there, that—'

Dmitri broke off as a siren sounded at the mine, a high-pitched whining noise that carried right across the valley.

'What's that?' Max asked.

'Watch,' Dmitri replied.

There was a brief silence, then the sharp report of an explosion – a series of explosions really. Max saw puffs of smoke erupt in a line across the base of the mountain as a dozen separate charges detonated, then there was a roar and a great chunk of rock broke away and collapsed in a cloud of billowing dust.

'They do that several times a day,' Dmitri said. 'Then the ore is taken by truck to the processing plant.' He pointed to a complex of buildings nearer the coast, a sprawling collection of metal sheds and chimneys that was as unsightly as the mine itself. 'They extract the platinum, then ship it out to a refinery in America where it's purified further.'

'It sounds complicated,' Max said. 'And expensive.'

'It is,' Dmitri agreed. 'But worth it to Rescomin. Look at what they've built here. All those processing sheds and offices, but they've also had to build a village for the workers. You see those concrete blocks over there – that's where they all live.'

'What are those pipes for?' Max asked, indicating a row of wide metal tubes that came up out of the ground and then snaked away to different parts of the site, white steam seeping out through valves in their sides.

'Thermal heating,' Dmitri replied. 'Like those hot springs we were in. They pump hot water up from underground and use it to heat the offices and workers' flats.'

'And that metal tower with the wheel on top? What's that?'

'The winding gear for one of the disused mine shafts. They used to mine underground here – there are old shafts everywhere – but the seams ran out so they turned to open-cast mining. The ore is less rich, but there's more of it, as you can see.'

Max let his gaze rove over the mine. In the gloom of dusk, the noise of the trucks and diggers echoing across the valley, smoke and steam and dust rising up to form a thick, noxious cloud, it seemed to him like a vision of hell. And his dad was somewhere in there.

He looked further east and saw high, sheer cliffs along the coast, lines of jagged rocks at the bottom over which huge waves were breaking, sending plumes of white water and spray up into the air. 'That must be Dead Man's Bay,' he said.

Dmitri nodded. 'Zaliv Myertvetsa. The first Russian settlers in Kamchatka called it that because it claimed so many lives. Dozens of ships were lost there, smashed against the rocks by the tide and currents. That's why they built the port seven kilometres south, in a more sheltered part of the coast. Dead Man's Bay is just too dangerous for boats.'

Max turned back to the processing plant, studying the buildings thoughtfully. 'You know the place well. Where do you think they might be holding prisoners?'

'I worked there for five months, went to every part of the site, but I never saw any prisoners, never heard of any.'

'That was last year. They'll only have been brought here in the past few weeks. Since Shadow Island was destroyed.'

Dmitri grinned. 'Since *you* destroyed it, you mean.' He looked hard at him, his eyes lighting up. 'You want to do that here? Burn the place down?'

'I just want to get my dad out. Are there any isolated buildings? Areas that are more secure, more closely guarded than others, maybe with cells or rooms that prisoners could be locked up in?'

Dmitri didn't reply. He thought for a moment, then said, 'Well, there *is* something. The bunker.'

'Bunker?'

'There's been a mine here for decades, since before the Second World War. Then during the Cold War the Soviets built an underground bunker – some kind of military installation, a listening post or radio station, something like that.'

'It's still here?'

'It was abandoned after the fall of communism, hasn't been used for years.'

'How do you know?'

'One of the old miners showed me. Took me down a staircase. It was just a wreck, an empty concrete shell with water dripping from the ceilings, mould on the walls.'

'Could Clark be using it again?'

'I don't know. It's possible, I suppose.'

'I want to take a look at it,' Max said. 'Can you show me?'

Dmitri nodded. 'Wait until night. Then we'll go there.'

# NINETEEN

The mine had vanished into the darkness, the pits and quarries hidden by the night, blending in so well with the landscape that they might not have been there. Everything was black, including the sky, which was heavy with clouds. Only the processing plant and the workers' accommodation blocks were visible, picked out by the floodlights that were dotted across the site.

Max and Dmitri climbed down off the ridge and cut through the forest to the road, which Dmitri said was deserted at night, no trucks or other vehicles moving along it. They didn't talk as they walked, but there was a silent bond between them. The antagonism of their initial encounter had all been forgotten. They were allies now, their friendship cemented by what had happened to their fathers. They had a shared purpose – a shared determination to find Alexander Cassidy, to find out for certain what had happened to Sergei Alekseev, then take their revenge on Julius Clark.

They made good time, covering the three kilometres to the mine in under forty minutes. As they neared the perimeter, Dmitri led them off the road onto an area of rough grass and scrub and crouched down behind a boulder. He took the plan of the site from his rucksack and shone his torch on the paper, partially shielding the beam with his hand.

'There's no fence or gate,' he said. 'The road just goes straight into the mine. This first building on the left, here, is the storeroom, where they keep all the supplies. Food, clothing, machine parts – everything from truck tyres to toilet paper. It all has to be brought in by ship. The only things that aren't stored here are the refined platinum, the fuel for the vehicles and the explosives. They're kept separately, in these buildings here.'

Dmitri pointed to three squares on the left-hand side of the plan, then his finger moved to the right. 'This is the main processing plant, the crushing mill and flotation tanks. These buildings are offices and the canteen for the workers. And here is the entrance to the bunker.'

'What's it like?' Max asked.

'Just a door in an old tin shed,' Dmitri replied. 'Inside, there was a lift, but it wasn't working. That's why we took the stairs down into the bunker.'

'Was the door locked?'

'Yes.'

'I can deal with that, I'm good with locks,' Max said,

feeling in his pocket for the piece of wire he still had with him.

Dmitri clicked off the torch and stowed the plan away in his rucksack, then stood up and headed across towards the mine. Max stuck close to him, feeling butterflies in his stomach. He was on edge, looking out for danger.

They rejoined the road for a few metres, then entered the site, pausing in the shelter of the storeroom to survey the ground in front of them. There was a wide open yard, illuminated by floodlights, and beyond that a cluster of concrete office blocks and the huge frame of the processing plant that had to be at least two hundred metres from end to end. Parked against the wall of the storeroom was a line of high-backed trucks and a couple of jeeps. Dmitri crept along behind them, then paused again, gesturing across the yard at an access road next to the offices. Max nodded. Dmitri checked there was no one around, then sprinted across the yard. Max went after him, listening to the soft pad of their feet on the ground, watching their shadows changing shape as they raced away from the lights.

They ducked into the cover of an office block and ran along by the wall where it was darkest. Dmitri turned right between two buildings and slowed, signalling to Max to do the same. They crept to the end of the wall and peered cautiously around the corner. On the far side of another floodlit yard was the entrance to the bunker. Max could see the door – a big, solid-looking metal panel with a keyhole on one side. As he watched, the door opened and two men – wearing uniforms like soldiers – emerged. Slung casually over their shoulders were sub-machine guns. They both lit cigarettes and smoked them, chatting idly to each other in Russian.

Max and Dmitri retreated, taking shelter behind one of the office blocks.

'I think you're right,' Dmitri said softly. 'The bunker is back in use again.'

'Can we get inside it?' Max asked.

Dmitri shook his head doubtfully. 'Not through that door, it's too risky. I've never seen guards around the mine before. With guns like that. They'd shoot us if we tried to get in.'

Max's stomach was churning, a mixture of nerves and excitement. His suspicions were correct. Something was going on in the bunker, something that needed armed men to guard it. That could only be Clark's brainwashing programme – nothing else made sense. And that meant Max's dad had to be down there. Max didn't want to delay. He wanted to find his father and rescue him. But the guards were a problem. How were they going to deal with them?

'You've got your rifle,' Max said. 'Could we burst in through the door and hold the guards up at gunpoint?'

'Bad idea,' Dmitri replied firmly. 'There are two of them and they have machine guns. I only have an old hunting rifle. And there may be more guards inside. It would be crazy to rush in.'

'Then what do you suggest? We *have* to get in there, Dmitri. It's vital. Is there another entrance?'

'I don't know. Maybe.'

'Maybe? What do you mean?'

'The old miner who took me down there, he said something about a back way, an exit that could be used in an emergency.'

'Did he say where it was?'

'Down one of the old, abandoned mine shafts.'

'Do you know which one?'

'No, but I suppose we could work it out. If we had to.'

'Dmitri, we *have* to,' Max said.

'It's risky.'

Max took hold of Dmitri's shoulders and looked him directly in the eye. 'My dad is down there,' he said fiercely, his voice low and intense. 'Julius Clark's scientists could be pumping him full of Episuderon, interrogating him right now. They might even have killed him. We can't afford to wait. We have to *do* something.'

Dmitri gazed back at him uncertainly. Now they

were here at the mine, his resolve seemed to be weakening. 'I'm not sure . . .' His voice trailed away.

'Well, I *am* sure,' Max said. 'Julius Clark murdered your father, Dmitri. He kidnapped him and gave him a dangerous drug that killed him. Do you want him to get away with that? Is that the kind of son you are?'

It was a harsh thing to say, but it had the effect Max intended. Dmitri's eyes hardened. He looked away for a moment, as if he were remembering his father, remembering the years they'd spent together. Then he gritted his teeth and nodded.

'No, Clark isn't going to get away with it. I'm going to make him pay.'

'The two of us together,' Max said. 'We can do it. Now let's take another look at that plan.'

Dmitri took the paper out of his rucksack and they studied it again by the light of the torch. Dmitri pointed to three or four printed circles in different parts of the site. 'Those are the old shafts.'

'Can you still get down them?' Max asked.

'I don't know. There used to be lift cages for taking the miners underground, but I don't know whether they're still there, whether they still work. They might have filled the shafts in.'

'How big is the bunker? What kind of area would it cover?'

Dmitri traced an invisible line on the plan with his finger. 'About that, I think.'

'So it spreads over here to the north of the site. That rules out those three shafts. They're too far away. It has to be this one here, near the workers' flats.'

Dmitri stared at the plan. 'I know that shaft,' he said. 'It's the oldest on the site, worked in the nineteenth century by miners looking for gold. It doesn't have winding gear or lift cages. The shaft goes horizontally into a rock face.'

'Let's check it out,' Max said.

'We'll need some equipment first.'

'For what?'

'You'll see. Follow me.'

They ran back along the access road and across the yard to the storeroom. Dmitri took a key from his pocket and unlocked the door.

'You have a *key*?' Max said incredulously when they were safely inside the building.

'I took one of the spares when I worked here,' Dmitri replied, grinning. 'I was a stores clerk for part of the time. That's how I know they won't miss all the stuff I steal. The record-keeping is terrible. Give me a second.'

Dmitri clicked on his torch and vanished into the depths of the warehouse. When he reappeared a few minutes later, he was carrying a coiled rope and a heavy steel crowbar. He passed the rope to Max. 'Best to be prepared,' he said.

Leaving the storeroom, they avoided the yard and went west towards the mine workings. Dmitri stopped outside a small one-storey concrete building that had no windows and a sturdy looking metal door. He jammed the crowbar into the narrow gap next to the lock and wrenched it back, breaking the door open.

'Wait here,' he said, handing the crowbar to Max and slipping into the building.

He was gone less than five minutes. When he came back his hands were empty.

'What were you doing?' Max asked.

Dmitri didn't seem to hear the question. He took back the crowbar and headed off, moving quickly but carefully round the far end of the processing plant. There was no one about. The plant wasn't working, nor was the mine. The only places showing a light in this part of the site were the workers' flats. Down below the flats was a bare rock escarpment about twenty metres high into which a hole had been cut. The opening was roughly the size of a standard household door and it was blocked off by a barred metal gate held closed by a padlock.

Dmitri shone his torch through the bars, revealing a passage that had been hacked out of the rock. It was less than a metre wide and only just high enough for a man to stand up in. Max examined the padlock – it was much newer than the gate, which had been eaten away by rust. He took the piece of wire from his pocket and used it to pick the padlock. Dmitri watched, impressed by his skill.

'That's pretty good.'

'I've had a lot of practice,' Max said.

He tugged on the gate. It was stiff, but it swung open with a piercing squeak that set his teeth on edge. He looked apprehensively into the opening. The passage sloped down slightly into the cliff. He wondered how long it was, what they would find at the bottom. His stomach was knotted again – he was venturing into the unknown and he sensed danger. Would this be the last lock he ever picked? Was his career as an escapologist coming to a close? He shook off his fears by thinking of his father. Alexander Cassidy was somewhere down there in the darkness. And only Max could save him.

'You ready?' he said.

Dmitri nodded. Max took the torch from him and stepped into the passage, the beam of light playing over the rock walls. Dmitri followed, pulling the metal gate to behind him. They walked in single file for thirty metres, the incline getting gradually steeper, then Max came to an abrupt halt, holding out an arm to stop

Dmitri. He was shining the torch straight down at a vertical shaft in the ground. He moved a little to one side so that Dmitri could step forward next to him. The shaft was about three metres in diameter and maybe forty or fifty metres deep. In the torchlight they could just see the bottom of it.

'This has to be it,' Max said. 'The emergency escape route from the bunker.'

'How would anyone get up it?' Dmitri asked. 'It's just a hole.'

Max shuffled cautiously forward to the edge of the shaft and crouched down, shining the torch around the sheer walls. On the near side, only visible if you leaned out over the opening, was an iron ladder bolted to the rock.

'That's how,' he said. He directed the beam lower and swore under his breath.

'What's the matter?' Dmitri said.

'Look.'

Dmitri stepped to the edge and gazed down. The iron ladder continued for only three or four metres, then stopped. The lower sections were no longer there. 'That's why I brought the rope,' he said. 'Just in case. You ever abseiled before?'

'Only a couple of times,' Max replied. 'On a school outdoor pursuits course.'

'I've done it a lot, with my dad. Up in the mountains near here. Let me go first.'

Dmitri put his hunting rifle and the crowbar on the ground. Then he lay flat on his stomach, his shoulders and arms hanging out over the edge of the shaft, and tied the end of his rope to the top rung of the ladder. He tugged hard on it a few times. It seemed to be holding.

'Light the way for me,' he said. Then he put the crowbar in his rucksack, slung his rifle around his neck, looped the rope under his left arm and around his back and finally kicked the rest of the coil down the shaft. It unravelled as it fell, the last few lengths landing at the bottom with a faint slap. He lowered himself over the edge and began to abseil down, paying out the rope slowly as he descended, his feet pressed against the rock wall. Max watched, shining the torch down the wall so Dmitri could see where he was going. He took it cautiously – one metre at a time – but it was clear that he knew what he was doing. His feet touched the bottom of the shaft and he let go of the rope and stepped away, looking up at Max.

'Throw me the torch,' he called softly.

Max let the torch fall and Dmitri caught it safely, then shone the beam back up the shaft. Max looked at the rope dangling from the top rung of the iron ladder. He wasn't sure about this. It was true that he'd abseiled before, but that was with a safety line tied around his waist and a proper harness, an instructor on hand to tell him what to do. And it had been in daylight on an easy rock face, not underground in the dark, down a deep shaft that was smooth and slippery with moisture. He looked down. Dmitri angled the torch beam away from his face so it didn't dazzle him.

'You OK?' he called.

'Yes,' Max called back, though he didn't feel OK. There was no room for error – one slip and he could plunge fifty metres to his death.

He knelt down on the edge of the shaft, then twisted round and lowered his legs into the opening. When his feet found the ladder, he descended a few rungs until he could grasp the iron side struts with his hands. The metal was cold and clammy. He could smell the damp, stale air in the shaft. He climbed lower, stopping when his feet reached the bottom rung. The ladder creaked under his weight and he thought for a moment that he felt it give a little. He went still. No, he must have imagined it. The ladder was as solid as the rock to which it was attached.

Very slowly, he took his left hand off the side strut and grasped the rope. Then he removed his right hand and pulled the rope around his back and under his armpit as Dmitri had done. He leaned out a little, letting the rope take his weight, and shifted his feet from the bottom rung to the bare rock below it. Bracing himself, his heart going like a triphammer, he leaned back further, so he was almost perpendicular to the wall, and began to abseil down.

He was gripping the rope so hard his knuckles ached and he could feel the tension in his muscles. He payed out the rope bit by bit, feeling it sliding over his back. Then he heard a sharp crack of metal breaking, felt a sudden lurch and he dropped a few inches and jolted to a stop. Had the rope slipped? He looked up and saw to his horror that one side of the ladder had come away from the wall. A bolt had snapped clean off and the ladder was now fastened to the rock at only one point. He glanced over his shoulder. He was still twenty metres from the bottom of the shaft.

'What's the matter?' Dmitri called up. He evidently couldn't see the ladder dangling from a single bolt.

Max didn't reply. He didn't want to speak, didn't want to open his mouth in case the movement caused the ladder to break free entirely. He inhaled slowly, staring up at the bolt. It was holding his weight now, but how much longer would it last? It must have been there for years: the metal would be old, brittle – it might fracture at any moment. The missing sections of ladder should have given them a warning, told them it wasn't safe, as they'd obviously come away and fallen off at some point in the past. And now the last remaining piece was about to do the same.

It was too late to try to climb back up. And too dangerous. Hauling himself up would put even more strain on the bolt than continuing his descent. So he kept going. He payed out a little more rope, trying to do it evenly, avoiding sudden jerks that might snap the bolt. His heart was in his throat. His life was hanging on that one tiny piece of metal. He dropped a metre, then another. The bolt seemed to be holding. He let out more rope and glanced down again. Dmitri was gazing up at him anxiously. He must have seen, or sensed, that something was wrong.

Max looked back up the shaft. He was so deep he could no longer see the ladder clearly. It was outside the direct beam of the torch, which Dmitri was focusing on the wall by Max's feet. He dropped a couple more metres, trying to go faster. That was a big mistake. His left foot slipped on the greasy surface of the rock and his body lurched downwards, pulling sharply on the rope. He heard the snap of metal again, felt the ladder come away from the wall, then he was falling backwards through space. Falling rapidly down towards the bottom of the shaft.

He heard Dmitri cry out in alarm, felt the cold air

rushing up past his face. He flailed his arms wildly, trying to slow himself down, but he kept falling ... Falling. Then he landed. He'd expected something hard, a sudden impact with the rock floor, but it was soft like a body, and he realized that Dmitri had caught him. The torch clattered away and the shaft was plunged into darkness.

Max felt Dmitri collapsing, both of them tumbling to the ground. His hip and shoulder thudded heavily onto the rock, sending a stab of pain through his body, a shower of stars across his eyes. The impact knocked the wind out of him. He felt as if he were suffocating. He tried to suck in air, but it was like a vacuum – there was nothing there. Then a trickle of oxygen seeped through the hoop around his chest, a trickle that quickly became a gush, then a flood. He could breathe! He filled his lungs and rolled over.

'Dmitri?'

There was a strangled grunt from close by. Max reached out with his hand and touched clothing, then flesh – Dmitri's face.

'You OK? Dmitri?'

'Yes.' The word was like a groan, squeezed out with difficulty.

Max scrabbled around on the ground, found the torch and clicked it on. Dmitri was lying on his side, struggling to breathe. Max helped him sit up and supported him as he gradually got his breath back. The ladder and rope were tangled up together at the side of the shaft – it was a miracle that they hadn't hit Max or Dmitri as they crashed to earth.

Max rubbed his hip and flexed his leg. He'd taken a bad knock, but nothing seemed to be broken. Dmitri, too, appeared to have come off without serious injury. He pulled away from Max and felt his limbs, massaging his bruises.

'Thank you,' Max said. 'That's the second time you've saved my life.'

Dmitri forced a weak smile. 'Are you hurt?'

'Just a few bruises. You?'

'The same.'

'We were lucky.'

Max shone the torch around the shaft. Set back half a metre into the wall was a metal door, orange with rust, that had to be the entrance to the bunker. Then he looked across at the rope and broken ladder again, and up to the top of the shaft. They'd managed to get down all right, but one thing was certain: they wouldn't be going back out the same way.

They took a few more minutes to recover, then they stood up and went to the door. It was locked. Max peered through the keyhole. Nothing beyond except blackness. The lock mechanism, like the door, was old and rusty. He could see immediately that he wouldn't be able to pick it, not with just a piece of wire.

'We'll have to use the crowbar,' he said.

Dmitri took the tool out of his rucksack and forced open the door. The lock broke with a crack that echoed loudly around the mine shaft and they paused, looking at each other, both thinking the same thing: what if someone in the bunker had heard the noise? Dmitri raised his rifle to his shoulder and nodded at Max, who pulled back the door and stepped rapidly out of the way.

The room inside was in darkness. Max lit it up with the torch and saw piles of rubble and rotten timbers on the floor, walls eaten away by decay. It was a disappointing sight. Had they got it wrong about the bunker? The place seemed derelict. On this evidence, it didn't look as if it had been used in years.

Dmitri lowered his rifle and they walked into the room. Max felt the temperature change at once. He'd expected it to be cold, like the mine shaft, but it was noticeably warmer. Dmitri felt it too.

'There's heating down here,' he said.

Max picked his way through the piles of rubble to another rusty door at the far side of the room. Running up the wall in the corner near the door was an enormous metal pipe, a good half metre in diameter, that radiated heat and gave off a low humming noise.

'That's the hot water being piped up from underground,' Dmitri said.

Max crouched down to look through the keyhole in the door and saw a faint glimmer of light on the other side. He straightened up, feeling a buzz of excitement. Heating, lights – there was definitely something going on down here.

They used the crowbar again to break the lock on the door, and waited half a minute before they pulled it open. There was a corridor outside, illuminated only by dim emergency lights. The floor and walls were bare concrete, the surfaces grimy and stained with damp and black mould. It was warmer still here and there were grilles in the ceiling that looked like air-conditioning vents. There was absolutely no doubt about it now: the bunker was back in use.

They moved cautiously along the corridor and round a corner into a more brightly lit area. It seemed deserted – no sign, or sound, of people. The walls and floors were rough concrete here too, and despite the air conditioning, there was a damp musty smell. The place had been cleaned up, a few cosmetic improvements made, but the years of neglect were still apparent. Max tried a door on his left, easing it open a couple of centimetres, seeing darkness inside, then stepping through, Dmitri right behind him.

Max clicked on the light and gave a gasp of shock. There was nothing cosmetic about the changes to this part of the bunker. He was standing in what looked like a brand-new laboratory. There were stainless steel workbenches around the walls, lots of computer terminals and complicated-looking machinery, and in the centre of the room was something that sent a shiver down his spine: a high-tech chair, like a dentist's chair, with a headrest and leather straps on the arms. A chair identical to the ones he'd seen in the laboratory on Shadow Island in which prisoners had been tied to be injected with Episuderon.

'What is this room?' Dmitri asked.

'It's where the brainwashing takes place,' Max replied quietly.

'How do you know?'

'Because I've seen something very like it before.'

Max was shaken by the contents of the room. It brought back vivid, disturbing memories of Shadow Island; of the prisoner he'd seen being drugged – the man he now knew to have been the Kurdish journalist, Arhat Zebari; of finding Consuela and Chris strapped to similar chairs and rescuing them just in time. He licked dry lips and swallowed, picturing his father being drugged and interrogated here.

'My father was killed in a room like this?' Dmitri said.

'Yes.'

Max turned to look at him. Dmitri's mouth was set tight, his eyes burning with anger. 'If there are prisoners here, we have to get them out,' he said. 'Get them out *now*.'

He spun round to leave, but Max put a restraining hand on his arm.

'We have to be careful,' he said. 'What about the guards?'

Dmitri slapped the stock of his rifle. 'I'll take care of the guards.'

Max stared at him. 'You'd shoot them?'

'You think they won't try to shoot us?' Dmitri retorted. 'Clark's men have tried to kill you before, you told me so. They've murdered my father. Who knows, they might have murdered your father too. And you're worried I might shoot them in self defence? Wake up, Max. It's them, or us.'

Max kept staring at him, realizing that Dmitri was right. There was no room for moral scruples here. Not if they wanted to come out of this alive. 'OK,' he said. 'But *how* do we get the prisoners out. What do we do with them then? We're in

Kamchatka, in a mine owned and controlled by Julius Clark.'

'I don't know,' Dmitri said. 'What about stealing a truck, heading inland to the main road?'

'But we'll still be in Kamchatka,' Max said. 'We have to get out of the country.' He paused. 'What about the *Reunion Star*? Do you know anything about it?'

'I've met some of the crew. They're mostly Americans.'

'Clark's men? Does he own the ship?'

'No, he charters it. The crew could help us.'

'Will the ship still be here?'

Dmitri nodded. 'It always takes at least twenty-four hours to load it. You think we can get the prisoners to the port and escape by sea?'

'You got a better idea?'

Dmitri thought for a moment, then shook his head.

'Then let's get moving,' Max said. 'We're wasting time.'

They went back out into the corridor and crept softly along it until they reached a junction like a crossroads, four corridors branching off in different directions. Were there guards down here? Max wondered. If so, where were they? Maybe they stayed up on the surface – like the two men they'd seen earlier – watching the entrance.

'Can you remember the layout of the bunker?' he whispered to Dmitri.

'It was different back then,' Dmitri replied. 'I don't recognize any of this. They must've built new walls, divided it up.'

Max glanced into the corridor to their right, saw doors evenly spaced along both sides. Offices, maybe, he thought. Then he noticed the small metal flaps in the doors, the light switches on the walls outside each room and remembered that the cells on Shadow Island had been just like that.

'This way,' he said.

He stopped by the first door and pulled open the metal flap, saw the faint outline of a small darkened room. He flipped the light switch. A man was lying asleep on a bed at one side of the cell. He sat up, shielding his eyes, and squinted across at the door; he seemed disorientated, but he didn't look as if he'd been drugged.

'We're friends,' Max said.

'Friends?' The man stood up and walked over to the door. 'What is this place? Why am I here? What's going on?' He spoke English with an Australian accent.

'You been here long?'

'A day, maybe two days. I've lost track of time.'

'We're going to get you out.'

Max stepped back from the door. He could probably

have picked the lock, but brute force was quicker. Dmitri jammed the crowbar into the gap and broke the door open. The man came out into the corridor. He was in his thirties and looked tough and competent, able to take care of himself.

'What's your name?' Max asked.

'Ken. Who are you guys?'

'Later,' Max said.

He went to the next cell, turned the light on and looked through the flap. Another man was inside, lying on a bed. Dmitri forced open the door and they went in. The man moaned and rolled over restlessly. Max shook him awake, clamping a hand over his mouth to stop him crying out.

'We're friends,' he repeated. 'If you want to get out of here, don't make a sound.'

The man sat up, staring at them with a dazed expression on his face, his eyes wide and unfocused. Max could tell he'd been drugged. They helped him up off the bed and although he was unsteady, he could walk unaided.

Max and Dmitri left him with Ken and moved on to the remaining cells. Two were unoccupied, but in the others they found a further five men and one woman. The woman and three of the men seemed fit and mentally stable, but the other two men were in a bad way, only able to walk with help. One of them was completely out of his mind, drooling at the mouth and sweating and trembling as if he had a fever.

But they didn't find Max's father. Max was distraught – he'd been so sure he was here.

'My dad, where is he? There must be more cells somewhere,' he said to Dmitri. 'I have to find my dad.' He was in a panic, suddenly at a loss as to what to do. 'Where would they be, the other cells? You have to help me, Dmitri. I *know* my dad's here.'

'Calm down,' Dmitri said evenly. 'We have to deal with these people first.' He nodded at the freed prisoners huddled together in the corridor. 'What're we going to do with them?'

'Can you find the stairs? The ones you came down before?'

'I think so. They were at the southeast corner of the bunker.'

'Which way's that?'

Dmitri looked around, working out the compass points, calculating the route they'd taken through the bunker.

'It's over there,' he pointed. 'Along the corridor and to the left.'

'Let's get everyone there,' Max said.

They gathered the prisoners into a group and explained what they were going to do. How they had to hide in the stairwell while Max and Dmitri went off to look for Alexander Cassidy, and any other prisoners they'd missed. Then they'd get to the surface, find a way to divert the guards and steal one of the trucks to drive to the *Reunion Star*. The Australian, Ken, immediately took responsibility for the others, delegating the task of helping the weaker prisoners to the strongest men. Then they headed off down the corridor and round a corner into a small vestibule with a pair of double doors leading off it.

'That's it,' Dmitri said.

Max pushed open the doors and saw an iron staircase rising up through a concrete well. He gestured to the others, beckoning them in, helping them with the two men who couldn't walk by themselves, then he and Dmitri went back out into the vestibule and returned to the crossroads, taking one of the other corridors to look for more cells.

To look for Max's dad.

They passed through a lobby, which had a lift at one side, and paused at the opening to another corridor. Dmitri put an eye around the corner and pulled back quickly.

*Guard*, he mouthed silently.

*Just one?* Max mouthed back, holding up a finger. Dmitri nodded.

Max took a look for himself. The guard was about five metres away, standing outside a door, his sub-machine gun pointing down at the floor; he looked bored, restless. Then he yawned and took a couple of paces along the corridor to stretch his legs. Max ducked back out of sight. He put his mouth to Dmitri's ear and whispered, 'He's coming this way. What do we do?'

Dmitri whispered back, 'Leave it to me.'

He gripped his rifle across his chest, stepped to the corner and waited, Max sheltering behind him. They heard the guard's footsteps coming nearer. He was walking slowly, his boots scraping on the lino. As his body drew level with the corner, he was staring straight ahead, completely off guard.

Dmitri lunged forward and hit the man hard on the side of the head with the butt of his rifle. The guard passed out and tumbled over. Dmitri darted forward, managing to catch the sub-machine gun before it could clatter to the floor, but the unconscious body still made a thud as it landed. Max and Dmitri froze. Had anyone heard the noise? They waited a few seconds, then ran to the door the man had been guarding. Dmitri gave Max his rifle and kept hold of the sub-machine gun. Max pushed open the door and the two of them rushed in.

The room was sparsely furnished, containing a table

and two chairs and nothing else. On one of the chairs, his back half turned towards the door, was Julius Clark. On the other, his wrists strapped to the arms, was a grey-haired, frail-looking man with a gaunt face and hollow eyes. He glanced up as Max and Dmitri burst in.

'Hello, Dad,' Max said, trying to keep his voice steady. 'I've come to take you home.'

# TWENTY

Julius Clark twisted round in his seat and stared at the two boys, Dmitri first. Then he recognized Max and his jaw dropped open in shock. The colour drained from his face. 'You . . . ?' he stammered. 'But you're . . .'

He started to get to his feet, but Dmitri forced him back down with the barrel of the sub-machine gun.

'Who's this?' he asked curtly.

'Julius Clark,' Max replied.

Dmitri's eyes opened wide, then his mouth tightened. 'The boss himself. That's a bit of luck.'

Max turned to study his father. He looked weak and desperately ill, his body emaciated, his skin so pale that with his grey, almost white, hair he seemed like a ghost.

'Is that really you, Max?' Alexander Cassidy croaked feebly. He was staring at Max in utter disbelief.

'It's me, Dad,' Max replied, distressed to see him in this state. 'Are you all right?'

The question came out automatically, but even as he asked it Max realized how stupid it was. Alexander Cassidy was clearly *not* all right. He was in a very bad way indeed. Max rounded furiously on Clark.

'What've you done to him, you psycho?'

Clark didn't reply. He was still gaping incredulously at Max.

Max turned back to his father.'Has he injected you with anything, Dad? A drug?'

Alexander Cassidy nodded vaguely. 'He . . . asked me . . . questions. Names . . . he wants names . . . the Cedar . . . Alliance.' His voice petered out. Just those few words seemed to drain him.

The anger welled up inside Max. He wanted to kill Clark for what he'd done to his father. But he controlled himself. His dad came first: he had to look after him, get him out of the bunker. Walking over to the chair, he bent down and unfastened the straps around his father's wrists. The skin was red and sore where the leather had chafed.

'Can you stand, Dad?'

'I . . . think . . . so.'

Max helped his father up from the chair. He felt terribly thin and fragile, his bones sticking out through his skin. He was breathing heavily from just that slight exertion.

'You died,' Clark said in bewilderment. 'Off the Golden Gate Bridge. I had your rope sabotaged. I saw it on television – the crate smashing into the sea, the divers going down to look for you and finding nothing. How can you be here?'

'It takes a lot more than that to kill me,' Max replied. He was worrying about his dad, wondering how they were going to get him out in his present condition.

Clark started to get up again, but Dmitri shoved the barrel of his sub-machine gun into the side of his head and he sat back down heavily. Behind his rimless spectacles, the tycoon's icy blue eyes were frightened.

'Who are you?' he said to Dmitri.

'You murdered my father,' Dmitri said calmly. 'Sergei Alekseev. You remember him?'

'I've murdered no one,' Clark blustered back. 'That's ridiculous. I've never heard of Sergei Alekseev.'

'He was a good man, a good father. He was trying to protect the environment, to stop greedy people like you destroying the world for profit. And you murdered him.' Dmitri put his sub-machine gun against Clark's head again. 'And now you're going to pay for it.'

'No!' Max cried out.

Dmitri's finger tightened on the trigger.

Max grabbed his arm. 'Dmitri, no.'

'He's a diseased animal,' Dmitri said, his eyes never leaving Clark's. 'And diseased animals need to be put down.'

'That's not the way,' Max said sharply. 'We're taking him with us.'

'With us?'

'He's got to stand trial for what he's done. Let the law deal with him.'

'He killed my dad,' Dmitri said. His voice was shaking with emotion, his teeth clenched together in a grimace of hatred. 'Why shouldn't *I* kill *him*?'

'Because we're not like him, that's why,' Max said. 'Put the gun down, Dmitri. Think about it. Is this what your father would have wanted? His son to turn into a killer in a foolish act of revenge? Yes, you're right, Clark's filthy vermin, but don't soil your hands on him. You're better than that.'

Dmitri didn't move. He pushed the gun barrel deep into the skin above Clark's ear. Clark was trembling visibly. Max watched, holding his breath. Then, suddenly, Dmitri pulled back, keeping the gun trained on the tycoon. 'Get up,' he ordered.

'Now, look,' Clark said, 'you've got this all wrong. I've never—'

'Get *up*!'

Clark rose unsteadily to his feet.

'You try to escape and I *will* kill you. You understand?' Dmitri said.

Before Clark could reply, the air was shattered by the

sudden deafening noise of an alarm bell. Max let go of his dad and stepped over to the door. He whipped it open and looked out. The unconscious guard was no longer lying in the corridor.

'Quick, we have to get out,' Max said. 'You first, Dmitri. The guards will be on their way.'

Dmitri pushed Clark in front of him, prodding him forward with the barrel of his gun, using the tycoon as a shield. Max slung Dmitri's hunting rifle across his back, then put his arm around his father's shoulders and helped him out of the room. Alexander was so weak he could barely walk. Max had to hold him up and half carry him along.

They went down the corridor, heading towards the stairwell, but they couldn't move very fast, not with Alexander struggling to even stand. He'd lost a lot of weight, but Max still found him a heavy burden.

They came out into the lobby by the lift. Alexander Cassidy stumbled and Max had to hang on tight to prevent him falling. Dmitri reached out with an arm to assist, momentarily taking his eyes off Clark. Then everything seemed to happen at once. The lift doors opened and three guards piled out, two with their sub-machine guns raised, the third – the man Dmitri had knocked out – with a pistol he must have got from upstairs.

Dmitri yelled out a warning, but he was off balance, his gun swinging sideways. Clark didn't hesitate to take his chance. He darted forward suddenly, breaking away from the group, shouting at the guards.

'Shoot them!'

But the tycoon was still in the line of fire. The guards had to wait a fraction of a second and that delay was enough for Dmitri to let off a burst from his own gun. He'd obviously never fired a sub-machine gun before because it jumped in his hands, the bullets spraying wide, missing Clark and two of the guards, but catching the third man in the shoulder, knocking him to the floor.

The other guards dived out of the way and Clark scuttled behind them, yelling at them again to shoot. Max and Dmitri grabbed hold of Alexander between them and ducked into the shelter of the nearest corridor. The route to the stairwell was cut off now, so they had no choice but to retreat. Alexander was breathing heavily, his feet trailing along the floor as Max and Dmitri almost dragged him down the corridor.

Dmitri had his head twisted round, looking back, watching out for the guards. A head appeared around a corner, then a guard stepped out, his sub-machine gun braced against his hip. Dmitri squeezed the trigger on his own gun and the guard threw himself sideways, firing a quick burst which peppered the wall only inches away from Max's head. Plaster showered down on him and he increased his pace, urging his father on.

'Hold on, Dad, we'll get you out of here.'

They turned sharp right into another corridor and paused. Dmitri let go of Alexander to peer back round the corner. A guard was creeping out cautiously. Dmitri squeezed his trigger again, but nothing happened. He swore violently.

'Out of bullets,' he snarled furiously. Those two bursts had emptied his magazine and he had no more ammunition. He threw the sub-machine gun down in disgust and took the rucksack off his back. 'Hold them off for a second,' he shouted at Max.

Max propped his father gently against the wall and unslung the hunting rifle, unsure what to do with it. He'd never fired a rifle in his life. Dmitri was rummaging in his rucksack, taking out a couple of small blocks a few centimetres square and a couple deep.

'What are those?' Max asked.

'Plastic explosives,' Dmitri replied.

Max stared at him. So that was what he'd been doing inside the windowless concrete building. 'You're going to blow the place up?' Max was horrified at the thought.

'We've no choice,' Dmitri said.

'Do you know what you're doing?'

'I watched the miners using it loads of times. They showed me how to set the detonators.'

'But what about—?'

'We're outnumbered, Max. We can't hold them off with just a hunting rifle and only a few bullets.'

'Dmitri—'

'Do you want to get out of here?' Dmitri barked angrily. 'Watch the corridor.'

He bent down, placing one of the blocks of explosives against the wall and adjusting the timer. Max cocked an eye round the corner. The guard was halfway along the corridor. Max raised the rifle to his shoulder, looked down the sights and squeezed the trigger. The barrel jerked up, the stock hammering back into his shoulder and the bullet shot away over the head of the guard. Max fired again, aiming lower, ready this time for the recoil. The guard crumpled to the floor, clutching his leg. *I hit him*, Max thought, appalled at the idea of shooting someone. At least the guard wasn't dead. He was crawling away to safety, leaving a smear of blood behind on the lino.

'Give me the rifle,' Dmitri said, snatching the weapon away from Max.

Max went back to his father. Alexander was sagging against the wall with his eyes closed. He was only semi-conscious, unaware of what was going on around him. Max slipped his arm around his shoulders and led him away along the corridor while Dmitri followed, walking backwards so he could watch their rear.

Max saw a doorway coming up on their left that looked familiar and realized it was the way they'd come in, the room next to the mine shaft. Then he saw a figure at the far end of the corridor. Two figures — guards who'd circled around to come at them from the other side.

'Dmitri!' Max yelled.

The Russian boy spun round and fired two shots in quick succession, neither hitting their target. The guards kept coming, aiming their sub-machine guns, so Max pushed his father through the doorway and leaped in after him. Dmitri hurled himself to the floor just as the guards opened fire, sliding along the concrete on his stomach. Then the plastic explosive detonated, blowing a massive hole in the wall. Lumps of debris flew through the air, and smoke and dust billowed out in a choking cloud, blinding the guards.

Dmitri scrambled through the doorway. He had the second block of explosives in his hand and was already setting the timer. He tossed it out into the corridor and grabbed hold of Alexander.

'Get back!' he shouted. 'Away from the door.'

They retreated deeper into the room, around the piles of rubble. The door to the mine shaft was still open, just as they'd left it, but there was no chance of escape that way. Dmitri dropped to the floor, pulling Max and his father with him.

'Take cover!' he ordered, putting one arm round Max, one round Alexander. Max hugged his father close, protecting him as the charge exploded outside. They heard an almighty bang, then the wall of the room shattered, severing the pipe bringing hot water up from underground. A jet of water shot out. If it had hit the three of them directly, the force would certainly have killed them. But it hit the ceiling first, then the deflected water surged down and across the room, sweeping them away. Max had never felt anything so powerful in his life. It was like a tidal wave, an unstoppable wall of water driving all before it.

The pressure was unbelievable. In seconds they'd been swept out through the door into the mine shaft and propelled upwards like corks in a fountain. The water swirled around them, over their heads and in their faces. It was hot, but not scalding hot. Max held his breath, hanging on tight to his dad and Dmitri, feeling the water shooting them higher and higher. He could see nothing in the blackness, but he sensed the walls flashing past, the waves foaming against the rock, then the flood hit the roof and changed direction. He was flung sideways along the horizontal passage, still clinging desperately to Dmitri and his father.

The pressure eased off as they got further from the shaft. The flow of water decreased. Max snatched a breath, held his dad's head above the surface. His leg scraped on rock and he was deposited heavily on the ground like flotsam washed up on a beach. Dmitri and Alexander were lying next to him, water lapping over their legs.

'Dad? Dad?' Max cried, trying to feel if Alexander was breathing. '*Dad?*'

Alexander gave a cough, then he was spitting out water, gulping in air. Dmitri, too, was coughing up water, getting his breath back.

'You OK?' Max asked.

'I think so,' Dmitri replied with a gasp. 'Your father?'

'He seems to be OK. Can you get up, Dad?'

Alexander gave a murmur of assent, too shaken to speak. Max stood up and helped him to his feet. They stumbled along the passage, pushed open the barred gate and stepped out into the open air. It was lighter here. Max could see his dad's drawn face, his hair slicked down by the water, his clothes dripping. Dmitri came out behind them. Max glanced up at the workers' flats. Had anyone heard the alarm bell, or the explosions? The bunker was a long way down. Maybe the noise had been inaudible on the surface.

'We can't walk to the port,' Dmitri said. 'Not with your dad like this. We need a vehicle.'

'What about the other prisoners?' Max said. 'We have to go back and get them.'

'Into the bunker? Are you out of your mind?'

'We can't leave them, Dmitri. Maybe it's safe now. Maybe the guards are all dead, or injured. You shot one, I shot another. Who knows what those explosions did to the others.'

'It's madness, Max. I lost my rifle in the flood. We're completely unarmed. We have a chance to get away now. We should take it.'

'We can't abandon them,' Max insisted. 'Let's go and look, at least.'

He didn't wait for Dmitri to respond. There was no time for discussion. He put his arm around his dad's shoulders and walked slowly away, quite prepared to do it on his own, if he had to. But Dmitri caught up with them before they'd gone five metres. Max was expecting him to argue, but he didn't. He just took hold of Alexander from the other side and helped Max carry him.

They went round the back of the processing plant and across to the storeroom. Alexander was groaning softly, as if he were in pain.

'He needs to rest,' Max said. 'All this is too much for him.'

'Over here,' Dmitri said. 'Not much further.'

They carried Alexander to one of the open-top jeeps, parked beside the line of trucks in the yard, and put him in the back, lying down on the seat.

'Stay with him,' Dmitri said. 'I'll go and check the bunker.'

'No,' Max said. 'My dad will be OK. I'm coming with you. We'll be right back, Dad.'

The two of them raced across the yard and along the access road next to the offices. As they turned right between blocks, they heard footsteps ahead, saw a shadowy huddle of figures coming towards them. Max stopped dead, thinking at first it was Clark's men. Then he saw that two of the group were being helped along and recognized the face of the man at the front as he passed through a pool of light. It was the Australian, Ken.

Max and Dmitri ran to meet them.

'You got out?' Max said in amazement. 'How?'

'Walked up the stairs,' Ken said phlegmatically. 'We heard the shooting, then the explosions. It seemed a good time to make a move.'

'And the guards?'

'There were none by the entrance. They must all have gone down into the bunker.'

'This way,' Max said. 'Quickly.'

He led them back along the road and across the yard to the trucks. 'What about keys?' he asked Dmitri.

'They usually leave them inside,' Dmitri replied. He pulled open the nearest cab door and peered inside. 'Yes, in the ignition.'

He went round to the rear and let down the tail-board. The able-bodied prisoners clambered inside, with the weaker ones being lifted up to join them.

'You OK to drive?' Dmitri asked Ken.

'Sure. Which direction?'

'Head down the road. It goes straight to the port.'

'Let me get my dad,' Max said. 'He's in one of the jeeps.'

He walked towards the vehicle and was almost there when two men burst out on the far side of the yard, one of them letting rip with a sub-machine gun. Max hurled himself to the ground by the jeep and glanced over his shoulder. Ken was scrambling into the truck cab, start-ing the engine. Dmitri was on the ground, snaking across towards Max. The truck pulled away, the tail-board still dangling down, the terrified prisoners crouching inside.

Dmitri wormed round the front of the jeep, yelling at Max to get in. There was another volley of gunfire. The bullets hammered into the bodywork of the jeep. Dmitri was behind the wheel now, turning the key. Max dived in beside him, crouching low as the Russian boy spun the wheel and the jeep sped away.

The two men were running across the yard, climbing into one of the other jeeps. Looking back, Max saw who they were: a uniformed guard – and Julius Clark.

'Hang on!' Dmitri shouted.

The jeep swerved violently out onto the road. Max could see the tail lights of the truck two hundred metres ahead of them. He looked back. The other jeep was racing out of the yard, Clark himself driving, the armed guard beside him. All the other guards must have been out of action, Max realized. That was good. Surely they could get away now. He lowered his gaze to his father who was sprawled out on the rear seat, his eyes closed. *We can do this*, Max said to himself. *It's only seven kilometres to the port, to the safety of the Reunion Star. We can get there.*

Dmitri floored the accelerator. The jeep bounced over the rough surface, kicking up stones and dust. They sped across the plain, the terrain flat for a distance, then the road started to climb, winding up the valley side. The truck slowed, struggling with the gradient and the bends. Dmitri had to slow too, the engine roaring as he changed down a couple of gears, the jeep headlights cutting across the trees at the side of the road, picking out the branches, the leaves silver in the beams.

Clark was slowing as well. He was sixty or seventy metres back, hunched over the wheel, staring forwards with intense concentration. The guard next to him was hanging onto the door handle, the barrel of his sub-machine gun resting on the dashboard – waiting for the right moment to shoot.

Dmitri spun the wheel to the right and the jeep skidded round a bend, nearly sliding off into the forest. Max let out an involuntary cry of alarm.

'You driven a jeep before?' he called across, almost shouting to make himself heard above the din of the engine.

'A few times,' Dmitri replied. He turned the wheel again, fumbling for the gears.

'You got a driving licence?' Max asked, and saw a flash of Dmitri's teeth. It might have been a grin, or a grimace.

'No. But at the mine no one cared. Come *on*, move.'

He was staring at the lorry in front, urging it on. They were nearing the top of the hill now. They rounded the final bend, then the road dropped away over the other side. The lorry accelerated. Max looked back again. Clark's jeep had closed the gap and Max could now see his face, his spectacles glinting faintly in the reflected light from the headlamps. The guard was lifting his sub-machine gun from the dashboard, getting himself ready. Max called out a warning. Dmitri gave a nod, glancing in his rear-view mirror, then veered across the road, swerving back and forth to disorientate the guard, make it harder to shoot.

Up ahead, the lorry was pulling away from them. Ken was driving like a maniac, taking bends at a dangerously high speed. In the back, the other prisoners were cowering against the walls, clinging on for their lives. Max took another look over his shoulder – the guard had put down his gun and was hanging onto the door handle again.

'How're we doing?' Dmitri asked.

'They've dropped back a little,' Max replied.

'Good.'

Dmitri put the jeep into another skidding turn, stones flying up and pinging on the doors. Then they straightened up and were out on the plain, heading for the river. The speedometer crept over seventy kilometres an hour. They could have gone faster, but the truck was in the way. Dmitri held back, watching his rear-view mirror all the time.

'Get down!' he yelled, ducking his head over the steering wheel.

A hail of bullets smashed into the jeep, shattering the

windscreen, the glass spraying out over the bonnet. Max crouched down in the footwell, peering anxiously back between the seats, relieved to see that his father hadn't been hit. Alexander was on his back, his head rolling from side to side.

'Keep down, Dad!' Max shouted.

There was another burst of gunfire. More bullets pounded the body of the jeep, punching holes in the metal. Dmitri drove almost doubled up in his seat, squinting over the dashboard at the road in front. They were on the causeway over the river: no edges to the road, just a two-metre drop to the floor of the plain, the shallow channels of water meandering underneath them.

The guard fired again and the jeep slewed to one side, Dmitri fighting desperately to control it.

'The tyre's blown,' he cried, trying to straighten up. But the jeep was heading inexorably for the edge of the road. Dmitri braked – too hard. The wheels locked and the jeep careered out from the causeway, flying through the air and crashing heavily into the river. Max clung on tight, the impact jarring through him as the vehicle ploughed through the shallows and bounced to a halt on a sandy bank. He pushed open his door and dived out, stunned to be in one piece, thinking first of his dad. Alexander had been thrown forwards onto the floor. He was lying behind the front seats groaning, trying to sit up.

'Dmitri?' Max called.

'I'm OK.' The Russian boy was hauling himself out on the other side. He didn't seem to be injured.

'Help me with my dad.'

Max whipped open the rear door and they lifted Alexander out, supporting him between them. They scrambled up the bank and across the undulating grassy meadow beside the river. Glancing back, Max saw that Clark's jeep had stopped on the road. The tycoon and the guard were jumping down over the edge, splashing through the water after them.

'Hurry!' Max said urgently.

The forest was only thirty metres away. If they could get into the trees, find cover, they might have a chance. They lifted Alexander's feet off the ground and ran, stumbling and tripping in the darkness, but somehow staying upright. The grass gave way to low bushes and scrubby undergrowth. Max and Dmitri forced a way through and plunged into the forest, ducking under the low branches, catching their feet on the tree roots. Almost immediately, the ground began to slope upwards. Carrying Alexander became even harder. Max and Dmitri had to slow down, panting heavily, but they kept climbing. They could hear Clark and the guard behind them, chasing them up the hill. Glancing back, Max saw the glimmer of a torch in the trees.

He was gasping for breath, so was Dmitri. Alexander, still only half conscious, was slumped in their arms. Max knew they couldn't move silently through the forest – it wasn't possible with his father so incapacitated. But stopping and finding somewhere to hide wasn't an option either. Clark was very close behind and he had a torch. He'd find them for certain.

They broke out of the trees into a clearing and Max paused, looking around, realizing he'd been here before. It was where he'd first met Dmitri, where they'd had their terrifying encounter with the bear. An idea suddenly came to him – a thin, improbable, hopeless sort of idea, but it was all he could think of. They couldn't keep running for much longer.

'The bear we met earlier,' he whispered to Dmitri. 'Does it live around here?'

'Up the hill over there,' Dmitri replied. 'It has a den in an earth bank.'

'How far?'

'Fifty, sixty metres. Why?' Then he guessed what Max had in mind. 'You mean . . .'

Max nodded. 'Quickly. One last effort.'

They picked Alexander up between them again and staggered across the clearing, Dmitri guiding them into the trees. A torch beam flitted across them and Max looked over his shoulder. Clark and the guard were in the clearing, only twenty metres away.

'There's the den,' Dmitri said, nodding away to his left.

Max saw the dark outline of the earth bank. He bent down, picked up a handful of stones and hurled them in a shower towards the bank. They stumbled on for another five or six metres, then stopped, too worn out to continue. They lowered Alexander to the ground, propping his back against a tree trunk, and sat down beside him.

The torch beam hit them full in the face. Max saw Julius Clark walking towards them. He was holding the torch in his left hand, a pistol in his right. Max felt a crushing sense of defeat. It was all over. They'd got so far, but now the game was up. They were at Clark's mercy.

The tycoon gazed at them triumphantly. Max knew they must have looked a pitiful sight: two exhausted boys and an invalid. They could hardly have been less of a threat.

'So I'm a diseased animal, am I?' Clark said, the insult obviously still rankling. 'A diseased animal that needs to be put down. Well, we'll see who gets put down now.'

He took a pace nearer, pointing the torch straight at Max.

'I should have killed you on Shadow Island. You've been a thorn in my side ever since. But not any more. You've pulled your last stunt, Max, performed your last escape. The show's over.'

'For us, maybe,' Max said, feeling too tired, too despondent to offer much resistance. 'But killing us won't save you. There are too many people who know what you've been up to. There are too many witnesses to your crimes.'

'You think so? I wouldn't be so sure, Max. I have a lot of powerful friends, a lot of influence with governments around the world.'

'Your friends will be caught too,' Max said. 'We have your secret files. Downloaded from your computer in Borneo.'

'*What?*' For a moment Clark seemed unnerved, unsure of himself. Then his confidence returned. 'You're lying. You couldn't have downloaded my files. You don't know the password.'

'VICTOR one,' Max said and enjoyed the look of shock on the tycoon's face. 'We've cracked the codes too. How else do you think I found out about Woodford Down Laboratories? You're going to jail, Clark. There's nothing more certain.'

Clark stared at him. 'If I do,' he said with a chilling smile, 'you won't be around to see it.'

'Max, what's happening?' Alexander asked in a frail, puzzled voice. 'Where am I?'

'You're with me, Dad,' Max replied gently. 'You're safe.'

He took his father's hand in his own and peered into the forest behind Clark, the earth bank a black shadow in the trees. Nothing moved. Not a branch, not a leaf. Max knew his plan had failed.

Clark raised his pistol, holding the torch beam steady on Max's face. Max gripped his father's hand tight, waiting for the end. They were together, at least. They'd found each other again, been reunited. That was one small, bitter consolation. He thought of his mum, hoping that somehow soon – maybe through the information in Clark's files – her name would be cleared and she'd be released from prison. But whatever happened, it would be too late for Max and his dad. Neither of them would ever see her again.

Then Max saw something move in the trees behind Clark's shoulder. He thought it was just a bush swaying in the breeze, but then the bush seemed to change position, come forward towards them. Max blinked, wondering if his eyes were playing tricks. But no, it *was* moving, changing shape. The bush was growing, shooting up from the ground and turning into a tree maybe half a metre wide and two metres tall, with a branch sticking out on either side. The branches whipped round with lightning speed, one catching the guard around the head, the other hitting Julius Clark. There was a crunch of bones snapping and the two men were hurled violently to the ground, Clark's pistol skittering away across the dirt.

Max choked back a cry of alarm as the bear fell on the tycoon's body, tearing it apart with its teeth. He watched for a few seconds with a kind of horrified fascination, then had to look away.

Dmitri was already getting slowly to his feet. 'Come on,' he whispered, pulling Alexander up.

'The guard . . .' Max began. 'Maybe—'

'He's dead,' Dmitri said bluntly. 'A blow like that, he would have died instantly. We can do nothing for him.'

Max stood up, trying not to look at the bear, but aware of it slavering and grunting, its jaws crunching.

'Come on, Max,' Dmitri repeated. 'We have to get to the ship.'

They hooked their arms around Alexander and crept away into the forest, heading back downhill through the trees. Max was in a daze, walking automatically, instinctively avoiding obstacles in his path. But all he could see was the vivid imprint of the bear coming out of the shadows, rising up and killing Julius Clark with a single blow of its massive paw, then falling greedily on the body, its mouth gaping. Max shuddered and tried to erase the pictures, but knew they would always be with him.

It took them fifteen minutes to reach Clark's jeep. The keys were still in the ignition. They laid Alexander down on the rear seat and climbed in. Neither of them spoke on the short journey to the port until they came over the final rise and saw the *Reunion Star* berthed alongside the quay.

'Thank God,' Max murmured. 'She's still here.'

But clearly not for much longer. The cranes were silent, their booms motionless. The forklift trucks were parked neatly by the warehouse, the stevedores passing around a bottle of vodka before they returned to their flats at the platinum mine.

Ken and the other prisoners were already on board. And Max and his father and Dmitri were obviously expected for there were two crew members on hand to help them up the gangplank and escort them to the bridge.

The captain, a big man with a dark beard and an air of quiet competence about him, was listening intently while Ken and the others – those that were fit enough to speak – told him how they'd been abducted and brought to Kamchatka. They broke off as the new arrivals came onto the bridge, Max explaining to the captain who they were. The captain stared at him, as if an extra-terrestrial had just come on board.

'*Max Cassidy?* The boy escapologist who died off the Golden Gate Bridge? Who was the lead item on every news bulletin when we left San Francisco?'

'That's me,' Max said modestly.

The captain shook his head in disbelief. 'This gets more and more incredible.'

'This is my dad,' Max said. 'He's not well. Please could you find him a bed, some medical attention?'

The captain snapped off an order to one of his officers, then turned back to Max. 'Is that everyone now? We're ready to sail.'

'Not me,' Dmitri said. 'I'm not coming.'

Max looked at him in surprise. 'You're not? After all that's happened, you want to stay here?'

'It's where I belong,' Dmitri said simply. He walked away across the bridge and down the stairs.

'Give me two minutes,' Max said to the captain and ran after Dmitri, catching him as he stepped off the gangplank onto the quay.

'You could come with us, you know,' Max said. 'To America, then home with me to England.'

Dmitri shook his head. 'I'm Russian. This is my home.'

'What are you going to do? Live in your cave, continue stealing food from the mine, drinking vodka in the hot springs? Is that what you really want?'

'No, I've had enough of that. You coming here, all that's happened, it's woken me up, made me realize what I should be doing. I'm going to take the jeep, drive to the main road and get back to civilization.'

'And then what?'

'I'll do what I always planned – take up the fight for the environment where my dad left off. Do it properly this time. There are other people like him, people who want to save what we have left of the natural world. Maybe I can do my bit to help them.'

Max held out his hand. 'Thanks for everything, Dmitri. I owe you my life. So do those people on the ship.'

'It was nothing. We were a team, Max.'

'Good luck.'

'You too.'

They shook hands. Then Max went back onto the ship and stood on the deck as the gangplank was raised and the vessel left port. Dmitri watched from the quay for a while, the *Reunion Star* heading out to sea, the figure leaning on the rail getting smaller and smaller, then he lifted his arm to wave one last time and walked across to the jeep. Max saw him climb in and start the engine. The jeep pulled off, turned out onto the road and disappeared up the hill.

Max felt an immense sadness, seeing Dmitri go, but he knew in his heart that this wasn't goodbye. They would see each other again, he was certain of that. He took a final look, then walked away across the deck in search of his father.

Dawn was breaking over the ocean. The shoreline was still dark, Dead Man's Bay hidden by the headland, but up the valley, beyond the forest, the snow on the top of the volcano was turning pink in the first rays of the new day.

# TWENTY-ONE

The long oak table in the conference room of the *London News Chronicle*'s offices was covered with neat stacks of paper, so many that barely a centimetre of the polished wooden surface was visible. Dan Kingston gestured at them casually, pulling out a couple of chairs so he and Max could sit down.

'Julius Clark's files,' he explained.

Max stared at the piles, some of them half a metre high. There must have been thousands of sheets of paper.

'This is all from the memory stick I brought back from Borneo?'

Kingston nodded. 'Your computer guy finished decrypting them last week. While you were, well' – the journalist smiled – 'let's say, otherwise engaged over-seas. They make for very interesting reading. A lot deal with the financial side of Clark's many businesses. Not the official, audited accounts he put into the public domain, but his secret accounts that detail the bribes and other payments he made to various people around the world.'

'What kind of people?' Max asked.

'Politicians, police officers, government officials. Wherever he did business, there was someone on the take. He spent millions every year on bribes, or bribes disguised as donations to political parties.'

'Including this country?'

'Oh, yes, he didn't neglect the UK. We've had a team of reporters going through every single document, checking and cross-checking all the information, making sure we're absolutely certain of our facts before we publish anything. It's sensational stuff, Max. Probably the biggest political scandal the world has ever seen. It's a global affair – here, the US, Europe, Russia, the Middle and Far East. No region is going to come out of it unscathed. In this country alone, we've identified sixteen Members of Parliament, four senior police officers, twenty-four civil servants and several employees of the security service who have received illicit payments from Clark or his companies. One of the MPs is a junior minister at the Home Office – the department that controls the police and MI5.'

'And the man I asked you about on the phone?' Max said. 'Have you found his name anywhere?'

'Rupert Penhall? Yes, Mr Penhall features prominently in the files. He had dealings with Clark going back at least ten years, possibly longer. And he has a numbered bank account in Switzerland into which Clark pays nearly two hundred thousand pounds a year.'

'Wow!' Max pursed his lips. 'That's a lot of money.'

'About two million pounds over that ten-year period.'

'And what did Penhall do in return?'

'We're still trying to establish exactly what he did. But he undoubtedly pulled strings for Clark, protected his business interests. Penhall has close connections with both MI5 and MI6. He has a lot of very powerful friends.' Kingston reached out to pick up a large, bulging manila envelope from one of the stacks of papers on the table. 'I made copies of the important bits for you. To give to your police contact. I'd appreciate it if you held off for a few days, give us a chance to run the story first.'

'When's it going in the paper?'

'From tomorrow. Then every day after that for the next week.'

'You have that much?'

'We could fill the paper for a year with what we've got.' Kingston grinned at him. 'You're a journalist's dream, Max. First all that drama in San Francisco and your escape from Kamchatka, now this. You're the most famous kid on the planet. Give it a few weeks and the public is going to be heartily sick of hearing your name.'

'What about Clark's fifth columnists – the people he kidnapped and brainwashed on Shadow Island and in Kamchatka?' Max asked. 'Is there anything in the files about them?'

'Plenty,' Kingston replied. 'Julius Clark was a control freak, an obsessive keeper of records. We have names, places, dates, everything we need to build a detailed picture of what he did: who he abducted, what their jobs were, how many died during the brainwashing, when the survivors went back to their organizations to work for him. There are hundreds of them – ecologists, scientists, lobbyists, lawyers, you name it – covering pretty much every environmental organization in the world.'

'You're going to expose them?'

'They need rooting out. Their employers have a right to know who they are, and the individuals concerned will need medical help to get back to normal, to wipe out the effects of the drug they were given. Kingston paused. He looked at Max and his tone became gentler. 'How's your dad?'

'Not too bad.'

'Is he still in hospital?'

Max nodded. 'The doctors say he's making good progress. They think he should make a full recovery, but it might take a bit of time.'

'That's good to hear.'

'He seems to have had a very high resistance to Episuderon. He's an extremely tough, resilient person.'

'I guess it runs in the family,' Kingston said dryly. 'And your mother? When's she coming out of prison?'

'It's going to be a few days yet. There's all the legal red tape to sort out, but it should be before the end of the week.'

'Good.' Kingston wagged a finger at him. 'And don't you forget who's getting the first exclusive interview with you all.'

Max grinned. 'I haven't forgotten.'

Kingston pushed his wire-rimmed spectacles up his nose and regarded Max pensively for a moment.

'And what about you, Max?'

'Me?'

'You've been through a hell of a lot, especially for a fourteen-year-old kid. How are *you*?'

'I'm OK.'

'Is that the truth?'

'Yes,' Max said. And it *was* the truth. At least, for the time being. He'd expected some kind of traumatic after-effects from what he'd been through – nightmares, cold sweats, depression. But they hadn't happened. He was sleeping well and he felt fine, both physically and mentally. Of course, he thought about Kamchatka and the Golden Gate Bridge, and Borneo and Shadow Island too, but the memories didn't disturb him – not deep down. He'd survived all the ordeals, come out the other side in one piece. That was good reason to be cheerful, not depressed.

There were other reasons to be happy too. Julius Clark, his greatest enemy, was dead and Rupert Penhall would soon have to answer for his illegal actions. But most importantly, Max had achieved his two most heartfelt desires – he'd found his father, and his mother would soon be a free woman again. Nothing could be better than that.

Dan Kingston was still looking at him. 'You're sure you're OK?' he said.

'Yes,' Max replied firmly. 'Thanks for asking. Thanks for everything you're doing. I appreciate it.'

'Are you crazy? I should be thanking *you*. You've given me the scoop of a lifetime.' Kingston glanced at his watch and stood up. 'I'm sorry, Max, I have to go. The editor will be yelling at me if I don't get back to my work. I've tomorrow's splash to write.'

'I look forward to reading it.'

'Keep me posted on your mum and dad. Oh, and one other thing: writing all this stuff about you has given me an appetite for escapology. The next time you do a show, I want to be there in the audience watching you in action.'

'I'll see what I can do,' Max said.

The unmarked police car turned in through the gates of the imposing, three-storey Georgian villa and came to a halt on the gravel forecourt. A second police car, containing two uniformed officers, followed close behind.

Detective Sergeant Kevin Richardson got out of the first car and paused, looking up at the white walls of the house, the stone columns and elegant portico along the front. It was an attractive building, with well-maintained gardens all around it. In this part of London, Richardson estimated, it would be worth several million pounds – and most of it paid for with tainted money.

He waited for the two uniformed officers to join him, then they went up the short flight of steps to the front door and rang the bell. A petite woman with highlighted blonde hair answered.

'Mrs Penhall?' Richardson asked politely.

'Yes.' She was staring at the two uniforms behind him, the beginnings of a puzzled frown on her forehead.

Richardson showed his ID. 'Is your husband in?'

'Yes, he is. What's this . . . Is everything all right?'

'Perhaps we could speak to him?'

Mrs Penhall stood back to let them enter. There was thick carpet on the floor, a curving staircase going up to the first floor. A boy about nine or ten years old, wearing a grey blazer and red school tie, came out into the hall and gazed at them curiously.

'Rupert!' Mrs Penhall called, then turned to the boy. 'Have you finished your breakfast, Sebastian? Quickly, hurry, or you'll be late.'

Rupert Penhall emerged from the kitchen, his plump face pink and freshly shaved. He had a mug of coffee in one hand, a half-eaten piece of toast in the other.

'For you,' his wife said.

Penhall looked at the officers. 'What is it?' he asked curtly.

'We'd like to speak to you, sir,' Richardson said. 'Is there somewhere more private we could go?'

'Private? Is this to do with work? Couldn't you have waited until I was in my office?' Penhall's voice was sharp and irritated.

'We need to speak to you *now*, sir,' the detective said.

'Oh, very well. This way.' Penhall led them across the hall to a study at the back of the house. There was a leather-topped desk and chair at one side of the room, shelves of books on the walls. The large picture window gave a view of a velvet lawn and beds of flowers and shrubs. He sat down behind the desk, still clutching his coffee and toast. 'What the devil is this all about?' he demanded. 'I'm in the middle of breakfast.'

Richardson took a photograph out of his jacket pocket and placed it on the desk. 'Do you know this man?'

Penhall glanced at the photo and turned pale. He looked up quickly. 'What the hell is going on?' he snapped.

'If you'd answer the question, please?' Richardson said softly.

'No, I've never seen him before in my life. OK? Is that all you came here for?'

'That's funny,' Richardson said. 'Because he knows *you.*'

'You're wasting my time.' Penhall pushed back his chair and started to get up.

'Sit down!' the detective barked.

'What!' Penhall glared at him indignantly. 'Look, do you know who I am? One phone call from me and you'll be out of the Met on your ear.'

'Sit down.'

Penhall hesitated, his gaze still fixed on Richardson, then he shrugged and slumped back down. 'You're making a very big mistake,' he said angrily, but his eyes were worried, his manner less assured now.

'His name is Ronnie Cook,' the detective said. 'He's

done time for burglary and grievous bodily harm. We have CCTV footage of him entering a house in north London and planting an explosive device in the gas cooker. You know the house I'm talking about, I think.'

'I have no idea what you're talking about.'

'Ronnie Cook says you paid him to plant the bomb.'

'And you believe him? A convicted criminal? Really, this is ridiculous.'

'He also says that you paid him to kill a man by pushing him in front of a lorry.'

'Oh, come *on*, this gets worse. You can't be serious?'

'Oh, yes, Mr Penhall, I'm very serious indeed,' Richardson replied. There was no trace of emotion in his manner, just a clinical professionalism. 'The man was my father, Detective Chief Superintendent John Richardson.'

Penhall gave a start. He licked his lips, then took a sip of his coffee to give himself time to think. When he spoke again, his manner was defiant. 'I don't have to listen to this nonsense. Who's your superior officer? I think I'd better speak to him.'

'You will,' Richardson said. 'As soon as we get you to Scotland Yard.'

'You're arresting me?' Penhall's mouth fell open in shock.

'On suspicion of conspiracy to murder and to cause

PAUL ADAM

an explosion, and taking bribes from Julius Clark.'

Penhall recovered himself, giving a dismissive shake of his head. 'Julius Clark? You mean the business tycoon? I've never even met the man.'

'We have his files,' Richardson said, almost smiling. 'Every penny he's ever paid you is itemized.'

Penhall stared at him, too stunned to speak for a time. Then he said, 'You can't do this. You can't arrest me. I have friends, important friends.'

'I know,' Richardson said. 'And most of them will also be under arrest by now.' He gave Penhall a formal caution and asked him to stand up.

Penhall's cheeks were flushed bright red with fury. 'This is outrageous,' he protested. 'I'm not coming.'

'Your wife and son are in the house,' Richardson said calmly. 'You can walk out of here with us of your own free will, or we can handcuff you and drag you out. Which is it to be?'

Max had dreamed of this day for two long years. Dreamed of the moment when he and his parents would be reunited. Now it had arrived, he felt un-accountably sick. There were butterflies in his stomach and his limbs were trembling. He couldn't remember when he'd last felt so nervous – even his shows didn't affect him quite like this.

367

They were in the reception area of Levington prison – Max, his dad and Consuela, who'd driven them all up from London. Alexander's doctors had allowed him out of hospital for a few hours only – he was still too frail to cope with more than that. He was sitting on a chair against the wall. He was thin and pale, but there was a glow of joy in his eyes. The prospect of seeing his wife again had given him a new energy.

Max glanced around impatiently. He hated this place, hated everything about it – the walls, the fences, the locked doors, the prison officers with their keys jangling at their belts. But at least it was the last time he'd ever come here. There'd be no more humiliating searches, no more waiting at the table in the visiting area, no more having to watch his mother's suffering. She was coming out. After two unbearable years of captivity – eighteen months in Santo Domingo and six in Levington – she was now a free woman.

There were footsteps in the corridor behind the barred steel gate at the back of the reception area. Max saw a large female prison officer approaching, a big, hefty woman whose bulk seemed to fill the entire width of the corridor, obscuring the smaller, slighter figure who was walking along in her wake.

Max went to his father and helped him up from his chair. The steel gate was unlocked and then Helen

Cassidy was stepping out, hesitating a little as if she couldn't believe this was happening. She smiled at Max and Alexander, her eyes filling, then she ran to them, her arms outstretched, enfolding them both in a tight embrace, hugging them close as the tears of happiness poured down her cheeks. Max could feel her arms around him, feel her sobbing.

'Oh, Alex, Max, Alex, Max,' she kept repeating, not even attempting to find any other words.

Then she pulled away and gazed at them tenderly, still smiling, still crying. She was wearing make-up for the first time in two years, a new summer dress and high heels that Consuela had brought up to Levington two days earlier – Helen's 'coming out' clothes, she called them.

'Oh, Alex.' Helen hugged her husband again and they whispered a few quiet words to each other. Then she turned to Max, pulling him into her arms.

'Oh, Max, I love you so much. I can't tell you how happy this makes me.'

Max hugged her back, choking with emotion, trying to hold in the tears, then giving up and letting them flow.

When Helen finally released him, she embraced Consuela, both of them weeping, then she lifted a hand to her face, feeling her damp skin, her smudged mascara. 'Oh, God, I must look awful,' she said. 'I can't go out like this.'

Max laughed. 'Well, it's good to get back to normal so quickly,' he said.

Fortunately, Consuela had come prepared. She handed Helen some tissues and a compact with a mirror so she could touch up her make-up.

'How do I look now?' Helen asked.

'You look great, Mum,' Max replied. 'Doesn't she, Dad?'

Alexander smiled at his wife. 'Yes, indeed. She looks very beautiful.'

'Are you ready?' Max said. 'I have to warn you, there are a lot of photographers and reporters out at the front.'

'Are there?' Helen looked horrified. 'Do we really have to go out that way?'

Max nodded. 'It won't take long. Just a few pictures, that's all.'

They went out in a line, Max in between his mum and dad, Consuela on the other side of Alexander, helping him walk. But as they emerged through the big wooden doors onto the prison forecourt, she slipped away discreetly, leaving Max and his parents centre stage.

There was a huge crowd of photographers and television cameras waiting for them. In the short time since Max's return from Kamchatka, his story had gone all around the world. The release of his mother from prison was a massive event and practically every newspaper, every television station on earth, wanted a piece of it.

The Cassidys posed patiently, holding hands and smiling as the flashbulbs exploded around them, answering a few of the questions that the reporters shouted out before Max, realizing his father was beginning to flag, brought the impromptu press conference to a close. A squad of police officers escorted them to their car, the photographers scrambling to get more pictures. Max sat in the front next to Consuela. His parents were in the back, still holding hands, bewildered by all the attention.

A police car led them down the prison drive to the road, then waved them past, turning sideways across the carriageway to stop the reporters and photographers following.

They didn't talk much on the journey back to London. It was as if they were waiting for the right moment to catch up with one another, to begin their lives together again.

Chris had stayed behind at Rusty's flat in the Docklands. Max and his parents were going to live there temporarily, until they found a place of their own to rent: the family home was still uninhabitable, but it was going to be rebuilt once the insurance payout had been settled. Chris had been busy preparing a small, low-key welcome-home party. He'd bought roast chicken, salads, cheese and freshly baked bread from a nearby deli and put a bottle of champagne on ice. Consuela looked around approvingly as they came into the flat, noting the places set at the table, the food neatly laid out, the glasses waiting to be filled. On the kitchen worktop, carefully placed so Max wouldn't miss it, was that morning's edition of the *London News Chronicle*. The front-page lead, by Dan Kingston, contained more revelations about Julius Clark's criminal activities, and in a side column was a related story about Rupert Penhall appearing before magistrates and being remanded in custody.

Consuela introduced Chris to Helen, then they broke open the champagne and drank a few toasts – to Helen, to Alexander, to Max, to being a family again.

Helen studied the table and turned to Consuela.

'There are only three places set,' she said in a puzzled voice.

'Chris and I aren't staying,' Consuela replied.

'*What?* But you must.'

'No,' Consuela said firmly. 'You need some time to yourselves.'

'But—'

'It's all decided. We'll see you later.'

As Consuela and Chris left, Helen and Alexander gazed uncertainly at each other and Max could see that he was going to have to take charge. He pulled out chairs and made his parents sit down. Then he joined them at the table and they linked hands. Max smiled at them. He'd never seen them so radiantly happy.

'OK,' he said. 'So where do we begin?'

Max regarded all his shows as important, but this one meant more to him than all the others put together. He was back in the London Cabaret Club, his usual venue, with a few new tricks and stunts prepared to stun the packed house. There was nothing exceptional about any of that. It was who was present in the audience that made this evening so significant.

Max could see them all in the front row below him: Isabella Gonzales, the young girl who'd done so much to help him in Santo Domingo; Ari, the Dayak boy who'd been his invaluable companion in Borneo; and Dmitri Alekseev, clean-shaven and smart, looking very different from the wild, vodka-swilling youth Max remembered from Kamchatka. All three of them had been flown to England by the *London News Chronicle*, which, nearly three months after Max's return, was still running stories about his incredible exploits.

Kevin Richardson and his wife were there too, and Max's best friend Andy and some of his schoolmates. So were Chris Moncrieffe, Rusty and Zip, Dan Kingston and Lucas Fisher. And sitting in the middle of the row was Helen Cassidy, watching her son perform at the London Cabaret Club for the very first time, her face alight with pride and joy.

'To end tonight's show,' Max said into the microphone, 'I'm going to call on the help, not only of Consuela, but of someone very special and close to me – the person who's taught me pretty much everything I know about escapology. Ladies and gentlemen, please welcome my father, Alexander Cassidy.'

There was an eruption of ear-splitting applause as a tall, grey-haired figure came out of the wings and walked slowly across the stage. Alexander Cassidy was looking a lot better. He'd put on weight, got some colour back into his skin. Although he hadn't yet regained his full strength, he was well on the way to making a complete recovery from his illness.

'Well, this is quite an evening, isn't it?' he said to the audience. 'I don't know about my teaching Max everything he knows about escapology. From what I've seen tonight, I think *he* could teach *me* a few things. If I ever get back into performing – and after watching my son, I may be having second thoughts about that – I can see

I'm going to have some serious competition on my hands.'

The audience laughed and Alexander beamed at Max. Then he turned back to the microphone.

'Let me tell you about this final stunt. It's so difficult that I have my doubts whether it's humanly possible for anyone to pull it off – even the Half-Pint Houdini. Consuela, would you bring out the equipment now, please?'

Consuela emerged from the wings pushing a metal trolley bearing an assortment of chains and manacles. She was wearing one of her usual dazzling show outfits – sequins on her red top, jewels gleaming in her hair, silver rings dangling from her ears – but with the additional sparkle of a diamond engagement ring on her left hand.

She left the trolley in the centre of the stage and stepped back. Alexander picked up a pair of handcuffs and showed them to the audience.

'Very shortly, I'm going to put these handcuffs on Max's wrists. Not one pair, but two. Then I'm going to fasten his ankles together with two pairs of leg irons. Chains will be wrapped around his body and secured with three padlocks, then he will be put inside a steel safe. Consuela, if you please . . .'

Consuela pulled aside a curtain to reveal a massive

safe, two metres square, its door swung open to show its formidable construction.

'This safe is used by jewellers and gold bullion dealers,' Alexander went on. 'Its sides are fifteen centimetres of solid titanium steel, the lock so complex that, to my knowledge, no locksmith on earth has ever managed to crack it. Once Max is inside, the safe will be winched into the air and suspended three metres above the stage. Then . . .' he paused. 'Then, well, after that it's all up to you, Max.'

Max came forward into the spotlight looking convincingly worried. 'How on earth am I going to escape from all that?' he asked.

His father smiled at him. 'You'll think of something, Max. You always do.'

# RESISTANCE
## BY CRAIG SIMPSON

*Short bursts of frenzied machine-gun fire filled the air and I saw the radio operator slump forward. The radio crackled. I could hear a German voice. A shiver went down my spine . . .*

### Norway, September 1943

For brothers Marek and Olaf, a hunting trip out on the frozen Hardanger plateau offers a brief chance to escape the German occupation. But returning home they witness the horror of their father's arrest by the Gestapo and the start of a brutal regime under the evil Lieutenant Wold. When their daring plan for revenge is foiled they are forced to seek refuge in the vast and unforgiving Norwegian wilderness.

Saved from an icy grave by Resistance freedom-fighters, fourteen-year-old Marek is captivated by their courage and determination. He may not be a crack shot like his brother, but he is quick-thinking, resourceful and a talented mechanic. With youth on his side, the Germans probably won't suspect him, which is perfect for a part in the ambitious attack planned by the group. But can he keep his nerve, especially when the final assault will throw his friends and family into the hands of the enemy?

'A terrific romp . . . fans of films starring Bruce Willis
(or David Niven) should love it'
***TES***

ISBN: 978 0 552 55571 5